W9-ASP-645

RED LINE

RED LINE

A MATT SINCLAIR NOVEL

by

Brian Thiem

CROOKED
LANE

NEW YORK

Copyright © 2015 by Brian Thiem

Published in the United States by Crooked Lane Books, an imprint of The Quick Brown Fox & Company LLC.

Crooked Lane Books and its logo are trademarks of The Quick Brown Fox & Company LLC.

The Library of Congress Cataloging-in-Publication Data is available upon request.

ISBN (hardcover): 978-1-62953-194-6
ISBN (paperback): 978-1-62953-373-5
e-ISBN: 978-1-62953-207-3

Cover/book design by Jennifer Canzone

Printed in the United States.

www.crookedlanebooks.com

Crooked Lane Books
2 Park Avenue, 10th Floor
New York, NY 10016

First Edition: August 2015

10 9 8 7 6 5 4 3 2 1

Chapter 1

The man heard a gasp from the backseat as he turned onto Fifty-Second Street. The girl named Samantha opened her eyes in a sudden panic. The eyes of the other girl in the backseat darted back and forth several times, as if she were trying to figure out where she was.

The man slowed the Cadillac Escalade at the parking lot of the emergency room. The lot was empty except for an ambulance, its back doors open toward the building. He spotted a camera and then a second one pointing downward, covering the parking lot and the wide glass doors that opened into the ER.

He jabbed the brake and stopped.

A uniformed security guard sat inside at a small desk. The man backed into the empty street and continued to the traffic light at Martin Luther King Jr. Way. A wide grass median divided the six-lane thoroughfare into northbound and southbound lanes. Above, the elevated tracks for BART rested on huge concrete pedestals that looked like giant gray mushrooms in the fog that rolled in nightly from the San Francisco Bay. Traffic was light. The digital clock on his dash read 4:02.

He turned right and stopped at the bus stop just north of the corner. A Plexiglas shelter covered the bus bench. He climbed out of the driver's seat and jogged around the front of the SUV to the passenger side, opened the back door and lifted the older girl, Jenny, from the car seat, wrapping his arm around her to hold her up, and placed her on the ground. He shuffled her to the bench and sat her down, then returned to the car and brought Samantha to the bench in the same manner. Samantha leaned against her friend, resting her head on the other girl's shoulder, her eyes locked open in a zombie-like stare.

The man slipped Samantha's cell phone out of her clutch purse and turned it on. He scrolled to *Mom* and pressed the number.

"Sam, where have you been? You've had me so worried."

He spoke slowly. "Ma'am, Samantha is with a friend named Jenny. They can't talk right now, but they need your help."

"Who is this? Is this some kind of joke?"

"Please listen carefully. The girls have taken some drugs and need to go to the hospital. Get something to write with and I'll tell you where they are."

"Who is this?" she demanded.

When he didn't reply, her voice softened. "Okay, I have a pen."

"Outside Children's Hospital in Oakland, at a bus bench on Martin Luther King Way, just up from Fifty-Second Street. If you can't get here fast, you might want to call the hospital and have them pick up the girls."

"I got it. Now, who is this?"

"A friend."

He pressed the end button, wiped the phone on his jacket lining, and returned it to Samantha's handbag. He scanned the area to ensure no one was watching. A car zipped by without slowing, and the driver didn't look his way.

"Girls, stay here," he said. "Your parents are on the way."

Samantha seemed to focus on him for a second, but then her eyes resumed their distant, Rohypnol stare.

He drove a block up the street and pulled to the curb. In his rearview mirror, he saw one of the girls poke her head out of the front of the shelter.

"Go back and sit down," he said under his breath.

She stood, looked straight ahead, and wobbled onto the sidewalk. She paused at the curb, and then stumbled, straight-legged into the street.

"No, no," he muttered.

A pair of headlights in his mirror grew larger, and car tires screeched on the asphalt. Then he heard the thud.

He jumped out of his SUV. The car stopped and two people got out. They bent over the form in the street. One yelled something. Seconds later, people dressed in blue, pink, and green hospital scrubs ran toward the accident.

He climbed into the Cadillac and drove off.

Chapter 2

Thirteen Months Later

Sergeant Matt Sinclair parked his unmarked Crown Vic behind the line of black-and-white Oakland PD cars. He stepped out of the car, swept his black suit coat back with his right hand to keep it from hanging up on the Sig Sauer .45 worn in a holster on his belt, and stood there, taking it all in.

A dozen uniformed officers occupied the street and sidewalk in front of him, some talking with citizens and others huddled in groups of two or three, pens and aluminum clipboards in hand. Sinclair glanced at his watch on his left wrist, slid a yellow pad from his folio, and wrote, *0552—Arrived at scene. Cool, clear/fog, dry, dark—but full moon, street lighting.* He took a deep breath, tried to relax the knot in his stomach, and then strode toward the uniforms.

A heavyset man with sergeant stripes on his sleeves hurried toward him. His bald head glistened under the streetlights. "Matt, good to see you back in a coat and tie," Jim Clancy said.

"Good to be back," said Sinclair. "How many more days to go?"

"Three months, eight days, two hours—but who's counting."

"Not gonna stick it out for thirty?"

"The day I turn fifty, I'm outta here. Twenty-six is plenty. What about you?"

"Shit, Jim, I got fourteen years 'til I hit the big five-oh."

"Fourteen years—assholes don't get that much time for murder."

Sinclair raised his notebook and prepared to write. "Did you drag me out of bed at oh-dark-thirty just to bust my balls?"

Clancy pulled a stack of assignment cards from his back pocket and looked at the notes he had scratched on the back of the cards. "An X-ray tech from Children's is walking to the parking garage after an overtime shift and sees a kid slumped on the bus bench. Thought it didn't look right. You know, white kid, not dressed like he belongs in Oaktown after dark. Calls to him, shakes him, gets no response, so he calls nine-one-one as well as a nurse buddy in the ER. We get the call at zero-four-fifty-eight. First unit arrives the same time as paramedics at five-oh-four. I get here about ten minutes later. They pronounce him at the scene. Body was cold. Paramedics figure he'd been dead at least an hour."

Sinclair looked up from his notepad. "Are you leaving out the obvious just to fuck with me?"

"No apparent cause of death—no GSW, no stab wounds, no obvious trauma. Don't even know it's a homicide. Right now, we're writing it up as an SC Unexplained Death."

"Great," said Sinclair.

He preferred callouts where the bodies were peppered with a half-dozen gunshot wounds to SC, or "suspicious circumstance," deaths. These they had to handle like homicides, which they sometimes turned out to be, but just as often, after spinning his wheels and wasting days of work, he'd get a call from the coroner saying the death was natural or accidental.

Clancy put his notes away. "We called homicide because someone tied the kid's wrists and ankles together with flex-cuffs. Come on, I'll show you."

Cars containing early morning commuters slowed to check out the activity and then sped off. The eyes of every officer followed Sinclair. He was an average-sized cop. Six feet tall, with a slender, athletic build. This used to be one of his favorite moments, like walking the red carpet. He remembered his first homicide scene as a young patrol officer thirteen years ago—street people yelling, friends and family of the victim wailing, suspects in the rear of marked cars pounding on the windows. Then two homicide sergeants pulled up—older men, nearly his father's age, dressed in dark suits and starched white shirts. They walked with a bit of a swagger, and their faces showed not a trace of worry, the sense that they had absolutely no doubt they would solve the case. At that moment, Sinclair knew he wanted to work homicide, to feel that confidence, to inspire that sort of respect, admiration, and awe.

Today, Sinclair felt like running back to his car and driving as far away as possible. What was he thinking when he'd asked to return to the unit? Was he fooling himself that he could go back as if the past year never occurred? He hoped the officers at the scene couldn't sense his anxiety. Cops could detect fear in people the way dogs did.

An officer raised the yellow tape, and Sinclair slipped underneath. The Plexiglas bus shelter was ten feet long and open to the street. It sat six feet back from MLK Way and a hundred feet north of Fifty-Second Street. A green metal bench filled half the enclosure. Behind the bus stop, a gray multistory parking garage for Children's Hospital took up most of the block.

Sinclair surveyed the concrete in front of him to make sure he didn't trample on any evidence and stepped into the shelter. The bus schedule was on one wall: Route 18, last bus at 11:32 p.m., first one at 6:28 a.m. A milk ad, *Help Me Drink Healthy*, hung beside it.

The victim was slumped sideways on the seat, his head resting against the side wall of the shelter. Sinclair tried to recall the position of the rape victim who'd been left on the same bench last summer. Arquette, Samantha, female, white, fourteen. Coincidence? Maybe, but the details of that investigation were lost somewhere in the fog of booze that surrounded him back then.

This boy was young, smooth-faced, wearing a black Stanford University T-shirt, blue jeans, and white sneakers. He looked to be about the same age as the older of the two girls from last summer.

"Little cool to be wearing just a T-shirt," said Sinclair.

"Sure is. It was already down in the fifties when I came on at eleven," said Clancy. "A lot warmer on the other side of the hills, though."

Sinclair leaned toward the body. "The flex-cuffs the department issues are a lot thicker than these things on his wrists. These look like electrical cable ties, like what you buy at a hardware store. We got an ID on him?"

"We didn't want to search the body until the coroner got here, but I had YSD check missing persons," said Clancy, referring to the youth services division. "He fits the physical—same clothing too—of a seventeen-year-old juvenile missing from Danville since about midnight. Danville

PD faxed the report and photo to us, and I got an officer en route to pick them up."

Too many patrol sergeants, especially the younger ones, thought simple tasks, like having YSD check the state missing persons system, was something only detectives could do. Clancy was old school and did whatever was needed to get the job done. "You got a tech and coroner on the way?" Sinclair asked.

"The tech is up the street scouring for evidence. Should be back in a minute, and I was waiting for your okay before calling the coroner."

"Do it," said Sinclair.

Clancy pulled out his cell phone, and Sinclair returned to his scene notes as a familiar voice behind him chirped, "Good morning, Sergeant Sinclair. We've missed you on these scenes."

Without turning, he replied, "Hey, Joyce, how's my favorite tech?"

Short, squat, and with bleached-blonde hair, Joyce Talbert looked nothing like the tall, leggy CSIs on TV, and although she had plenty of seniority to work the day shift, she had worked as a civilian crime scene technician for fifteen years on the midnight shift by choice.

"I wish I had something for you, but I haven't found any evidence to point to a suspect. I snapped loads of photos of the vic and the scene. I'll print the Plexiglas around the body. Maybe we'll get lucky and our killer leaned against it and left a perfect palm print."

"We can dream," said Sinclair.

"I'll go through the trash before I leave and see if there's anything interesting." She nodded at a green metal trashcan just south of the bus stop.

"Just in case our man left a beer can in there with his prints on it or a Kleenex with his DNA?" Sinclair said.

"Right, and when I find it, I'm sure the lab will have your suspect's name before lunch."

With the criminalistics section's backlog of DNA cases, Sinclair knew that even if they were fortunate enough to find DNA evidence, they'd be lucky to get results in a month. "Any profound insights?"

"Me? You're the legendary homicide detective," she said, a grin spreading across her face.

The legend Sinclair once was had begun dissolving four years ago in the streets of Baghdad and Fallujah. The military had called him back to active duty with the Army Criminal Investigation Command. A year later, he returned to homicide a changed man. The department welcomed him home as a war hero, but he didn't see it that way. The values of duty, honor, and country, which the Army had instilled in him years ago, seemed quaint and idealistic. His wife saw his change—mood swings, sleep problems, hypervigilance—yet stuck by him as long as she could. When she suggested he get help, he insisted there was nothing wrong with *him* and packed his stuff and moved out. Six months later, she filed for divorce. He didn't care. He stopped caring about everything last year after he killed a murder suspect he chased into an abandoned house when he should have waited for back up. Once he stopped caring, it was easier to justify hitting the bar instead of working his cases, easier to jump in his car when he was so drunk he could hardly walk.

As Sinclair scanned the faces of the uniforms at the crime scene, he knew everyone welcomed him back with no ill feelings. Maybe he was the only person he needed to seek forgiveness from.

Clancy ducked back under the crime scene tape and announced, "Coroner's ETA is ten minutes. We're still holding onto the X-ray tech who found the vic. You wanna talk to him?"

Sinclair skimmed the handwritten statement taken by one of the officers. He didn't know anything more. "No, let him go."

"We've pretty much finished the canvass of the area. The only open business nearby is the hospital, and we talked to the folks in the ER and security. The people in the houses down the street were asleep and saw nothing."

A tall, lean officer made his way toward Clancy and handed him some papers. Clancy paged through the missing person report to a photocopied picture and held it alongside the victim's face. "Well, at least we know who our victim is."

Sinclair shuffled to the back of the taped-in crime scene area to get out of the commotion and read the report: *Missing Person: Caldwell, Zachary W., male, white, 17, 5'11", 145, blond, blue. Last seen by his parents at 2030 hours when he left his house to meet some friends for coffee. His school night curfew was 2200, and according to his mother, he was never late. His mother, Brenda Caldwell, called the Danville Police at 2230 when he didn't come home or answer his cell. Brenda called the police again at 2400 when Zachary had not yet returned, and they dispatched an officer to take a report.*

The Danville officer had met with Brenda and Zachary's father, Paul Caldwell, at their residence. Brenda's occupation was listed as homemaker, and Paul was a surgeon at Oakland Children's Hospital. The parents described Zachary as a straight-A student who never drank or used drugs. He was also a school athlete—lacrosse, swimming, and golf. He never missed curfew on weekends, when he was allowed out until midnight, and they said there were no indications of any personal issues that would prompt Zachary to run away. The report listed three boys who met him at Starbucks, but all three said he left alone at about 2145 to return home. Officers searched the area around Starbucks and found Zachary's car, a black 2010 BMW 328i convertible, parked on a side street a block away.

Sinclair got the Danville watch commander's number from the YSD desk officer and punched the numbers into his cell phone. "Your missing person's report says you guys found the BMW. What did you do with it?"

"Nothing so far," replied the watch commander.

"I need you to tow it with a hold for OPD and search the area between where it's parked and Starbucks."

"Search for what? Did you find our missing juvenile?"

"Yeah, we found him."

"Dead?"

"Yeah, dumped in our city but probably killed elsewhere, so look for any evidence that might relate to an abduction or homicide."

"Nothing good ever happens when I talk to you fellas in Oakland," the Danville officer said. "Whenever one of our citizens ends up in your city, they're raped, robbed, or shot."

"Job security," said Sinclair. "Do me a favor and keep this quiet. I want to be the one to tell his parents."

"You think they did it?"

"Wouldn't be the first time," said Sinclair.

Chapter 3

The sky was beginning to turn light and overpower the yellow sodium-vapor streetlights when an attractive woman in civilian clothes made her way through the uniforms toward Sinclair. Sinclair remembered the first time he saw Cathy Braddock. He was a rookie, starting his tour of duty on the night shift. A hard-bodied young officer right out of the academy, wearing a pair of tight jeans and a revealing tank top, caught his attention as she walked out of the locker room at the end of her shift. He was admiring her backside when a veteran cop poked him in the ribs. "Tread lightly, kid. Her father and grandfather were both Oakland cops. That makes her part of the family, not some tossup for you to add to your list of conquests."

Since then, Braddock had added a husband, two kids, and twenty pounds as she worked her way from patrol to sexual assault and finally to homicide, where she took Sinclair's slot when he was kicked out of the unit six months ago. A plastic clip contained her thick, chestnut-colored hair, and her only makeup was pink lip gloss. The jacket of her brown pantsuit was at least a size too large but still couldn't conceal the bulge from the Glock on her right hip.

"Sorry I'm late," she said. "Phil told me you'd always beat me to the scene."

When Sinclair transferred to homicide five years ago, Phil Roberts was his training officer. They remained partners until Sinclair was demoted, at which time Phil became Braddock's trainer and partner. When Sinclair returned to homicide, Phil transferred to the intelligence unit, and that left Sinclair as the senior partner of the team and Braddock's training officer for the remainder of her yearlong probation. Sinclair missed Phil. They had the best clearance rate in the unit, solving 80 percent of their cases. Now he was stuck with training a rookie homicide detective.

Sinclair looked at his watch. "The one-hour rule is the outside limit. Good detectives make it to the scene a lot quicker."

When Sinclair was new in homicide, he would have slept in his clothes if that was what it took to get to a scene before his training officer.

"Understood. I'll do better next time," she said, biting her lip.

He briefed her on the scene and then said, "I'll be the primary on this one—just shadow me and follow my lead."

"This isn't my first dead body."

"It's your first with me. I'll give you more leeway when I think you're ready. Besides, I haven't had a fresh case in six months, and I don't want the guys to think I'm dumping a shit case on my rookie partner."

A large van with the sheriff's department seal on the sides crept toward the scene. "Here comes the meat wagon," said Sinclair.

Two older men stepped out. They wore rumpled sport coats and ties a decade out of style. Their title was coroner's investigator, but to the police, they were little more than body snatchers. The forensic pathologists, the medical doctors who did the autopsies, rarely left the morgue.

Charlie Dawson smiled broadly as he approached. "Sergeant Sinclair, I heard you were back."

"Charlie, have you met my new partner, Cathy Braddock?"

Braddock extended her right hand. Sinclair reached out and pushed it back down.

"Nice to meet you, Sergeant." Dawson made no attempt to shake hands. "You're a lot better looking than the other homicide dicks."

"Watch him. He's a dirty old man," said Sinclair, winking at Dawson.

As Dawson's partner set up the gurney and body bag, Dawson and Sinclair traded information, each of them scribbling notes in their respective notebooks. "I'll handle the next of kin notification on this one," said Sinclair.

"You hate the sobbing and *Oh Lordy, Oh Lordy* wailing," Dawson said.

"Yeah, well, this kid ain't your average dope-dealing, parolee murder victim. His suburban mom and dad might know something and actually believe talking to the police isn't taboo."

"Doc Gorman's already got two bodies waiting, so he probably won't get to this one until late morning," said Dawson.

"Call me when he's ready to start."

The body snatchers gloved up and approached the bench. Talbert stood to the side, snapping photos with her Nikon. A uniformed officer stood to the other side and took notes. Sergeant Clancy stood in the back watching.

Braddock fished a pair of latex gloves from her pocket, pulled them on, and then handed another pair to Sinclair.

"I don't plan on touching anything," Sinclair said without looking at her.

She put them back into her pocket and moved in to get a better view.

Dawson and his partner lifted the body and laid it on a white sheet spread on the sidewalk. As they did, the body released a pungent odor, and Sinclair heard Braddock catch her gag with a soft groan. The putrid smells—body gasses, feces, urine—filled the air, but Sinclair had long ago become accustomed to the smell of death.

Dawson went through the kid's pockets, dropping items into a plastic bag: key ring, cell phone, loose change, and wallet. He ran his hands over the victim's clothes. "No rings, no watch," he said. He removed a necklace with a shiny pendant from the kid's neck. "Medallion on neck chain," he said, dropping it in the bag.

Dawson lifted the victim's shirt and did a cursory look. "Let's roll him," he said. His partner grabbed an arm and pulled the body onto its side. Sinclair remembered a homicide a few years ago, when they were baffled as to the cause of death until the coroner rolled the body and pointed out a tiny, nearly bloodless entrance wound in his back. The autopsy showed a .25 caliber bullet embedded in his heart and the entire thoracic cavity filled with blood. However, this body had no such wounds.

They grabbed the corners of the sheet and lifted the victim into a body bag and onto the gurney. Dawson announced, "No rigor, so probably been dead less than four to six hours." As they tucked the arms into the bag, Dawson looked up. "Sergeant Sinclair, look here."

Sinclair looked at the crook of the right arm and saw several purple bruises and a series of fresh injection marks spotted with dried blood. "Danville boy turns into a junkie for a day," Sinclair said but not believing it.

"The doc'll have to say for sure, but these bruises seem consistent with someone tightly gripping his arm," said Dawson. "You can almost make out where the fingers pressed into the flesh. And whoever was working the needle wasn't very good at it. Looks like he missed the vein a bunch a times. Accidental OD?"

"Hands and legs bound, arm grabbed tightly, syringe jabbed and missed before it got the vein," Sinclair said, thinking aloud. "If drugs killed him, I don't think the kid did it voluntarily."

Dawson zipped the body bag and wheeled the gurney to his van. Sinclair reached into his coat pocket and pulled out an inexpensive cigar. He clipped the end of the Dominican corona and lit it with an old Zippo lighter he'd bought years ago in a dust-filled Army PX tent in Baghdad.

Braddock shot him a look. "Isn't smoking at a crime scene a no-no?"

Sinclair glared back at her. "And why is that, Sergeant Braddock?"

"Because it could contaminate the scene," she answered.

A BART train clattered along the elevated track above him, carrying business-suited workers from the East Bay suburbs to San Francisco offices. Once it passed, he said, "Yes, I'm sure a cigar ash on the sidewalk will contaminate the scene." He continued to meet her eyes. When she looked away, he continued. "The other reason cops and *new* detectives are told not to eat, drink, or smoke at a crime scene is so they don't transfer some contaminant, such as blood, from their hands to their mouths. You probably noted that I didn't touch anything out here and sure as hell didn't shake hands with a coroner investigator, whose hands have been who-the-fuck-knows-where."

The tightness had returned to his stomach. He knew he shouldn't take it out on Braddock, but having to work with her pissed him off. He needed to ease back into the job. Pick up a few easy cases. Keep a low profile for a while. Not have to worry about and carry a rookie.

Sinclair left her standing there and ambled up the street to a cluster of three officers. After chatting with them for a while, he visited a cop who was sitting in a car writing his report and another who was directing cars and pedestrians around the scene. Phil had taught him the value of walking around and being accessible to the uniforms. Occasionally one would say, "I didn't put it in my report because I didn't think it was important, but—" and then provide a tidbit that proved invaluable. Besides, Sinclair enjoyed talking with the street cops. Although he was a sergeant, he still thought of himself as one of them.

Sinclair finished his stroll just as the sun broke over the horizon, an orange glow through the fog that still hung thick over the San Francisco Bay and downtown Oakland. This wasn't the kind of case he needed his second day back in the unit. The old Sinclair would have relished the challenge, but with all he'd been through, he would have preferred a simple domestic homicide—a mom-and-pop, as they called them—with the wife dead at the scene and the husband sitting in the kitchen crying when officers arrived. Or maybe a gang drive-by. Even if there were no leads on it, a week later, no one would care. This one was going to require work and skill.

"Officer Ramirez is the RO on this," said Braddock, identifying him as the reporting officer, the patrol officer responsible for writing the crime report. "I told him to get a supplemental report from everyone on the scene, then head downtown and get started on his report."

"And don't leave until Sergeant Braddock or I review it," Sinclair said to Ramirez.

"Yes, sir," Ramirez said. After a pause, he asked, "Any theories, Sarge?"

"Do I look like Sherlock Holmes?" said Sinclair. "Detectives that come up with theories before collecting the facts often end up going down the wrong path."

Sinclair took several puffs on his cigar. He didn't know enough to come up with a theory yet, but he didn't believe in coincidences. There had to be a connection to the two girls from last summer. He'd seen victims killed in the same locations before, usually a drug corner, where bodies from warring narcotics gangs littered the streets for weeks until eventually the police locked up the shooters or one side wiped out the other. He wondered if this kid was the one who raped Samantha Arquette or if his death was retaliation, like he'd seen in drug turf wars. Or maybe he and the girls were friends, and the same suspect was responsible for both crimes. Too many possibilities this early.

Sinclair met Ramirez's stare. "All I do at this stage is observe and collect information. It's not glamorous or exciting. So to answer your question—I have no idea who killed this kid or why—but I sure as hell intend to find out."

Sinclair strode to his car, and Braddock scurried to catch up. "Leave your car here and ride with me," he said.

"Where're we going?"

"To tell the mom and dad the bad news and see how they react."

Chapter 4

Braddock climbed into the passenger seat, her arms filled with a briefcase, handbag, and notebook. Sinclair accelerated off before she closed the door. She swung her briefcase into the backseat, buckled her seatbelt, and stared at Sinclair.

"Thanks for making me look stupid back there."

"Act like a homicide detective and I'll treat you like one." Sinclair weaved through the city streets to the freeway onramp.

"Like you—a friggin' ass?"

"If you're gonna work homicide, you have to learn to say fuck."

"I can say fuck when it's necessary."

"Good for you," said Sinclair, unable to prevent himself from grinning.

"Don't give me that condescending crap."

"Shit," Sinclair corrected.

"So that's the first lesson from my new training officer, how to say shit and fuck."

"You're learning."

"I didn't ask for this either," she said. "I was quite happy working with Phil."

"Phil was *my* partner long before anyone considered you for homicide."

"You left. That's not my fault."

Sinclair hadn't found out Phil was gone until he stepped into the office yesterday. Braddock was junior. They should've transferred her when Sinclair returned to the unit. Instead, they offered Phil a plum assignment in intelligence. Maybe what really burned him was Phil accepting the transfer. Phil said he needed a change. Homicide had worn him down. Lieutenant Maloney could've shuffled the teams and let Sinclair work with one of the other guys. Sinclair wondered if the lieutenant had asked, and no one wanted to partner with him.

"The chief's looking for a reason to strip me of my stripes permanently. I know that." Sinclair merged into the morning commute traffic on the 24 Freeway. "Instead of getting a partner like Phil, who could maybe keep me from stepping on my dick, I get stuck with someone who *I* need to watch over to keep her from stepping on her . . ."

"Real cute, Matt."

Sinclair smiled. "I'll try not to embarrass you in front of the other cops."

"I'm not a bad cop, you know."

Sinclair knew Braddock's reputation was that of a damn good cop. She was in the academy class after his and spent her first seven years in uniform. She worked the toughest parts of town and never let her gender or size stop her from handling every call on her beat or making her share of arrests. Whenever another officer called for assistance, she was one of the first to arrive and jump into the fray, even when the assholes were twice her size. After patrol, she worked as an investigator in the Sexual Assault Unit and as a supervisor when she made sergeant. She was known to be damn good at it, so when the slot opened in homicide, she was the top candidate.

"Call Danville, tell them we're on our way. And run the parents. They're probably clean, but you never know."

While Braddock made the calls, Sinclair pulled his cell phone off his belt and made the required notifications to the homicide lieutenant and the police chief's chief of staff. He gave both the same rundown, both asked the same questions, and he gave both the same responses. "No, we have no suspects at this time," and "No, we don't know what the motive is."

Sinclair's phone clicked while he was making the notifications. One voicemail: Liz. His relationship with Elizabeth Schueller, a reporter for Channel 6 News, had started six months ago when she was after the inside scoop on a high-profile murder he was working and invited him out for a drink. He agreed—what man wouldn't? She was the most beautiful television personality in the Bay Area. Everyone knew Liz flirted with cops and prosecutors over drinks to get a story, but she was known as a tease—nothing more. After a half-dozen drinks, Liz invited him back to her place, and they had been together—if you could call it that—ever since.

Sinclair saw Braddock was listening to someone on her phone and taking notes. He pressed the button for Liz's cell phone.

"Hey, Matt, I'm lying here in bed, curled up with your pillow between my legs."

"I'll be here for a while. Looks like a homicide."

"Typical Oakland murder or one my viewers would be interested in?"

"Victim's a righteous citizen. My partner and I are driving out to Danville to interview the parents right now."

"So you can't talk now, huh?"

"Right."

"Call me later with the inside scoop. Love ya."

As Sinclair returned his cell phone to its belt case, Braddock looked up from her notebook.

"So, you're still doing the sexy Channel Six reporter."

Sinclair glared at Braddock. Very intuitive for hearing only half of the conversation, he thought.

"She's gorgeous. Heck, if I wasn't a happily married woman, I could be attracted to her myself."

Sinclair rolled his eyes and then glanced at Braddock to see if she was serious.

She giggled. "Gotcha."

Chapter 5

Sinclair got off the freeway at Camino Tassajara Road and drove west toward Blackhawk. In 1975, a land developer named Ken Behring had bought the former 4,200-acre horse ranch and began building houses and the exclusive Blackhawk Country Club. Eventually, about 2,000 houses were built, including many large estates, one of which was the 28,000-square-foot Behring estate. During the 1990s, the overnight millionaires from the technology boom snapped up the lesser estates, the "McMansions," as fast as they could be built.

Braddock juggled two phones and a notepad on her lap as she spoke. "Brenda Caldwell has no rap sheet and her CDL is clear, not even a ticket in the last five years. Paul is clean too. His bio on the Children's Hospital website says he's board certified in neurological surgery, med school at USC, did his residency at Mass General in Boston. He was on the staff at Children's Hospital in Philadelphia until he came to Oakland in 2007. I found his house online. Four bedrooms, three and a half baths, four thousand square feet. It sold in 1997 for seven hundred thousand, and last sold in May 2007 for two point one million. That must be when the Caldwells bought it."

When Sinclair had worked with Phil, any information they needed beyond what existed in law enforcement systems or what they could get with a phone call waited until they returned to their desks.

"What kind of phone is that?"

"You're kidding, right?"

Sinclair took a closer look at her phone. "I'm not a total dinosaur. Lots of crooks have iPhones, so I know how they work, but the department issues—"

"That archaic phone that can survive an earthquake but can't do much more than call and text. Is that really your only phone?"

"It's worked out so far."

Sinclair flashed his badge, and the guard at the security shack waved them through. He parked behind a marked Danville car, and a female officer immediately exited and approached. "My sergeant told me to stand by and assist you any way I can."

"Wait here. If we need you, we'll call," said Sinclair.

Braddock said something to the female officer then scurried to catch up. "People said you became less of an asshole when you quit drinking, but I'm not so sure."

"Huh?"

"Out here, they don't have murders every day, so this is a big deal. You dismissed her like she was a meter maid."

"I'm here to investigate a murder, not nurture some Mayberry cop's self-esteem."

"Ever think someday we might need the local's help?"

"I sure hope not."

The brick walkway traversed a perfectly manicured lawn and ended at an immense oak door. Sinclair pressed the doorbell and heard a musical tone—probably something by Bach—echo throughout the house. He ran his hand through his hair and straightened his tie. The door opened, and a slim man wearing glasses and a dress shirt with the top two buttons undone stood there.

Sinclair swept back the corner of his suit coat to reveal the badge clipped to his belt. "Dr. Caldwell, we're with the police department. My name's Sergeant Sinclair. This is my partner, Sergeant Braddock."

Sinclair intentionally avoided mentioning Oakland or homicide. He'd let them think they were still investigating a missing juvenile.

"Have you found my son?" His eyes were bloodshot. Sinclair sensed worry and a sleepless night.

"May we come in?"

The doctor led the way across a marble-floored foyer with a soaring staircase, past a formal living room and dining room. Neither seemed to get much use. A great room took up the back of the house, sofas and coordinated chairs surrounding a TV and fireplace on one side and a large kitchen with the requisite granite countertops and stainless steel appliances on the other.

A plump woman wearing black leggings and an oversized T-shirt sat at a round table that matched the maple kitchen cabinets. The report said Brenda was forty-two. She still had a pretty face, but Sinclair suspected she was slimmer when she snagged the doctor and got pregnant with Zachary. In front of her was a coffee mug and a pile of used tissues, many with black streaks from her mascara.

"Would you officers like some coffee?" she asked.

"That would be nice," said Sinclair. Had she not offered, Sinclair would have requested coffee to give her something to do, something that would shake up her display of grief—real or rehearsed. She poured two mugs and set out a container of half-and-half and a canister filled with packets of white, pink, blue, and yellow sweeteners. Sinclair sat down with his black coffee while Braddock fiddled with cream and sugar.

For homicide investigators, the next-of-kin notification was secondary to their investigation. Sinclair needed to rule the parents out as suspects and gather as much information as possible before they were overcome with the shock of their loss. He jumped in.

"Have you heard from any of his friends or anyone at all since you made the report at midnight?" Sinclair asked.

"No," replied the doctor. Brenda shook her head.

Sinclair focused on Dr. Caldwell, watching every microexpression in his face. He glanced at Braddock, pleased she was doing the same with the wife.

"Does he have any friends in Oakland? Any reason he'd go there at night?"

"None that I know of and certainly not after dark," said Dr. Caldwell. "Why do you ask?"

"Did you have a fight with Zachary or did he do anything that required you to discipline him recently?"

The doctor looked bewildered and turned to Brenda. She said, "No, Zack is a perfect son."

Sinclair continued to focus on the father. "Dr. Caldwell?"

"I'm not home as much as my wife, but the answer's no. I never have to push him—he's self-motivated." His eyes darted to Braddock, then back to Sinclair. "Are you suggesting that our son ran away because of something we did?"

Sinclair sensed anger or maybe just indignation in Dr. Caldwell's response. He ignored it.

"I'm not judging here, but I need to ask—does Zachary have any friends who are into drugs or the fast life?"

The doctor's face relaxed. "No, Zack associates with other kids like him. Good kids. If he were into drugs, I'd know."

Sinclair had heard all parents say that. They're the last to know.

"Is there any reason for your son to be in Oakland—say around Children's Hospital?"

Dr. Caldwell's face twisted—surprised or perplexed. "You know that's where I work. I'm a physician—a surgeon. What exactly is going on?"

There was no right reaction for parents when learning of their child's death. Some burst into tears, some threw things, some attacked the person doing the notification, and some sat there stoically and without a trace of emotion. No particular response indicated guilt or innocence. Sinclair had learned to trust his instincts, which he found more reliable than a polygraph machine.

"I'm sorry I had to ask these questions." He pulled two business cards from his shirt pocket and slid them across the table to Zachary's parents, carefully studying their faces. "My partner and I are with the Oakland Police Department—Homicide. I'm very sorry to inform you . . ."

The coffee mug slipped from Brenda's hand onto the table with a clunk. She grabbed at it and knocked it to the tile floor where it exploded in a hundred pieces. She pushed back her chair and jumped up.

Braddock put her hand on Brenda's shoulder and gently pushed her back into her chair. "Let me take care of it."

Dr. Caldwell took a deep breath. "Zachary's dead?"

Sinclair nodded. "I'm sorry."

Braddock grabbed a roll of paper towels off the kitchen counter, tore off a handful of pieces, and began sopping up the coffee on the table. Then she squatted and swept the pieces of broken cup into a pile.

"How?" Dr. Caldwell asked in a steady voice.

"We don't know yet, but we're treating it as a homicide."

Brenda grasped Dr. Caldwell's right hand with both of hers. "You mean he was murdered?" She fought back tears.

"We believe so," said Sinclair.

Dr. Caldwell slid his chair toward his wife and put his arm around her. She buried her head into his chest and sobbed.

Chapter 6

Sinclair parked in one of the two slots reserved for the homicide standby team in front of the Police Administration Building, a nine-story rectangular building of glass and steel. When the PAB opened in 1962, on the edge of what was then skid row a half mile from the center of Oakland's downtown, the modern, sleek, and clean police station was the anchor for the area's renewal. Although the building suffered major damage during the Loma Prieta earthquake in 1989, and engineers determined it should be demolished and rebuilt, City Hall could never come to a decision to allocate the money. More than two decades later, with a minor retrofit, the building still housed most of the department's officers and civilians, all of whom prayed they wouldn't be inside when the next big one hit the Bay Area.

As Sinclair slammed his door, Braddock pulled her car into the space behind him. Sinclair had wanted to leave the Caldwells' house immediately after he broke the news to them, letting the Danville officer handle the emotional aftermath. However, Braddock quietly took the lead, and after thirty minutes of consoling words and gentle pats on their arms, she received Zachary's laptop computer, an index card containing his passwords, a list of his closest friends, and an assurance they would call her if they heard anything useful. Sinclair kept his mouth shut and stayed out of Braddock's way.

The homicide office was on the second floor. A side door at the top of a flight of stairs led from the street to the back hallway of the Criminal Investigation Division and into homicide. The walls were painted a shade of blue that psychologists in the 1970s thought promoted calm and tranquility, although it never seemed to work for Sinclair. A few years ago, pipes in the ceiling had burst and flooded the room with water and sewage, destroying everything except for their files, which officers were able to salvage. City workers brought the grey metal desks and file cabinets that had graced the PAB's offices for its first fifty years back out of storage. In between the new ceiling panels and florescent lights above and the new floor below, the office looked little different from what it did in the sixties.

Sinclair swept into the office and halted at Connie Williams's desk. "Will you hold, please?" she said into her phone, then handed him a stack of pink memos. Connie was a stout woman with straightened black hair, a copper-colored complexion, and full lips. "Eight messages, the first one's urgent."

"When're you gonna leave that old goat you're married to?"

"Honey, it's taken me forty years to train him. Besides, you like them skinny girls. I'd surely be too much woman for you."

Connie had been hired by the city at a time when they were still called clerk typists and had been the homicide admin for thirty years. Sinclair grinned. "I'd be willing to try."

"I transferred your phone line to me, so let me know if you want it back," she said to Sinclair. Then she punched the flashing button on her phone. "Sorry for the wait, so how may I help you?"

Sinclair continued past the seven empty desks belonging to the homicide suppression team and caught the lieutenant's eye as he passed his office door. "I'll be right in, Lieutenant," he said. Four of the other eight homicide investigators assigned to the unit sat at their desks. Their eyes followed Sinclair as he dropped his briefcase on his desk.

"Seventeen-year-old boy from Danville, dead on a bus bench at Fifty-Second and MLK, hands and feet bound, no gunshot or stab wounds," Sinclair announced to satisfy them.

Sinclair filled his dark blue coffee mug, an outline of a dead body printed on one side and "Homicide: Our Day Begins When Someone Else's Ends" on the other, and headed to the lieutenant's office. Seated in the glass-walled office behind a gray metal desk twice the size of Sinclair's was a flabby man in his late forties with thinning hair. Carl Maloney's sole investigative experience had been working Internal Affairs, so when he was given the coveted homicide commander position, everyone knew it was a reward for his loyalty to the chief. Nevertheless, Sinclair liked him because Maloney didn't pretend to know anything about homicide investigations and seldom told his people how to do their jobs.

Sinclair eased into a vinyl-covered chair in front of Maloney's desk. "We talked to the parents," he said. Braddock slipped into the chair next to him. "According to them, the kid's an angel. We stopped at the Starbucks where the kid left his car last night and talked with the Danville cops. So far, they got nothing. We figure the vic either left there with someone willingly and things later went bad, or someone snatched him."

"What makes it a homicide?"

Sinclair knew that people at City Hall and the chief's office wanted someone to blame every time another homicide number was added to the yearly tally, and as the messenger, the homicide lieutenant was often that person. Sinclair explained the bruising, needle marks, and attire. "The boy had no prior drug use. Hands and legs zip-tied."

Maloney looked past them for a moment. "Let's wait until we see the autopsy. The chief's office is getting questions already from the head of the hospital's department of medicine, so keep me apprised."

Sinclair got up and took a step to the door as Maloney added, "Have you finished your press release?"

"I haven't even sat . . ."

"I'm not about to tell you who you can date, but it created problems during your previous tour in homicide when Channel Six reported on murders before we even put out a press release." Maloney's chair creaked when he leaned forward. "Let's just say I'd appreciate it if we avoided that problem this time around."

"I'll get it done first thing, Lieutenant."

★

News from the Oakland Police Department

At 0458 hours (4:58 a.m.), Oakland Police officers and emergency medical personnel were dispatched to a report of an unresponsive person on a bus bench in the 5200 block of Martin Luther King Jr. Way. Upon arrival, they discovered a male juvenile with no apparent signs of life. Paramedics pronounced him dead at the scene. The victim, whose name is being withheld pending notification of next of kin, has been identified as a seventeen-year-old Danville resident. There were no visible signs of trauma, and the cause of death will be determined following an autopsy later today by the Alameda County Coroner's Office. Anyone with any information is urged to call Sergeants Sinclair or Braddock of the Oakland Homicide Unit at (510) 238–3821.

Sinclair e-mailed the release to the twenty people on the distribution list and printed three copies. He slid one into his file, dropped one on the lieutenant's desk, and then handed one to Connie and stood next to her as she read it.

"We've already notified the parents, but Danville PD wants time to notify the school so the grief counselors can do their thing," he said.

"The only thing in here that will pique the media's interest is the Danville reference. Other than that, teenage boy found dead in Oakland isn't news. You'll let me know when you release his name or call this a homicide?"

"Sure will."

"And you'll let me know if you want to start talking to the vultures yourself?" Connie said. "And you know I'm not including Ms. Schueller with my reference to reporters being vultures."

"Of course."

"Coroner called a second time. They're starting." Connie returned to a foot-high stack of reports on her desk.

Sinclair walked the two blocks to the county building, buzzed himself in through the main office, and walked down the stairs to a small room that led to the morgue. He pulled a cloth gown over his clothes and donned a paper cap, facemask, glasses, and booties. Then he pushed through the double doors. Despite the powerful ventilation fans that noisily sucked out the air, the smells of formaldehyde, antiseptic, and decaying flesh immediately filled Sinclair's nostrils. New police trainees would sometimes rush back out and vomit the first time they entered the room during the academy, but it took a body that had ripened for several days to bother Sinclair.

Dr. Gorman stood over a naked body laid out on one of the six stainless steel tables. "Good morning, Sergeant Sinclair," said the gray-haired man as he peered over his broad nose through a large magnifying glass. "I see three separate injection sites that apparently entered a vein on the right arm and at least five additional ones that missed the vein. I'll remove and examine this tissue further under the microscope. If you allow me to play detective for a moment, I'll say it would be odd for a right-handed person to inject himself in the right arm."

"How do you know he's right handed?" Sinclair asked.

"Excellent question."

Most pathologists who took up this specialty had difficulty dealing with people and realized a doctor didn't need a bedside manner when his patients were dead. But not Gorman. He was social, had a dry sense of humor, and regularly spoke like a professor. "Our subject's family doctor contacted the office first thing this morning and forwarded his medical file. The subject had a school sports physical a month ago. Neither the subject, in his personal history questionnaire, nor the examining doctor noted any health or medical issues. I personally spoke to the physician, and he doubts the subject had ever used an illegal substance."

"So someone else injected him."

"You will have to figure that out, but permit me to present several observations. If you look here," Gorman said as he cut into a purplish bruise just below the injection marks. "Young, healthy men don't bruise easily. The bruises are shallow, and since they are not well developed, I suspect they were caused close to the time of death. I further suspect the hand that grasped him was quite powerful, probably an adult male."

"Someone held his arm when they shot him up?"

"That would be a reasonable deduction. Look here." Gorman pointed to a spot on the body's right chest where a ruler lay between two marks. "These two abnormalities appear to be abrasions combined with burn marks. In a sense, they are burns. The tissue between the two marks is also disturbed. Are you familiar with electroshock incapacitant devices?"

"You talking about a Taser?"

"Precisely, but these injuries were likely caused by a contact device, commonly referred to as a stun gun. The abrasions are consistent with skin contact by the probes during a brief struggle that probably ensued between your assailant and our deceased. I read a number of medical journal reports around the time of the JonBenét Ramsey incident. Some experts suspected the marks on that little girl's body resulted from a stun gun, which initiated quite a volume of forensic research about them. To incapacitate a person with a stun gun requires maintaining contact between the victim and the charged probes for at least three seconds, maybe longer for a healthy male such as our subject here."

Sinclair had seen dozens of stun guns. Along with tear gas, they were legal for anyone except convicted felons and could be bought at thousands of places around the state. Although Dr. Gorman was probably right about the assailant being a strong male, Sinclair could think of several scenarios where a smaller, weaker person could hold a stun gun to Caldwell for three seconds, so this theory only told him that his suspect was *probably* a relatively strong man—not a hell of a lot to go on.

Sinclair stepped back as Gorman grabbed a scalpel and made a Y-shaped incision across the corpse's chest, another across the top of the chest, and a vertical cut from the neck to the pubic bone. A coroner's assistant stepped in with long-handled pruning shears. Although Sinclair thought of the lifeless forms lying on the autopsy tables as no more human than he thought of a hamburger as a big, brown-eyed cow, the sound of the ribs and breast-bone crunching grated on him like the sound of a drill in a dentist office.

Gorman lifted off the breastplate—the sternum with attached ribs—exposing the thoracic cavity, and scooped out a beaker of blood and divided it between three plastic jars with printed labels. He pulled out the organs one at a time and placed them on a wood cutting board that was resting on the corpse's thighs. He poked, prodded, and sliced each one and finally cut a piece, placed it into another labeled jar, and discarded the organ in a stainless steel pan. He spent more time with the heart, carefully turning it over in his hands and cutting sections away while examining it closely.

"There's no evidence of heart disease or trauma to indicate an immediate cause of death," Gorman said. "My determination will have to wait for the toxicology results."

"Can you rush that? It would be nice to know what killed him."

Gorman plopped the heart into the pan and looked at Sinclair. "I've given you all I can at this time. Toxicology results take up to six weeks for a reason. Very strict protocols must be followed."

Sinclair sighed. "I know, Doc. It's just that if some doper ended up unconscious in the ER, the hospital would draw blood and within an hour know whether he ODed on cocaine or barbiturates. My vic's a doctor's kid. He was found next to a hospital. It would be nice to know if he died from street drugs or something that came from the hospital."

Sinclair pulled off his mask as he headed for the door.

"Sergeant," Gorman called out.

Sinclair turned.

"My son is a pathologist at Children's Hospital. He and Dr. Caldwell are friends. Their wives socialize and their sons attended school together. If someone were to advise you of preliminary toxicology results, with the understanding they were unofficial, is it possible to guarantee that such information would never appear in a report and never be attributed to the source?"

"I deal with confidential informants all the time. I would never betray one." Sinclair untied the gown and reached in his shirt pocket. "I'll leave my card just in case someone needs it."

Chapter 7

Men and women dressed in suits alongside others in shorts and T-shirts scurried along the sidewalks between the PAB and the county courthouse on the opposite side of Washington Street. Others jaywalked across Seventh Street, disappearing into one of the bail bonds agencies or the storefront lawyer offices.

Sinclair walked past police transportation, where a hundred police cars filled a lot under the steady drone of traffic on the Nimitz Freeway overhead, and spotted a Channel 6 News van down the block, just beyond the side door to homicide. He had called Liz when he left the coroner's office, trusting she would make their meeting appear as a chance encounter to avoid any appearance of favoritism.

A stunning blonde swung her long legs from the passenger seat of the van and lowered herself onto four-inch stilettos. She tugged her form-fitting skirt down and adjusted her pink blouse so that just a touch of cleavage showed. Although she didn't quite stop traffic, a number of pedestrians stopped to watch her.

"Sergeant Sinclair, do you have a moment?"

Sinclair wondered what it would be like to embrace and kiss his girlfriend when meeting in public and not worry about her perfect makeup. He looked up and met her eyes. She liked standing two inches taller than him.

"You look gorgeous, as always."

"What can you tell me?" Her smile remained, but the voice was all business.

"I'll give you his name on the record, but the rest of this you didn't get from me."

"Fair enough," she said, pulling a reporter's spiral notebook from her Prada handbag.

Sinclair gave her a quick rundown.

"Will you do an on-camera?"

"Only what's in the press release."

She waved toward the van, and a broad-shouldered man walked their way cradling a heavy video camera. He was at least as tall as Liz in her heels, with sandy blond hair that nearly covered his ears. Sinclair could tell he maintained the three-day stubble he sported on his face with an electric trimmer.

"Matt, this is Eric. He's our new cameraman."

"I've heard lots about you," Eric said. His ice-blue eyes gave Sinclair the once over.

Most camera operators were disheveled middle-aged men who wore baggy cargo pants and T-shirts stretched across big bellies. This guy looked like he could work on the other side of the lens.

Eric turned to Liz. "How about the police building as background?"

On camera, Sinclair recited the same verbiage from the press release, adding Zachary's name. He looked into the camera, ignoring Liz's smile, which would make most men say more than they intended.

"You spoke to his parents. How are they taking this?"

Although he thought, *How the hell do you think they're taking it?* Sinclair played along. "They're quite distraught, as one would expect. I do request that the media respect their privacy for the next few days." Sinclair knew they would edit his last sentence out and stick a microphone in their faces as soon as they could, but he could later tell the Caldwells he'd asked the media to leave them alone.

"Zachary lived in Contra Costa County. Do you know what he was doing in Oakland at that time of night?"

"No, but if anyone saw him or knows anything that might help, please call Oakland Police."

Sinclair looked from the camera to Liz. "I gotta get back to work."

Liz swept her hand across her throat, and Eric lowered the camera.

"Thanks, Eric. I'll meet you back at the van."

Once Eric was out of earshot, she reached out and brushed her fingertips across the back of Sinclair's hand. He felt the sexual energy in her touch.

"Your new camera jockey's a step up from your last one."

"If you like that tall, rugged, handsome look," she said. "Jealous?"

Sinclair smiled. "Should I be?"

"No way. I'd blend in too much with another blond. I contrast better with the moderately tall, dark, and handsome types. Besides, even in my CFM pumps, he's taller than me, and you know I can't have that."

"CFM?"

"That's what these shoes say to the male world."

"You're going to give me a heart attack."

"Coming over tonight?"

"I'll try."

"You know, my pumps are just doing their job when they flirt with other men."

She winked as he turned toward the stairs.

★

Sinclair told Braddock about the autopsy and then wheeled his chair alongside hers to look at the laptop computer open next to her desktop monitor. "Facebook, Braddock?"

"Zachary's account. There's a hundred postings and comments about his death over the last two hours, but none before the school announced his death. Nothing useful so far, but I'll continue to monitor it. If any of his friends know anything, they'll probably start posting."

Braddock clicked the mouse a few times and a Twitter homepage appeared. "He has two hundred fourteen fol-lowers. Last night at eight-twenty-nine, he tweeted this."

Sinclair read the message on the screen: *HW dun G4C ★$.*

"Huh?"

"*Homework done, going for coffee at Starbucks.* After that, three replied saying they'd see him there. When we inter-view his friends, we'll need to ask everyone their screen names."

"Like asking a gangbanger his street name," Sinclair said. "How many people could have seen his tweet?"

"All two hundred fourteen of his followers."

"One of them could be our killer."

"It's possible, but that's a lot of people to identify and eliminate," she said. "Then there's Facebook, where he has over four hundred friends."

"On Facebook, you have to approve someone as your friend before they can see your postings, correct?"

"Yeah, but look how easy it is," Braddock said as she switched to her desktop computer, where a Facebook profile of a young girl popped up.

"Who's this?"

"It's one of the profiles I created when I worked child exploitation. Her name's Mandy, she's fourteen. The pedophiles loved her. I got the photos to create her identity from a Kmart back-to-school flyer. An hour ago, Mandy requested to be friends with twenty of Zachary's Facebook friends. Already, seven of them approved her."

Sinclair leaned back in his chair. "Great," he sighed.

"I made a list of kids we might want to talk to today. Those Zachary met for coffee, others his mother says are his best buds, and a few of his online pals. We should try to catch as many as we can at school before it lets out."

"Let's roll in five," he said.

Sinclair stepped into the lieutenant's office and briefed him on the autopsy. "With the addition of the stun gun, I see no way around making this a number," said Sinclair.

"The chief won't be happy."

"Remind him it wasn't you who killed this kid."

"I don't take it personal, Matt. It goes with the job." Maloney picked up an interoffice envelope from his desk, slid out several pages of paper, and handed them to Sinclair. "This is your copy. The department was served this morning, exactly one year from the day of the shooting."

Sinclair recognized the paperwork, the federal district court letterhead. The department, the chief of police, and Sinclair were being sued in federal court for unlawful death, civil rights violations, and an assortment of other official-sounding offenses. He noted the name of the plaintiff—Alonzo Moore's mother.

"I guess I shouldn't be surprised."

"The city gets sued on even the most righteous shootings," said Maloney.

"And mine was far from that."

"I told you that at the time."

"The chief won't be happy."

"The city attorney'll call you. Don't worry about being listed as a defendant. That's just a formality. It's the deep pockets they're after."

On the way back to his desk, Connie handed him a fat magic marker and a quarter sheet of paper. Sinclair wrote 76 on the paper, circled it, and added his and Braddock's initials on the bottom right. He removed 75 from the bulletin board and stuck the current number in its place. The city was on pace to top a hundred murders again for the ninth year out of ten. Still, it was way behind the early nineties, when one year Oakland hit 175. He guessed you could call that improvement.

The tradition of posting the most recent homicide number on the board had been around as long as Oakland had a homicide unit. To politicians and media, the number of murders was a barometer they used to measure the department as well as the overall condition of the city. When reporters or department brass called the unit for the current number for the year, as occurred several times a day, whoever answered the phone merely had to glance at the board. All numbers the standby team accumulated remained on the board during the week they were on call, which told the lieutenant with a glance if the team was becoming overwhelmed. When investigators solved a case, they put a diagonal red line through the corresponding number and stuck it back on the board for a few days. Sinclair knew a red line on *76* was a long way away.

He shrugged on his coat, stuffed the case packet in his briefcase, and followed Braddock to the door. Maloney waved him back into his office.

"I just got off the phone with the chief. He's wondering if you're up to this."

"What did you tell him?"

"He ordered you to test."

"Right now? That's bullshit, Lieutenant. We're up to our ass—"

"It's in the contract, Matt."

"I know exactly what's in the contract," said Sinclair. "The department can order me to test any time it wants for a fucking year. One dirty test and I lose my stripes for good and work the rest of my days in whatever bullshit do-nothing job the chief determines. He's fucking with me and you know it."

"It doesn't matter," said Maloney. "The city physician's expecting you. Stop there on your way to Danville."

Chapter 8

The man spotted Susan's car in the parking lot for the Lafayette Ridge Trail as he drove up Pleasant Hill Road. It was the second of her regular running trails that he checked. He turned around in the Springhill Elementary School driveway and parked beside her Lexus SUV.

He had followed Susan Hammond enough to know her routine. She'd leave the law office where she worked with her husband around one and drive home to Lafayette. One day she went to a nail salon, another she got her hair done, another she went shopping. At four every day, she'd drive to a trail and take off on a run. She'd return to her car in forty to fifty minutes, grab a Gatorade, and walk for five minutes to cool down. She'd then drive straight home. She was a creature of habit, which made his task easy.

His watch read 4:50 when Susan jogged down the dirt trail from the ridge. For a woman in her midfifties, she was amazingly fit, but like many avid runners, she seemed to be all skin and bones. Her thighs weren't much bigger than his arms, and she didn't have much in the way of a butt or breasts under her yellow nylon running shorts and tank top. She slowed to a walk the moment she hit the pavement and clasped her hands behind her neck to allow her chest to fully expand with each breath. Peering through the side window of the van, he saw the sweat glistening off Susan's body as she came toward him.

The chirp of the Lexus's door lock was his signal. He yanked open the side door and launched himself out of the van.

She turned toward him, startled. "Hey—" slipped from her lips as he grabbed her and pushed the stun gun against her ribs. She fought hard for such a thin woman, but he pressed the trigger until she went limp. He held her against his chest as he scanned the area for anyone watching.

He pulled her into the van and shut the door. He zip-tied her arms and legs, duct-taped her mouth, and then fastened her arms to one seat bracket and her legs to another with additional zip ties, a lesson he learned when Zachary began kicking on the drive from Danville to the bus bench. He climbed into the driver's seat, merged onto the 24 Freeway, and headed to Oakland. Just before the traffic slowed several miles from the Caldecott Tunnel, Susan recovered from the electrical shock and started to struggle, but he turned around in his seat and offered her another taste of the stun gun.

Twenty minutes later, he pulled into the parking lot of the Golden State Motel at Fifty-Fourth and San Pablo. He had found the place his first day in Oakland. Most of the twenty rooms in the two-story tan stucco building were rented by the week to prostitutes, pimps, drug dealers, and hustlers. It was the kind of place where people didn't get involved in anyone's business, unless it was to buy crack, a stolen television, or a girl by the act, the hour, or the night. Exactly the kind of place he had been looking for.

He parked the van in front of his room and crawled into the back. He flicked open a heavy lock-blade knife. "Listen, I'm going to release your legs so you can walk. If you struggle or try to run, I'll stick this in your heart. Understand?"

She nodded. He cut her loose and hoisted her out of the van. Once he was sure no one was paying attention, he walked her into room number eight and strapped her to a wood chair with additional zip ties. He slid a chair in front of her and sat down. "You must be parched. Promise not to scream and I'll bring you a drink."

She uttered "okay" through the tape covering her mouth.

He opened a small refrigerator on the other side of the room and returned with a Powerade and a Coke. "Your pick," he said.

She nodded at the sport drink.

"Remember, if you try anything, I *will* hurt you." He pulled the tape off her mouth and cut the tie that bound her left wrist to the chair. He twisted off the top and handed her the bottle.

She lifted the bottle to her mouth, took several long gulps, and brushed her hair from her face with a shaking hand. Her voice quivered. "Why? Why are you doing this?" She took several more swallows, dribbling some of the liquid down her chin as her hand trembled.

He took a sip of the Coke. "It's not personal."

"Not personal?" she said, tears rolling down her cheeks. "You kidnapped me and tied me to a damn chair."

"It has nothing to do with you."

She threw the bottle at him. The plastic container bounced harmlessly off his chest.

"You're crazy," she screamed. "Let me go!"

He tore a fresh strip of duct tape off the roll and tried to stick it over her mouth, but she slapped his hand. He grabbed her head, but she twisted away. With her free hand, she batted at his hands. He reached around the back of her head, grabbed a handful of hair, and yanked her head back. "Enough," he yelled.

He slapped the tape over her mouth and tied her wrist back to the chair. He glared at her for a few counts. "Just sit there while I take care of some things," he said as he left the room.

He turned on the water to the tub in the dingy bathroom, opened a small duffle, and set out various items on the sink. When he returned to the bedroom, Susan's eyelids were beginning to droop. He pulled the tape from her mouth.

"Wha' di' you give me?" she slurred.

He pulled a bottle of diazepam oral solution from his pocket. "Liquid Valium."

He cut the cable ties and removed Susan's clothes so they would be clean and dry when he redressed her. The sight of her naked body aroused him no more than it would if he were a surgeon operating on a patient. He carried her limp body into the bathroom and lowered her into the tub. She moaned like a drunk.

He picked up a scalpel from a pack of a dozen he'd ordered on the Internet and knelt beside the tub. "You'll hardly feel this," he said as he grabbed her right wrist.

She tried to jerk her arm away, but her effort was weak—no match for his grip.

He probed for her pulse with two fingers, then took the scalpel and cut deeply into the tissue lengthways. Most people who attempted suicide by cutting their wrists, he learned, fail because they cut across, and the wrist bones prevents the cut from going deep enough to sever the radial artery. He had done it right. A spurt of blood shot out every second, coinciding with the beat of her heart. He did the same with the other wrist.

He laid both arms at her sides under the water. "We don't want the blood to clot. You'll just drift into a peaceful sleep and it will all be over."

He dragged a chair into the bathroom. She slipped deeper into the tub as her body grew limp. Her head, resting against the back of the tub, rolled to the side. Her eyelids drooped but remained open. Her pink skin faded and the water turned from light pink to red. Her eyes finally lost their focus and dulled as he sat there watching the last of her life ebb from her body.

Chapter 9

It was dark by the time Sinclair and Braddock returned to the office. Everyone else was gone for the day. They opened their takeout on their desks. Sinclair bit into his half-pound cheeseburger, and Braddock cut the grilled chicken in her Caesar salad into bite-size pieces with a plastic knife.

"Do you want to talk about it?" Braddock asked.

"Talk about what?" Sinclair stuffed several French fries into his mouth.

"About our little stop at the city physician."

Sinclair was sick of people asking. For twenty-eight days, the counselors at the Merritt Peralta Institute tried to force him to identify how he felt every minute. He had one emotion down pat. The one that came up when people demanded he pee in a cup whenever they snapped their fingers, when bureaucrats with gold badges made him jump through hoops to get the job done, and when he looked at one body after another at the morgue.

"I've known others who drank more after they returned from the Middle East," said Braddock. "You must've seen plenty over there."

Sinclair had seen plenty. Long periods of dull routine and boredom, interrupted by an IED blowing up a Humvee directly in front of him. More routine, interrupted by a ricocheted bullet from an AK-47 hitting the soldier next to him. More routine, interrupted by an RPG round pinging off the roof of his SUV. It was a dud—he lived another day. He'd lost count of how many times he was under fire and learned to sleep through explosions from mortar rounds going off inside his compound. Until one firefight, after which he never again slept through the night.

"Yeah, I guess," he said.

"I heard they awarded you a Silver Star. What was that for?"

Although the chain of command for the Army Criminal Investigation Command, to which he was assigned, had recommended him for the Silver Star, the Department of the Army downgraded it. Sinclair's partner, a fellow CID agent, was also awarded two medals for the same battle, but they were handed to his wife along with a folded flag at Arlington Cemetery. Four MPs, half of the squad that was providing security for Sinclair's CID team, died that day, too.

"It was actually a Bronze Star," he said. "The army put some fancy language on the citation, but all I did that day was to try to stay alive and keep some other soldiers from dying until help came."

Sinclair looked at his half-eaten hamburger. Even though it was his first meal since the phone call woke him fourteen hours earlier, he was no longer hungry.

While Braddock ate her salad, he listened to his voicemails and organized the pages of interview notes into files. He and Braddock had interviewed nine kids at the high school and five more at their homes. During most investigations, Sinclair had to fight the urge to blame his homicide victims, but the truth was most were involved in something that led to their death. So far, it looked like the Caldwell kid was an exception. He was a straight arrow.

After rattling around through the unit file cabinets, Sinclair called across the room to Braddock. "Whatever happened to my old case packets?"

"Connie filed those you cleared, and the lieutenant reassigned your open ones to Phil and me."

"What about—"

"Samantha Arquette?" Braddock interrupted. "The girl on the bus bench a year ago?"

"You know the case?"

"Phil assigned it to me last month."

"I dropped the ball on that one," said Sinclair. Along with a few others around that time, he thought.

The way he'd been assigned Samantha Arquette's death eight months ago had pissed him off. Plenty pissed him off back then. Ever since he killed Alonzo Moore, Sinclair had been coming to work with a hangover nearly every day. The fog in his head finally cleared around ten, about the same time the fog burned off over San Francisco, and by three or four, all he could think about was getting off work and having a drink. Lieutenant Maloney had called him into his office at 3:30. Officer Kyle Newman, a sexual investigator, was there and told him about the Arquette case. Fourteen-year-old Samantha and her mother, Jane, were visiting Jane's old college roommate, Donna Fitzgerald, in San Francisco. Samantha and Donna's daughter, fifteen-year-old Jenny, went to Berkeley for the day. Early the following morning, an unknown male left the girls on a bus bench, and Samantha walked onto the street and was hit by a car. She suffered numerous fractures, internal injuries, and a serious head injury.

The hospitals found a cocktail of drugs—Ecstasy, animal tranquilizer, and Rohypnol—in both girls as well as evidence of vaginal rape. Because of the date rape drugs in her system, Jenny had little memory of the events. Samantha never regained consciousness. A month later, still in a coma, she was transferred to a hospital in New York, where she died. Sinclair knew the felony murder rule meant a death that occurred during the commission of certain felonies, such as rape and robbery, even if not directly caused by the suspect, was first-degree murder, and since the transportation of the girls after the rape—known as asportation in legal terms—was part of the crime, the rapist was accountable for consequences that occurred during that transportation. And the victim didn't need to die right away; the death was a homicide as long as she died from her injuries within a year and one day of the act.

Although technically a homicide, it was a shit case. Newman had worked it for five months and got nowhere. Even if Sinclair busted his ass and was lucky enough to make an arrest, the suspects would probably turn out to be juveniles or college kids with no prior record. They'd claim—in words supplied by their lawyers—that young people have sex when partying. They would say that the girls seemed older and that, when the girls later passed out, they did the right thing and took them for help. Sure, they made mistakes, but the death was accidental. It wasn't as if they grabbed some girl off the street, raped her, and cut her throat. Although not a defense for the crime, the mitigating circumstances would play with a judge and jury. Even if

Sinclair identified the suspects, the DA would likely plead them out to a few years at most. Sinclair had plenty of other cases to work, ones with promising leads, ones that would land the killer in prison for twenty years or for life.

During the subsequent months, Sinclair had done little more than go through the motions on the Arquette case. His heart wasn't in it. Each night after work, he'd down a dozen drinks at the Warehouse or polish off a fifth of bourbon at home. Mrs. Arquette called him several times a week, always first thing in the morning. He was in no mood to listen to her reminisce about her daughter and beg him to do more. Hers wasn't his only open case. It wasn't the only one he wished he could solve. It wasn't the only one he felt guilty about for not doing more.

After he crashed his car and went through several days of detox at the treatment center, his head began to clear. But the guilt remained.

Braddock dropped her salad container in the trashcan and pulled the Samantha Arquette case packet out of her desk. "The case was cold by the time it was handed off to you. There wasn't much to go on."

"Bullshit," said Sinclair. "I should've solved it."

"I was working sexual assault when this case came in on a Monday morning. Samantha was still at Children's and hadn't regained consciousness. Newman and I talked to Jenny at ACH, but the last thing she remembered was meeting some boys on College Avenue—the hippie area she called it—and going to a frat party. She had the classic symptoms of Rohypnol amnesia. Her description of the boys was all over the place. One minute a blond, the next an Arab. She thought they went to a bedroom in a frat house, but then thought they were raped in People's Park inside some hippie tent. Both mothers said the girls were virgins, and the sexual assault exams were consistent with that."

One of the things Sinclair liked about homicide was his victims were dead. He hated going to Alameda County Hospital and interviewing victims as Braddock did. He pulled Newman's investigative report from the case packet and paged through it. Newman had hit every fraternity at the University of California with photos of the girls, but nothing panned out. It was rush week, the weekend before classes began, and every fraternity had some kind of party going on. Newman continued trying to talk to Jenny Fitzgerald until, finally, her mother told him to stop calling. Jenny was in therapy and her mother wasn't about to allow the police or courts to interfere with that.

Sinclair scanned the report he had written back then. He'd asked the lab to resubmit the DNA profiles from the rape kits—both girls had semen and hair evidence—but both turned up negative, which meant the suspects' profiles weren't in the system. That supported his assumption they were college kids. He had sent flyers to the UC Police, and they distributed them around campus, but no tips came in.

"Homicide's supposed to solve the tough ones," said Sinclair. "I did no more than Newman."

"We have a second chance."

"A year ago, Arquette and Fitzgerald got left on the bus bench. Last night, Caldwell. What's the connection?"

"Why must you call these kids by their last names?" asked Braddock.

"Didn't they teach you in your report writing classes that we list victims, suspects, and witnesses by their last names?"

"I'm not talking about in a formal report. I'm talking about between me and you. Their names are Samantha, Jenny, and Zachary. You don't need to dehumanize them."

"If I humanized every homicide victim, I'd go crazy. Thinking of them as numbers on the board, last names on a report, is what allows me to do this job."

"Thinking of them as someone's children is what makes me *want* to do this job," she said.

"Feeling isn't healthy in this job," said Sinclair.

"I had met Jenny. I sat by Samantha's bedside. I talked to the mothers. Those assholes not only raped those girls, they stole their innocence. Now there's Zachary. There must be a connection beyond the bus bench."

"I don't believe in coincidences," said Sinclair "Tomorrow we'll do a full background on all three of them and see if any commonalities pop up."

"Sounds great."

Sinclair looked at his watch. Nine o'clock. "Go home. The next case is yours, and you need to be fresh when the phone rings at oh-dark-thirty with a dead crack dealer in East Oakland."

"What about you?"

"I'll be a few minutes behind you," said Sinclair. "I'm just gonna clear this paper off my desk."

Sinclair brought his case log up to date and filed the reports, statements, and other papers in the Caldwell case packet. He grabbed the Arquette packet from Braddock's desk and opened it. On top was a legal pad with Braddock's log, beginning with an entry last month: *Case reassigned to Braddock.* Her notes followed.

Sinclair started at the original crime reports and statements the patrol officers took from people at the scene and hospital. He found the call records from Jenny's phone, but not for Samantha's. It was a pain in the ass to get a search warrant for phone records, so he understood if Newman had tried to go through the family instead. Often, Sinclair just checked the call log on the phone, if he could get his hands on it. He scanned the property record. A tech had recovered items of bloody clothes and a rape kit from the hospital, but there was no mention of a phone. One more thing he had missed when he worked the case.

His cell phone vibrated. The text read, *On my way home.* He replied *OK*, stuffed everything back into the case packet, and returned it to Braddock's desk.

Just before he flicked off the lights, he stopped. He returned to Braddock's desk, pulled the legal pad out of the Arquette packet, and flipped to the end of Braddock's notes. He wrote today's date, followed by: *Case reassigned to Sinclair,* and put the packet in his desk drawer.

Chapter 10

The steam fogged the shower door, but Sinclair could still make out Liz's lean, shapely body under the spray of water. Elizabeth Schueller, a natural blonde, had the same perfect body that won her runner-up in the Miss California pageant when she was a journalism student at UC, Davis, eight years ago. He watched as she arched backward to rinse the shampoo out of her hair, pushing out her chest and stretching her flat stomach.

He set his cell phone and gun on the nightstand and hung his clothes in the closet space she had set aside for him. Then he cracked open the shower door and stepped inside. She wiped the water from her eyes, smiled broadly, and without saying a word, pulled him in and kissed him long and hard. She wiggled into his arms, pressing her slippery body against his. Sinclair drew in the minty smell of her breath.

"I know where I want you tonight," she whispered.

"Now?"

She pulled her head back and looked into his eyes. The playful look. "I'm in charge tonight. Dry yourself off and get in bed. I'll be there in a minute."

When she climbed into bed, Sinclair sat up to meet her, but she pushed him back down. "Just lie there," she ordered.

She took her time with him, touching, kissing, and licking. Finally, she straddled his hips and slid onto him. She rocked slowly back and forth. She bit her lower lip, her eyes locked onto his as if she were trying to communicate something without words. Finally, her eyes went to the ceiling, her back arched, and a guttural moan came from deep inside her. She smiled and said, "Your turn."

A few minutes later they lay on their sides, Liz's back against his chest. He pulled her tight, nuzzling the nape of her neck.

"How's it feel to be back working the murder police?" she said.

"I'll let you know once I figure it out. At times, I felt like my first day in homicide. My new partner and I had a rough start, but I think she'll work out."

She wiggled her butt against him.

"You have a great ass," said Sinclair.

"Hundreds of squats and lunges a week."

He kissed the back of her neck and breathed in the scent of her hair. Something floral, maybe jasmine, he thought. He cupped one of her breasts. "And perfect boobs."

"They should be. I had the best plastic surgeon in San Francisco."

He was no longer shocked at how openly Liz talked about her breast implants—much the same way he might talk with another cop about a new pistol purchase.

"Having to get surgery . . . didn't that make you feel . . ." Sinclair paused, searching for the right word. ". . . exploited?"

"Modeling is all about marketing a commodity. A five-foot-ten swimsuit model needs C cups. I made myself into the commodity they wanted. Businesses do that all the time." Sinclair felt her body tensing in his arms. "I could have spent ten years working my way up the ladder to even get an interview in broadcast. Had I come from a rich, connected family, my daddy might have gotten me a job. Instead, I used what I had to get the interview. Whatever it takes."

Liz twisted in his arms to face him. "It's not like you didn't do whatever you had to do to get into homicide. You still do whatever it takes to solve your cases."

"I wasn't judging you," he said, massaging her shoulders until she relaxed.

She stroked his face and kissed him lightly on the lips. "Sorry I got defensive. I know how hard it must be for you going back to homicide after everything you've been through."

"I guess we're both a bit defensive."

"And overly sensitive," she said.

"Yeah, that's me," he said, "a sensitive man."

She laughed.

Liz was right about one thing. He *had* done whatever it took to get to homicide. The crazy hours. Working the worst parts of the city. Pushing to make the big arrests and taking risks that could have gotten him fired or killed too many times. When the emotional pain got too great, he calmed them with bourbon. When the nightmares kept him awake, he drank them away. He wondered if it was all worth it.

"Do you ever worry about what you might have to do to become the next Amy Robach or Natalie Morales?" he asked.

She shifted her body back into his. "Whatever it takes," she whispered.

"Good for you." He kissed the back of her neck, and her breathing slowed as she drifted into sleep.

When he and Liz had started dating, he accepted that he was part of her whatever-it-takes. He knew the inside scoops he fed her helped her get noticed as more than merely a pretty talking head. Although he never compromised a case, he still sold himself. Sure, maybe they used each other, but he rationalized it by acknowledging that nearly every man would do the same.

He knew Liz was initially attracted to him because he was safe. He was recently divorced and his tough-cop, bad-boy persona conveyed he wasn't looking for a long-term commitment. But Sinclair had come to realize Liz wanted more than just his homicide tips. Deep down, she was insecure and craved love as much as anyone. Sure, she stuck with him after the car crash, but still he knew what they had was temporary. She had mentioned Barbara Walters, who had married three times and had a series of relationships with married senators and other prominent officials, as someone who never allowed love or relationships to interfere with her career.

Liz never considered she could have both; however, Sinclair had. It seemed a lifetime ago when he got married and discussed children and growing old with someone. But he couldn't put Iraq behind him and instead immersed himself in his work. He assumed his wife would let him deal with the war in his own way and on his own timetable and would stick around until he grew tired of homicide and took a normal assignment. A good marriage required a lot of time and energy. His relationship with Liz required neither.

He wondered now if he had lost his own whatever-it-takes motivation. That drive that took him to the top of the homicide ranks, that singleness of purpose to go through any barriers, to stop at nothing to take a killer off the street. He used to have it. That was why he hadn't given up on bringing Alonzo Moore to justice, even after his cases fell apart in court. His drive and tenacity was what had made him a great detective. But it also came with a price, and after he killed Moore, he began to question whether he went too far.

He was drifting off when his cell phone buzzed.

Chapter 11

Sinclair jockeyed his car into a space between two marked units and spotted a broad-shouldered man with a gold badge on his uniform striding toward him. As the midnight-shift watch commander, Lieutenant Beck was responsible for all uniformed police working the city at night. He was in his midforties but sported a buzz haircut like most of the twentysomething officers working under his command.

"You got here quick," said Beck.

"I was close."

"You had the one from last night?"

"Yeah, that was mine."

"It doesn't take a homicide detective to figure out this is the same guy," said Beck.

Beck had spent his entire career in uniform, but like many command officers, that never stopped him from thinking he was an expert at investigations, even though he never even investigated a residential burglary as a detective.

The yellow tape cordoned off an area twice the size as the previous night, and twice the number of patrol officers roamed the area. Several greeted him as he walked by. Sinclair slid under the tape. Talbert was snapping photos.

The body, dressed in running clothes, was laid out on the sidewalk in front of the bus bench.

"Paramedics got here before us," said Beck. "They found her on the bench in a sitting position. Put her on the ground to check vitals and start CPR, but rigor already present. Pronounced her."

"Any ID?"

"Paramedics felt something in the back pocket of her shorts, but we're waiting for the coroner before we disturb the body. I already called them."

"It used to be patrol waited for homicide to arrive and make that decision," said Sinclair.

"Seemed like a no-brainer to me, Sinclair. Two bodies the same place in two days might generate media attention. Figured we'd clean this up and get out of here quick."

Sinclair glared at him. "We stay as long as it takes."

"Whatever," Beck replied. "I also called the chief's office and PIO. Figured we'd get ahead of this."

Involving the department's public information officer and the police chief before Sinclair even made it to the scene meant he'd have a slew of people getting in his way. "What else did you say? Since it's my case, it would be nice if I knew at least as much as the chief."

"I told him it looks like we have another well-to-do victim, just like last night."

"We don't know who she is yet, right?"

"No, but look at her. Manicure and fancy haircut. She didn't get highlights like that at Supercuts, and the diamond on her left hand is at least two carats. My wife's pressuring me for a bigger one, so I notice these things."

Sinclair crouched and looked at her ring. Maybe Beck wasn't totally useless.

"The chief said he was coming here himself and told me to call your lieutenant," said Beck.

"That's fucking great."

"I'm just doing my job, Sinclair. I didn't ask him to come."

"You're just doing it too well, Lieutenant. What else?"

"Last bus of the night came by eleven thirtyish, driver sees a woman sitting there not moving. All the drivers are spooked after yesterday, so he calls it in. I got a unit at the bus yard getting his statement. Checked missing persons reports, but no similars. Doing the normal canvass of the area. Nothing so far."

Talbert slung her camera around her neck and stepped forward once Beck finished.

"Talk to me, Joyce," Sinclair said.

"Haven't found anything of value. I'll print the shelter again. Got some close-ups of the vic, and I'll get more when the coroner gets here and rolls her."

"Did you finish your report from the last one?"

"I was gonna finish it up tonight, but they sent me on this as soon as I hit in-service on the radio."

"Should I get another tech here?"

"I can handle it. I won't go home until I have both reports finished and on your desk."

The coroner's van arrived and Charlie Dawson stepped out. After he and Sinclair exchanged information, both coroner investigators gloved up and ducked under the tape.

Dawson extended the corpse's arms, showing Sinclair long, deep cuts in both forearms. "Classic suicide cuts," Dawson said. He twisted the arms around, showing a band of superficial cuts and abrasions around both wrists.

"Flex-cuffs—just like the last one," said Sinclair.

"Same thing on the ankles."

Dawson rolled the body and pulled two cards from a Velcro-closed pocket of her shorts. He held up a driver's license and Kaiser medical card. "Strange things for a jogger to carry around with her."

"Not entirely," said Sinclair. "Older guys do it all the time. Jogger has a heart attack or accident, they know who she is and where to take her."

Braddock slid under the tape and joined the group surrounding the corpse. "You beat me here again," she said to Sinclair.

"I was closer."

Braddock smiled knowingly.

"Here's something else interesting," said Dawson, running his hand over purplish coloring on the back of the legs. "Appears to be postmortem lividity, but not fully developed."

"Which means?" asked Braddock.

"The body was in a sitting position with the legs extended, sort of like someone sitting on a bed, for at least several hours after death," said Dawson. "If the body was in a chair or on that bench, for example, with the feet lower, the blood would pool into the lower legs. But that's only a guess. The doc'll have to say for sure."

"You mind if we hold onto the ID cards?" asked Sinclair. "I want to get them printed."

"No prob. Just get me all the info."

Talbert held out a plastic envelope and Dawson dropped the cards inside.

Sinclair copied the pertinent information into his notebook. "The woman's got a Lafayette address."

"Another rich place," said Dawson. "Just like the Danville boy."

"I live there," said Sinclair "And I'm sure as hell not rich."

"Yeah, right," said Dawson. "I know how much overtime you homicide dicks get."

Dawson rolled the body back over and placed paper bags over the hands. "Broken nail on the right hand. Maybe she scratched him and got some DNA."

Dawson removed a medallion that was hanging around her neck and dropped it into a bag his partner was holding.

"Wait a minute," said Sinclair. "Let me see that."

The pendant was a peace sign about the size of a half-dollar and made out of sterling silver or silver-plated. It hung from a cheap-looking chain.

"Didn't the boy have one of these?" asked Sinclair.

Dawson shrugged his shoulders.

"I'm sure of it," said Talbert as she punched buttons on her camera. "Look."

Sinclair, Braddock, and Dawson peered at the LCD display—the same medallion against the background of a black T-shirt.

Sinclair knew the moment he got the call that two bodies at the exact same place in two days was no coincidence. The medallion verified it. The cheap jewelry didn't match the rest of her appearance. He felt the hairs on the back of his neck begin to rise.

Sinclair and Braddock stepped back as the coroner investigators brought out a gurney and packaged the corpse.

"Can you run it down for me—when you arrived, who told you what?" asked Braddock.

"I know you're up and would normally be primary, but this is definitely linked to the Caldwell case," he told Braddock. "That makes this mine too."

Sinclair read the disappointment in Braddock's face. She didn't see it as dodging a bullet. "But, hey, we're a team," he said. "So we win or lose together."

Beck broke in. "One of my officers has something that may interest you."

They moved to the other side of the yellow tape, where a young black officer with a cherub face stood.

Officer Rose said, "This might be nothing, but a half hour before we were dispatched on this, I got a call on a nine-four-nine vehicle two blocks away. The caller was a neighbor who said she lives next door to a drug house, and a black van circled the block for ten minutes and then stopped in front of the house. I figure that if I were a killer and wanted to transport bodies, a van would be a perfect vehicle for it."

"Makes sense," said Sinclair. "Did she get a license number?"

"It came back to a Tyrone Hayes with an address over on Adeline."

"I know Hayes," said Braddock. "Big man. Gentle smile, soft spoken, but mean as hell. He did time for a series of rapes back in the nineties. He was a tennis-shoe pimp who liked to pick up young girls, drug and rape them, then turn them out."

"Not a very impressive pimp if he had to make his rounds on foot instead of in a fancy Cadillac," said Sinclair.

"A year or two ago, the sexual assault unit conducted home visits on all two-ninety registrants on this beat after a rash of home invasion rapes," said Braddock. "Hayes mean-mugged and threatened every male officer on our team but turned on his charm with me. Tried to impress me by saying that he branched out when in prison and found that young male asses were as good as girls."

"Sounds like a sicko," said Sinclair.

"The creep's sick enough to do this," said Braddock.

Sinclair turned to Rose, "I'm guessing you didn't spot the van."

"We cruised the area, but it was gone. The woman didn't see the driver. I drove by Hayes's house—the van was parked out front, but the house was dark. I ran him out. He's still a registered sex offender and on parole. Didn't see much value in knocking at the door and jamming him up, so we figured we'd keep a lookout for him rolling some other night."

"Do you want to go by and talk to him?" asked Braddock.

Sinclair shrugged. "Can't hurt. It's not like we have anyone else to talk to."

Chapter 12

Sinclair stood at the corner of an old Victorian house on a street that fifty years ago was predominantly Italian. A few late-model German cars were intermingled with older American ones on the street, indicating gentrification was taking a foothold in the neighborhood. Braddock and Officer Rose's beat partner, a bow-legged officer who wore black gloves with the fingers cut out, stood on the front porch. Rose covered the back. Since Braddock had history with Hayes, it made sense for her to make contact.

Braddock rapped at the door. "Tyrone, this is Sergeant Braddock. I'd like to talk with you."

A door banged at the rear of the house.

Rose yelled, "He's coming out the back."

Rose ran around the corner, out of Sinclair's view. Sinclair opened the chain-link gate and sprinted down the walkway. When he reached the backyard, he saw Hayes lumbering across the dark yard toward the back fence with Rose a step behind.

Rose caught him at the fence, but Hayes shook him off like an annoying insect.

Rose drew his expandable baton and snapped it open with a flick of his wrist. He swung low and connected with Hayes's knee with a solid thud.

Hayes howled in pain and rushed Rose, wrapping him up like a three-hundred-pound lineman does to a running back. He grabbed Rose's baton and yanked it from his hand and flung Rose to the ground. Rose struggled to his feet as Hayes swung a fist the size of a ham hock at his head.

Rose straightened and turned his shoulder into the punch. The blow knocked him off his feet and into a row of unkempt shrubs.

Rose lay still. Sinclair's first instinct was to rush to the downed officer to check on him, but it had been drummed into him during training exercises and reinforced on battlefields from Baghdad to Oakland that you had to neutralize the threat before you could attend to the wounded.

Sinclair stopped ten feet from Hayes, his hand on his pistol, and yelled, "Police! Freeze!"

Hayes stared at him. Black eyes inside a head the size of a bear's. Drops of sweat dripped off his broad nose. His nostrils flared as he sucked in huge breaths.

He threw Rose's baton to the ground. "Go ahead, shoot me, motherfucker."

The threat of a gun only worked with rational people. It was of no value when the person didn't care about living or dying or knew the cop wouldn't use it.

Hayes stepped toward him. Sinclair danced back a step.

When a cop had to wrestle with a suspect, his gun was a liability. If the suspect got his hands on it, the cop was dead, so Sinclair knew he had to protect his pistol while trying to fight a monster that outweighed him by nearly a hundred pounds.

Hayes lunged toward him and swung a roundhouse punch toward his head. Sinclair skipped back onto his left foot and parried the blow with his hand as it passed by inches in front of his face.

Hayes's momentum, along with Sinclair's parry, pulled Hayes off balance and left his right side exposed. Sinclair pivoted on his left foot, cocked his right foot into his thigh, and with years of training behind him, unleashed a side kick to Hayes's rib cage, just under his right armpit.

Hayes grunted and doubled over. Slowly, he straightened up again and took a step toward Sinclair. Sinclair stepped into him with his left foot and threw a straight punch into Hayes's face. Sinclair heard the satisfying crunch of bone. Hayes dropped to his knees, looked up at Sinclair for a second, and then collapsed to the ground.

Chapter 13

An hour later, Sinclair and Braddock returned to the murder scene. The body was gone, as were half of the officers. Lieutenant Maloney, dressed in a navy blue sport coat and tie, was talking to a tall black man wearing black slacks, a black polo, and a black windbreaker. Even though regulations required those on duty to wear a uniform or a coat and tie, the chief of police figured he could wear whatever he wanted when he visited a crime scene at night. The arrogance of the chief thinking his rank afforded him special privileges irked Sinclair.

"The man you went after isn't the killer, but you decided to smash his face anyway," said Chief Clarence Brown.

Sinclair wanted to point out the obvious: that had they known Hayes wasn't involved, they wouldn't have wasted their time with him, but he kept his mouth shut. After Sinclair had taken Hayes down, Rose's partner handcuffed him while Braddock attended to Rose and called for ambulances. Paramedics suspected Hayes had several broken ribs, a broken nose, and a fractured cheekbone. They transported him to the county hospital with a police escort. One of Lieutenant Beck's district sergeants arrived, took

Sinclair's statement, and did the use-of-force investigation and paperwork, required any time an officer puts a suspect in the hospital.

Meanwhile, Braddock had searched the Ford van and interviewed Hayes's mother and uncle, both of whom had been in the kitchen drinking coffee when the police knocked at the door. The mother said Hayes was at the Salvation Army the night Zachary was killed and had been home since midnight. It was Mrs. Hayes's brother who had driven the van to the crack house an hour ago to pay Hayes's drug debt so the local dope dealers would leave the family alone. Braddock verified his alibi for both nights with a few phone calls.

"Chief," said Braddock. "Tyrone Hayes has a ten-page rap sheet. He's the size of a refrigerator. If I was in Matt's place, I would've had to shoot him."

"And the story lead would say, *Petite female detective attacked by convicted serial rapist—forced to shoot to save her life.* Instead, we'll see, *Sergeant Sinclair, with three notches on his gun already, kicks and punches man in the face during homicide investigation.*"

Sinclair focused on Brown's shaved head glistening under the streetlights, wondering if he waxed it to create that shine.

"How's the officer?" Brown asked.

"His name is Officer Rose," said Sinclair. "He's getting X-rays of his shoulder at the hospital. It didn't look good, and he twisted his ankle when he fell."

"What's the meaning of these necklaces that your lieutenant told me about?"

"We don't know yet, Chief." Sinclair wasn't about to tell him about his theory, only to hear the chief challenge it as guesswork and speculation.

"Who is this woman? Is there a connection between her and the doctor's son?"

"All we have so far is CDL info on the woman. We don't know any connection."

Chief Brown ignored Sinclair and turned to Maloney. "I don't need to tell you that this shit will hit the fan by morning and people will want answers."

"I understand, sir."

Brown stepped toward Sinclair. Sinclair's eyes were level with Brown's chin, and he looked up to meet the chief's glare.

"If you can't put a red line through these cases quickly, I'll have them reassigned to someone who can."

Brown craned his neck and took several whiffs.

Sinclair felt his anger rising. Every captain and lieutenant cowered before this man. Sergeants and officers kept out of his way even though they were usually too insignificant for the chief to bother. But this was personal. First the urinalysis, now this.

"You want me to walk a straight line, Chief? Or maybe stand on one foot and recite the alphabet?"

"Don't forget who you're talking to, Sergeant."

Their eyes locked. Sinclair despised him. He hated the power he had over him. He hated how he made him feel. But he knew he couldn't win this showdown.

"I just want to do my job. I haven't had a drink in six months and have no desire to."

The second part was a lie. At that moment, he wanted nothing more than a few swigs of bourbon. It would calm the rage he felt, dissolve the fear. It would allow him to say exactly what he wanted to that arrogant, condescending prick.

"Then do it. And do it right," Brown said as he turned. "Lieutenant, with me," he growled at Maloney.

Chapter 14

The man made a U-turn on MLK Jr. Way and jumped on the freeway toward San Francisco. The Bay Bridge tollgate had no lines and he quickly accelerated to speed. The San Francisco skyline filled his windshield as he passed Treasure Island, the location of a former naval base. He sucked in the cool night air through his open window as his van passed by the skyscrapers and wound into the heart of the city. He traveled for ten minutes on city streets until he reached his target. The second-floor apartment was dark. A Mini Cooper sat in the driveway, indicating she was still working the day shift and would be asleep for several more hours. After having checked on her for several weeks, he had her schedule down.

From there, he drove back over the Bay Bridge to the old warehouse and produce district of Oakland. He counted six floors up and two from the side of the luxury condo building. The lights were off, so this woman too was probably asleep, just as she should be. A Ford Crown Vic shot out of the underground parking garage of the building and sped down the dark street. He knew where it was going.

A dim light glowed in the front window of the third house he visited, high in the Oakland hills. Based on his previous drive-bys of the house, he figured the doctor was working his normal night shift and the wife was asleep. Satisfied that his next three targets hadn't changed their routines, he pointed the van toward West Oakland.

He parked in the motel lot and buzzed the office door. The twenty-year-old night manager looked up from a pile of open physics textbooks and peered through the thick plastic window. The skinny Indian's paisley shirt looked like a Goodwill store reject. The heavy aroma of curry filled the air.

"Good evening, Mr. Smith."

When he'd checked into the Golden State Motel three weeks earlier, he told the motel owner, Mr. Patel, he had no ID or credit card but could pay in cash. The middle-aged man grinned slyly and said it would be $300 a week in advance, plus a $200 nonrefundable deposit for having no identification. Patel stuffed two of the hundred-dollar bills directly into his pocket. On the registration card, the man wrote the name John Smith, a phony address in New York as his home address, and a driver's license number he made up.

"I'd like to pay for another week," he said as he slid three hundred-dollar bills through the opening.

"Thank you, sir," the night manager said, examining each bill closely. "Would you like the maid tomorrow?"

He didn't want the intrusion of the weekly maid service but didn't want to do anything that might draw attention. "That will be fine."

Once inside his room, he went straight to the bathroom. As the last of the woman's life drained out of her yesterday afternoon, he had sat there watching and thinking. Six hours had passed and the water had seeped through the brittle, rubber plug. He ran the shower over her body for ten minutes, yet the body still had a red hue. He had left her in the bloody water too long. However, once he dried her off and laid her on the bed, it was hardly noticeable. She looked to be asleep. No pain etched her face. She had gone peacefully. Once she was dry, he had combed her hair and dressed her in her running clothes before loading her in the van and delivering her.

He inspected the bathroom carefully. There was no blood in the tub or on the floor. The towels were wet but not blood soaked. He hung them on the rack. The bed sheets were still damp, but they would be dry by the time the maid came. He took some soda cans and old newspapers out of the trash can and scattered them around the room and checked the drawers to make sure he still had some clothes there. He locked the door on his way out. After surveying the inside of the van to ensure nothing was visible, he locked the doors, set the alarm, and slipped through the fence and across the field to Fifty-Fifth Street carrying a well-worn backpack.

Praise Baptist Church sat among small single-family houses on Marshall Street a block north of Fifty-Fifth. A white wooden structure, it looked more like it belonged in a quaint New England village than the East Bay. Tucked behind the church were a small parking area and the minister's house. He had met Reverend Cecil Little, an elderly, gray-haired black man, while reconnoitering the neighborhood, and the reverend was more than happy to allow him to park his car there for a modest donation to the collection plate each Sunday. He even gave him a church bumper sticker, which the man slapped on the back of the van among all the other stickers. He figured it helped the van fit into the neighborhood better.

Now he climbed into the new Volvo S80 sedan and left this part of his life behind.

Chapter 15

Sinclair and Braddock walked up a curved, brick walkway to the front door of the sprawling ranch-style house in the Happy Valley area of Lafayette. Large, leafy trees graced the neighborhood, unlike newer developments where bulldozers razed the land and developers added pencil-thin saplings that took decades to mature. It was similar to the neighborhood on the other side of Lafayette where Sinclair had lived with his ex-wife—quiet and serene, an area that felt more country than suburb. Braddock had checked the address on her phone on the way there. Single story, twenty-nine-hundred square feet, four bedrooms, three baths. Built in 1954, worth 1.2 million today.

The only streetlights in the neighborhood were on light posts in front of each house. The wealth in this area was more understated than Blackhawk, where the Caldwells lived. Sinclair could see lights on inside as he pressed the doorbell. The porch light came on a second before the door opened. The man was in his midsixties, with a noticeable belly under the dress shirt that hung outside his trousers.

"Mr. Hammond," said Sinclair, pausing long enough to allow him to deny it. "I'm Sergeant Sinclair, this is Sergeant

Braddock. May we come in?" Sinclair swept aside his suit coat to show the sterling silver badge on his belt.

"Is this about my wife?" He slurred his words but answered what would have been Sinclair's next question.

"Yes. Can we talk inside?"

Hammond led the way past a spacious kitchen to a living room with dark, glistening hardwood floors. A piano sat against one wall and a brick fireplace flanked the wall opposite. Windows and French doors covered the back wall. Hammond dropped into a plush chair. An open book and a glass filled with an amber liquid rested on the end table. He closed the book and picked up his drink.

Sinclair watched closely as Hammond took a long swallow. He remembered how it felt when the liquor warmed his throat as it went down.

"I've been reading the same chapter for the last hour," he said. "She's never done this before."

"You mean . . . ?"

"Not come home."

Sinclair opened his notebook and asked the basic questions: name, birth date, address, phone numbers, employment. "What kind of law do you practice?" Sinclair asked.

"Personal injury and medical malpractice. One partner does family law and the other business—mostly contracts."

Susan worked mornings at the law office, he told Sinclair. Most days, she and her husband would have lunch together, after which, she would go home to take care of the house and her "ladies' appointments—you know, manicures, pedicures, hair, facials, and whatever else women do." Hammond paused and took another pull on his drink. "I'm surprised you came. Your dispatcher said they don't send officers out for adults missing less than forty-eight hours absent foul play."

"When did you call it in?"

"Around seven."

Braddock pulled her cell phone from her purse and left the room. A moment later, she returned and said, "Nineteen-oh-three, call came from their home phone number. I requested they put out a comm order on her car."

Hammond looked at her funny.

"That means a communication order, something that's sent electronically to other departments and broadcast over police radios to get officers looking for her car."

Hammond nodded and drained his glass. Sinclair could nearly taste the booze—something with an oaky fragrance. "Can I get either of you something to drink?" Hammond asked.

"Coffee?" Sinclair suggested.

"I'd have to figure out where it is. Susan always—"

"Sergeant Braddock will help you. Meanwhile, you don't mind if I look around, do you?"

He shrugged and led Braddock toward the kitchen. Sinclair anticipated an objection, Hammond being a lawyer and all, but Hammond didn't appear the least bit suspicious of Sinclair's request. A man whose wife was missing wouldn't be. Sinclair was prepared to tell him that it was standard procedure to search the house on all missing persons reports, which it was. Too often, cops found missing children hiding under beds or in closets when their mothers swore they checked the house before calling the police. When working patrol, Sinclair once found a piece of mulch in a missing child's bedroom. That led him outside where he found footprints in the shrub bed and a jimmied window.

The child had been abducted by the estranged stepfather. Another time he noticed a fresh deposit of dust on a closet floor and an empty space on the shelf above where a suitcase had been. The wife left on her own accord—no foul play involved. He never knew what he'd find in a house until he looked.

Whenever Sinclair searched the home of a homicide victim, he seldom knew what he was looking for. Sometimes it was what was *not* there that was important. Other times, it was an overall feeling that he got for the victim after seeing her habitat—an organized or sloppy personality; her taste in clothes; what she ate; whether she smoked, drank, or used drugs. Even though his gut told him Russell Hammond was not involved, he would keep an eye out for anything that would change his mind.

The first bedroom contained an antique white desk and bookshelf, sewing machine, and a small couch. A Coach handbag hung from the doorknob. Nothing interesting inside. The next bedroom was Russell's office and contained a heavy oak roll-top desk, high-backed leather chair, and bookshelves. A guest bath followed, fancy towels that weren't meant to be used hung on racks. It reminded him of the guest bath in the house he used to live in with his ex-wife. Farther down the hall was a comfortable-looking but sterile guest room.

The door at the end of the hall opened to a master suite. The king-size bed was neatly made and covered with as many pillows as the guest room bed. A stack of novels covered one nightstand. A John Grisham novel was on the other nightstand alongside a pair of drugstore reading glasses. The closets were neatly organized with an equal distribution of men and women's clothes. The bathroom cabinet held the usual assortment of toiletries and a few prescriptions: Viagra, Flomax, a statin for high cholesterol. None with Susan's name.

A sliding glass door led onto a brick patio and past that a rectangular pool surrounded by fruit trees and manicured shrubs. He jotted down a note to ask about a gardener and pool service. Sinclair walked across the patio and opened a sliding glass door that led into a family room. Huge stone fireplace against one wall. A sectional sofa in front of it. A bar stood in a corner opposite the fireplace. Sinclair studied the assortment of bottles: good bourbons, Kentucky whiskey, single malt scotches, brandies, and cognac—nearly forty bottles in all. He picked up one to study the label. He'd seen Stein Oregon Bourbon at his old liquor store for sixty dollars a fifth. He could get four bottles of Jim Beam or Jack Daniels for that price. And at the end of his drinking, four was always better than one.

Sinclair wondered if it was even worth staying sober. Back at the crime scene, Maloney had taken him aside once the chief left and told him the chief still felt insulted by the arbitration ruling that returned Sinclair to homicide. The chief called Sinclair a loose cannon, saying his investigations resulted in too much collateral damage too often. He ordered Maloney to issue Sinclair an official reprimand for insubordination for the way he spoke to him. An oral reprimand was an official slap on the wrist, documented with a written notation in his file. Normally, orals weren't a big deal, but Sinclair knew it was the beginning of the process of documentation and file building. An oral reprimand, a letter of discussion, a written reprimand, a one-day suspension, and then *boom*—demotion or termination.

He wasn't about to let the chief win. He put the bottle back and followed a door into the garage. A new Lexus sedan took up one space. The other stall was empty. He popped the trunk of the Lexus LS and glanced through the plush interior. Nothing.

Braddock poured Sinclair a cup of coffee as soon as he came into the kitchen.

"Mr. Hammond had lunch with Susan," she said, glancing at her notes. "He spent the afternoon at his desk, typical paperwork and phone calls. Left at five, got home quarter to six. Susan wasn't here. He called her cell. It rang then went to voicemail. He called several of her friends. I have a list here."

Braddock looked at Sinclair. She shook her head.

Sinclair took a business card from his shirt pocket and slid it toward Hammond. "I have some bad news for you. We found your wife."

The alcohol probably delayed his reaction. He looked from the card to Sinclair and back to the card. "What?"

"I'm sorry, Mr. Hammond, but your wife is dead."

"Dead?" Hammond stared at Sinclair, apparently hoping he had misunderstood.

Sinclair nodded.

"No," Hammond howled. Then the tears came.

Sinclair sat quietly while Hammond regained his composure. Then he suggested Hammond call a friend or relative. While waiting for Hammond's brother to arrive from the next town over, Sinclair asked the standard questions about enemies, suspicious people, and unusual occurrences but got nothing from Hammond that pointed toward who would want to kill his wife or why.

Chapter 16

Sinclair found two of the uniformed cops from the crime scene standing in the dark hallway outside the homicide office.

"Either of you know how to make coffee?"

They met Sinclair's look with blank stares.

"I don't drink coffee," the younger officer said.

Sinclair sighed. "We depend on you guys, especially after hours. If you get here before us, get the door key, come inside, and start the coffee. Your fellow officers drink it, and if we have witnesses or suspects to interview, we need them awake. And I need coffee, so if you don't want me on your ass the moment I walk through the door, have the coffee ready."

"Sorry, Sarge," said the senior officer.

Sinclair turned his computer on and hung up his coat as he heard one officer giving the other a step-by-step class on coffee making. Sinclair was amazed at how many of the young cops stood in line at Starbucks several times a day yet had never made a cup at home.

He and Braddock had left the house when Hammond's brother arrived. Within minutes, they got a call saying the

East Bay Regional Parks Police had found Susan's SUV. They met several officers in the parking lot of a hiking trail. Susan's car was unlocked and a cell phone sat in a cup holder next to an unopened sport drink. Nothing in the car looked disturbed. The park police officer found the key on the ground underneath the car, and Sinclair figured the killer surprised her and she dropped it during a struggle. He might have grabbed Zachary as he approached his car too, Sinclair surmised. Another similarity was that both cars were in secluded spots where an abduction wouldn't be noticed. Sinclair felt a pattern developing and pieces fitting together.

Sinclair grabbed an empty case packet out of the office supply locker and wrote *Hammond, Susan, 5200 MLK Jr Way* and the date on it. He was posting number seventy-seven on the board when Braddock came through the door.

"Good job, you guys." She smiled at the officers as she plucked her coffee mug off her desk. "Nice to see you know the priorities."

Sinclair shot a glance at the officers, and they winked at him. Braddock took a sip and said, "I had Talbert print Susan's phone so we can handle it. I'll start recording calls, contacts, calendar entries, and anything else I find on it."

Sinclair said, "After I check a few things in the Arquette packet, I'll begin doing the same with Zachary's phone." As much as he hated the laborious process of comparing every detail of their lives in search of a match, if he could find a place where their lives intersected, it might tell them something about the killer. But first, he had to satisfy the gnawing feeling about the peace medallions he'd had ever since he saw one around Susan's neck.

Sinclair went through Samantha's case packet, removed a CD, and slipped it into his computer. One hundred fourteen photos. The first twenty showed the bus bench and a girl—must have been Jenny Fitzgerald, he figured—being attended to by paramedics. The next fifty showed the roadway where the traffic collision occurred and a pool of blood from every possible angle. Twenty shots showed the car, most focusing on the damage to the front where it struck the girl.

He turned to the tech report, titled as a 901 Injury/ Auto-Ped. The narrative said that when the tech arrived, the pedestrian (Arquette) had already been transported from the scene. At the scene, the tech recovered bloody clothing that the paramedics had apparently cut away as they examined her for life-threatening injuries. The tech cleared the scene and went to Children's Hospital to take photos of the victim's injuries and collect any additional evidence.

Sinclair tapped his mouse and went through fifteen photos of a small, battered, blonde girl wearing a blue-and-white gown lying in a hospital bed. Her face was so badly swollen he had trouble seeing where her nose ended and her mouth began, except for a respirator tube taped around her mouth. In a photo that showed a close-up of Samantha's face, Sinclair noticed a chain around her neck. He clicked through four more photos until he came to one showing her face. Sinclair enlarged it on the computer screen and zeroed in on a shiny object on her chest just above the hospital gown.

"Bingo," he said.

Braddock wheeled her chair alongside Sinclair. "Well, I'll be . . ."

They both stared the photo. A peace medallion, exactly like the ones on Zachary and Susan.

Chapter 17

Sinclair was at his desk digesting reports when Sergeant Lou Sanchez walked in the door at ten to seven. Sanchez was in his midforties and had been in homicide for eight years. He had short, curly black hair and wore the plastic-framed prescription glasses with shatterproof lenses the department was required to offer for safety reasons but that most officers declined. Sanchez spoke slowly and deliberately, and although others thought he translated his thoughts from Spanish to English before he uttered a word, Sinclair knew it was part of his disciplined personality, unlike Sinclair, who often spoke before thinking.

Sanchez hung up his coat, filled his coffee cup, and stared at the bulletin board where the fresh number hung. "I see you had another one." He looked deeply into both interview rooms and bent down to look under the tables. "I see no witnesses here. Have you already booked your suspect?"

"You got it, Lou," said Sinclair. "Five eyewitnesses—all pointed out dude. Dude surrendered, cracked after five minutes, confessed to this murder as well as every unsolved from the last decade."

Braddock joined in. "Dude insisted he didn't want a trial—waste of time, he said, with me and Sinclair doing the investigation—so we drove him straight to San Quentin. Already settled into his new bunk on death row."

Dan Jankowski, Sanchez's partner, burst through the door. A big, red-faced man, weighing nearly three hundred pounds, Jankowski's booming voice knew only one volume. "Sinclair," he bellowed, "what the fuck are you and Lady Braddock doing here so early? You don't start 'til eight. No, don't tell me, another fine citizen of Oakland met his maker last night."

"Look at the board, Dan," said Sanchez, mimicking a heavy Spanish accent. "Two numbers, neither with red lines."

"You know what that means, amigo," said Jankowski.

"I think I do, partner. The coach might be getting the A-team warmed up in the bullpen."

Sanchez and Jankowski took their coffee to their desks and continued their banter as they fired up their computers and checked voicemail.

When Sinclair returned to homicide two days ago, the other guys welcomed him back but still kept their distance. He was tainted. Just like cops would be suspicious of a man who claimed he was a law-abiding citizen yet hung around with convicted felons, the other investigators were afraid of becoming sullied by getting too chummy with him. However, as Jankowski and Sanchez laughed and joked about his open murder cases, Sinclair knew they were no longer concerned with what the brass might think. The camaraderie of the unit was stronger. He was starting to feel like part of the family again.

After they had their laughs, Jankowski and Sanchez crowded around Sinclair and Braddock's desks. Sinclair gave a brief rundown of the three murders. When he showed them the photo of the medallion around Samantha's neck, they raised their eyebrows.

"What can we do?" asked Jankowski.

Sinclair explained his plan to copy contact and calendar events from each victim's phone or computer and look for commonalities.

"I'd help, but my fingers are too fat to work those new smartphones," said Jankowski. "Besides, they're smarter than me."

The oldest investigator in the unit, Jankowski was on his second tour in homicide. When he first came to homicide in the early nineties, they still typed investigative reports on IBM Selectrics. If he had his way, he still would. Sanchez, on the other hand, was the computer whiz of the unit. After high school, he joined the Marine Corps with visions of becoming a recon sniper, but instead, they trained him in computer technology and communications. Whenever investigators had a computer problem, they turned to Sanchez, who could solve it in minutes, instead of having to wait days for someone from the city's IT department to venture out of City Hall.

"It'll take you forever to do this by hand," Sanchez said. "Give me the phones and computers. I'll set up an Access database, download the computer and phone data into it, and have it automatically search for matches."

Jankowski said, "Last month, my nerd partner cracked a case by finding our suspect doing some Facebook thingy right next to where our victim was withdrawing money from an ATM. All that with his computer."

The rest of the unit flowed into the office, stopped at the coffee pot, and made their way to Sinclair's desk to inquire about the latest murder. At eight sharp, Lieutenant Maloney rolled through the door, and Sinclair and Braddock met him with a copy of the press release.

Maloney looked up from the paper, his face more haggard than earlier. Sinclair told him about the peace sign necklace in the Samantha Arquette photos.

"Jesus H. Christ," he said. "You're telling me we have a maniac out there killing people and hanging peace signs around their necks?"

Maloney picked up his phone and called the chief's secretary, asking to get a meeting with him and the deputy chief for the Bureau of Investigations. When he hung up, he said, "I'm pulling you off standby."

"Lieutenant," Sinclair objected, "we've only got two more days. If we get another one, Cathy can handle it. She hasn't had one yet."

A homicide team worked standby for a week, during which time they handled every new murder that occurred. Occasionally, too many cases or a high-profile murder would overwhelm the team, requiring the next team in the rotation to take over. But it was a matter of pride for investigators to handle every murder during their standby week, so Sinclair had to make his pitch.

"I need your full attention on this. Jankowski and Sanchez will take over standby. Until they get something, they'll assist you. This latest development will certainly get City Hall jacked up."

Sinclair headed straight to Jankowski and Sanchez to apologize and take their jabs. Jankowski's chair squealed as he leaned back. "I was thinking about telling you how the coach benched you 'cause you couldn't hit the pitching. Truth is, the boss made the right call. I'll enjoy helping catch this asshole."

Chapter 18

Sinclair entered the morgue as Dr. Gorman was pulling the stomach out of the body cavity.

"I started without you." Gorman set the organ on a cutting board that rested on the corpse's thighs. "We have a fit, healthy woman who did not die of natural causes. The external shows marks consistent with a stun gun, just as with the Caldwell subject, located on her left, frontal chest region at rib number ten. The distance between the probes is the same as on the previous subject, which indicates the same device may have been used."

Sinclair looked at the marks as Gorman continued. "Superficial lacerations and abrasions present on both wrists and ankles, similar to what we saw on Caldwell yesterday. If the DA were to ask me in court, I would say they are consistent with a victim struggling against flex-cuff restraints. We also have some bruising on the left arm. My guess is someone grabbed her arm very tightly. The nail on her left-hand ring finger is broken, so I took scrapings and clippings of all nails. It's always a long shot, but you might get some DNA."

"Did your people tell you about the peace medallion?" Sinclair asked.

"Yes, they did, and that's the reason I'm paying special attention to those areas I've mentioned. However, I'm not allowing that commonality between these two victims to influence my findings."

"Did you find any syringe injection marks?"

"No, and I closely examined obvious locations. Now we come to what is the probable cause of death. Both wrists show deep lacerations longitudinally along the radial artery, severing it in several places in each arm. The instrument was a very sharp, thin-bladed cutting instrument."

"Scalpel?" asked Sinclair.

"The cuts are consistent with a scalpel incision; however, I cannot exclude an extremely sharp knife. Suffice it to say that the nature of these cuts would likely cause sufficient hypovolemia to result in death unless direct pressure or other methods were applied to stop the hemorrhage."

"Meaning?"

"A state of decreased blood volume. The average body has about five liters of blood. If a hemorrhage results in a thirty to forty percent blood loss, we call that a Class Three Hemorrhage. That is the critical stage, where if life-saving measures are not initiated, unconsciousness and death will likely occur. Above forty percent, a loss of about two liters of blood volume, is fatal. I'll know more once I complete the autopsy and run some tests; however, I suspect the cause of death will be as a result of hemorrhage from the severed arteries."

She bled to death, thought Sinclair. "Anything else I need to know?"

"The cuts are clean and precise. No hesitation marks as are common in suicides. I can't imagine a victim remaining still while someone cuts her wrists, and based on the other autopsy, I intend to do a full tox to see if she was sedated before the cuts occurred."

"Do you have some tox info from the boy's autopsy?"

"Sergeant Sinclair, as you know, tox results take six to eight weeks," he said and picked up his scalpel. As Sinclair was walking out the door, Gorman asked, "Have you checked your voicemail lately?"

Sinclair looked at his watch. Eleven-fifteen. "Not for two hours."

"You may wish to do so."

★

Connie handed Sinclair several phone messages when he passed her desk. "They announced a press conference for noon, and five minutes later, everybody started calling to get the scoop. I told them that's why we have press conferences—so we don't have to talk to every reporter one at a time."

"Thanks," said Sinclair, shuffling through the messages.

"One man insisted he had a vital tip and would only leave it on your voicemail, so I connected him."

Sinclair filled his coffee mug, picked up his desk phone, and entered four numbers. He recognized the voice immediately. "Sergeant, this is a confidential source who cannot reveal his identity. Please keep this to yourself and wait for the official results before you use it. Caldwell's blood and urine contained a concentration of morphine at least five times the level necessary to cause death. Since heroin is metabolically converted to morphine in the body, there is no way to distinguish between pharmaceutical morphine and heroin entering his system; however, using chromatographic processes, additional substances that are the by-product of heroin were identified. This is preliminary and not conclusive, but it appears the boy was injected with heroin, which as we both know is not available medically in the US."

Sinclair leaned back in his chair and took another gulp of coffee. Gorman's information was interesting, but he'd have to find a way to use it without revealing its origin. The kid was no junkie, and nothing else pointed toward a typical drug-related murder. The question was, who would want to shoot Caldwell up with heroin and why?

Sinclair stepped over to Sanchez's desk. Cell phones and a laptop were arrayed among a rat's nest of cords on his desk.

"This will take some time," said Sanchez. He pulled a flash drive from a laptop and inserted it into his computer. "I have all relevant information from the phones. Once I convert it to a format compatible with the PC, I'll populate the correct fields in the—"

"Sinclair," Lieutenant Maloney yelled from his office.

Glad to escape the computer gibberish, Sinclair left Sanchez's desk and stuck his head into Maloney's office.

"I know—press conference," Sinclair said. "Whose brilliant idea was that?"

"The PIO recommended it to the chief. Said we should, quote, *get out ahead of this*, and the chief agreed."

"I think the PIO found a justification to put his head in front of a bunch of cameras."

Sinclair saw Maloney looking at his hands as he kneaded his left hand with his right.

"Let me see that," Maloney said.

Sinclair held out his hand, showing two swollen knuckles. "From my little fight last night."

"Should you get X-rays, be sure it's not broken?"

"It's just bruised. I'll be fine."

"That's another reason we don't punch people in the face."

"I know, their heads are harder than our hands."

"Talk with the PIO and make sure he knows what *not* to say." Maloney went back to his computer screen, signaling the conversation was over.

Sinclair trudged down the service stairs into the PAB basement and into the locker room, where he shaved and washed his face. He pulled his shoeshine kit from the bottom shelf and polished his wingtips, removing the debris and scuffs from the fight with Tyrone Hayes. He took a pale blue shirt from its plastic dry-cleaner bag and a burgundy tie from the top shelf of his locker. Sinclair had planned to leave Liz's place early enough to change clothes in the locker room before work, but the call-out disrupted that. He hated wearing the same clothes two days in a row, especially when he ended up on camera both days, since doing so signaled he spent the night some place other than his home.

Ten minutes later, Sinclair stood beside a podium with the Oakland PD logo. A dozen microphones, each with the name of a radio or television network in letters or numbers, were arrayed on top of the podium. The pressroom on the seventh floor buzzed with the conversations of thirty reporters and camera technicians. Sinclair recognized many of them. Liz, with her cameraman Eric at her side, chatted with a male reporter from Channel 4, the NBC affiliate. She flashed him a smile and returned to her conversation.

The only other department representative in the room was George Thomas, the public information officer.

Thomas was pretty-boy handsome. A light-skinned black man with shiny black hair, he wore a bright blue tie and a dark suit that was tailored too closely for someone who carried a gun, which Thomas seldom did. He looked more like a newscaster than a cop. The chief of police was absent along with any other ranking members of the department.

Thomas stepped behind the podium. "Good afternoon," he said, pausing until the room quieted. "I regret that the chief and mayor are not available for this press conference because they are engaged in a marathon planning session with other law enforcement agencies and city staff to coordinate resources to address the recent violence and to ensure the safety of our citizens. I will begin with an overview of the murders and the crime prevention strategies the department has planned so far. I will then turn the briefing over to Sergeant Sinclair, the lead investigator from our Homicide Division, to discuss the status of the investigation."

Thomas placed a poster board with photos of Zachary Caldwell and Susan Hammond on an easel adjacent to the podium and read a prepared statement. Standing behind Thomas, Sinclair wore his best poker face as he watched the cameras zoom in on the photographs and back to him and Thomas. After Thomas answered a few questions about the victims' backgrounds, he said, "I will now turn it over to Sergeant Sinclair."

Sinclair slid behind the podium and scanned the crowd. A baritone-voiced reporter for KCBS, the top news radio station in the Bay Area, shouted above the others. "Are these murders related? Is the same person responsible for both killings?"

He could feel every camera on him and knew he would be on every local news show and likely network news nationwide. "The killings are similar and may be the work of the same suspect."

"Well, are they or aren't they?" shouted an Asian man from the *San Jose Mercury News*.

"If I knew for sure, I would've said so."

Sinclair could never cut it as a PIO. A departmental spokesperson would never admit not knowing something, and Sinclair couldn't talk in circles and say nothing as he'd seen the PIO do. Sinclair paused as reporters yelled over each other. Then he calmly pointed to a tall brunette reporter from Channel 7 with her hand up.

"Sergeant, can you tell us if the victims have anything in common? Did Mrs. Hammond know Zachary?"

"We're looking into it. If any citizens know of a relationship, I'd appreciate a call."

Sinclair ignored the two reporters who yelled out questions and called on a middle-aged man from Channel 5, the CBS station. "You've neglected to say how they were killed."

"In an active investigation, it's necessary to withhold certain evidence. The murderer might be reading the newspapers and watching the news, so I don't want to tell him everything I know. What I will say is, both victims were likely killed elsewhere and then deposited on the same bus bench. We call this kind of murder a *body dump*." Sinclair saw the print reporters writing in their notebooks. He visualized "body dump" in the headlines tomorrow and was pleased he could give them a bone that wouldn't jeopardize his investigation. "I will say, however, that neither died from gunshots."

More hands shot up, but before Sinclair could call on one, a reporter from the *San Francisco Chronicle* shouted, "It sounds like you're withholding evidence that shows the incompetence of your department. You're asking the public to trust you, yet you won't provide any information that allows the people to make their own judgment. Don't you think the public has the right to know?"

Sinclair had learned the hard way how some reporters try to provoke investigators into saying something spontaneously. It might look good on the front page, but responses to that kind of provocation would land him in front of the chief's desk—the last thing Sinclair needed. If he uttered one stupid comment in a fifteen-minute interview, the dumb comment was the ten-second sound bite that made the air or the lead of the newspaper article.

"Mr. Nesbit," Sinclair addressed the reporter by name. "The public's right to know covers public safety issues, not ongoing criminal investigations. After we arrest and charge a suspect, our investigation becomes public record. You'll have to wait until then to judge the competence of our work."

The room was silent for several seconds. Sinclair knew that most of the journalists in the crowd didn't like Nesbit much more than the cops did and enjoyed seeing him spanked. Nevertheless, many secretly admired his brashness. He saw Liz's hand among the sea of raised hands and called on her.

"Elizabeth Schueller, Channel Six News," she said in her on-the-air TV voice. "Can you tell us what the department is planning on doing to protect the citizens in the Bay Area?"

Sinclair looked at her for two counts, wishing he could thank her for the softball she tossed him. "I cannot speak for the rest of the department, but what I'll be doing is real simple—I'm going to find the man responsible and put him behind bars. Now if you'll excuse me, I've got murders to investigate."

Two minutes after Sinclair sat down at his desk, John Johnson pulled up a chair beside him. Johnson had worked the crime beat for the *Oakland Tribune* for forty years and was the only reporter who had free access to the homicide office. The investigators considered him as much a much a part of the homicide family as their fellow detectives.

"You handled the vultures well," said Johnson. "Nesbit's always been a prick, but you need to watch him. Some of the TV types were miffed that Channel 6 splashed the victims' pictures in little teaser shots a few hours ago, yet no one else got them until the press conference. They all know about you and Liz, so you best be careful. If she's the only one who gets exclusives, it'll give Nesbit even more reason to trash you in the *Chronicle*."

"I appreciate the warning. The San Francisco liberals love his antipolice stance."

Nesbit had written every dirty detail about his shooting, drunk driving accident, and demotion and even wrote about Sinclair's divorce as if he were one of Hollywood's bad boys. One article he wrote for the *Chronicle*, "Rising Homicide Star Falls," belonged in one of the rags displayed in grocery store checkout aisles.

"Don't be surprised to see your past rehashed in articles Nesbit writes about these murders. He'll disguise it as background and the editors will probably let it in."

"Will they ever forget?" Sinclair asked, not expecting an answer.

"I'll try to slip in the good stuff you've done in my articles. Most of the TV reporters like you. They want to keep communication open, so they won't screw with you. But you can't hold the wolves at bay forever."

Chapter 19

Sinclair hated Bay Area traffic. With no freeway north of the Bay Bridge, the only way to get through San Francisco was on city streets clogged with cars, trucks, and buses. Whenever he swung into the right lane to avoid a car turning left, he ended up behind a bus that stopped in the middle of the lane to load and unload passengers. Sinclair and Braddock crept from red light to red light on Geary Boulevard, inching their way toward Presidio Heights.

"How'd you and Jankowski do with Susan's husband?" Sinclair asked.

"Jankowski acts all gruff, but he's just a big teddy bear," she said. "Mr. Hammond was more than cooperative with everything we asked for."

"Anything enlightening?"

"We downloaded her address book from her laptop, and Hammond even gave us a Quicken file with their check and credit card information. Jankowski got him to sign releases so we can get updates from his bank, the phone company, and any other businesses we think of later."

"He's awful trusting for a lawyer."

"He's not like the defense attorneys we deal with. He wants us to find who killed his wife. He acts like he's got nothing to hide, so either he truly doesn't or he's a great actor."

"I'd still keep an eye on him. He's a lawyer and they teach lawyers how to lie in law school," said Sinclair.

Sinclair hoped all the background work on the victims would pan out. Although he wasn't optimistic, there was no other avenue to pursue; nothing pointed to a motive or a suspect. Phil had told him on one of their first cases, "When you don't have a suspect or any idea why your victim was killed, investigate the victim. The reason for the murder often lies with him."

"What do you think the chances are of Mrs. Fitzgerald letting us talk to Jenny?" Braddock asked.

"We've got to give it a shot. I should've taken a close look at the two girls when I first got the case."

Sinclair hoped that if he got to the bottom of what happened to the two girls and how they ended up on the bus bench that night, he might find the key to the last two murders. Earlier, he had called two phone numbers he had for Jane Arquette, but both were disconnected. He called the NYPD detective who was assigned the case when Samantha died in the Manhattan hospital, hoping he had contact info for Jane, but only reached his voicemail. He doubted Mrs. Fitzgerald had softened since the last time they spoke, but his best chance was meeting her face-to-face. Sinclair had tried to call her husband, who was one of the top executives in the commercial real estate division of Wells Fargo Bank, but his executive assistant took a message and called Sinclair back later to say it was a family matter, and he'd have to go through Mrs. Fitzgerald to talk to Jenny.

Sinclair turned onto Arguello Boulevard and looked for a parking space. He pulled onto the sidewalk in front of the single-car garage. "Unbelievable," said Sinclair. "You pay millions of dollars to live here and you can't even find a place to park."

"It's worth three million. Thirty-five-hundred-square-foot house on a twenty-five-hundred-square-foot lot."

Sinclair craned his neck to view the top of the three-story house. "Can't be much room for a backyard."

"Probably the size of a couple of jail cells."

They took the stairs to the front door and rang the bell. A slender woman with a brunette ponytail, wearing yoga pants and two layered tank tops, opened the door.

"Mrs. Fitzgerald," said Sinclair, "My name is—"

"You're Sergeant Sinclair," she interrupted. "My husband's office said you called."

"May we come in and talk?"

"There's nothing to talk about," she said, folding her arms across her chest.

"We'd like to speak to Jenny."

"She doesn't remember anything."

"It's important. There're new developments."

"My only concern is protecting my daughter."

"Just asking her a few questions shouldn't harm her."

"You're not my daughter's psychiatrist."

Sinclair felt a hand on his arm as Braddock gently pushed him to the side. "It's nice to see you again, Mrs. Fitzgerald," said Braddock. "We would never do anything to harm Jenny."

Mrs. Fitzgerald smiled. "I remember you from the hospital. Cathy, isn't it?"

"Yes, and you're Donna, right?"

Mrs. Fitzgerald smiled again.

"I'm in homicide now," Braddock said, "and Jenny's case is special to me. Maybe if just I talk—"

"Do you have children of your own?"

Braddock smiled. "Two."

"You're lucky. That's one of the many things Jane and I had in common. Back when we were freshmen together at Brown, we talked about getting married and having two or three children. Along with the perfect career, of course. But we both only had one. I tried, but Jenny's all I have and I'll do anything to protect her."

"I'm sorry, and I do understand. I want to be with my son and daughter every second of the day to make sure . . ." She trailed off and then said, "But I also need to protect the thousands of other Jennys and Samanthas out there. That's why I'm here. And your daughter could help."

Tears welled in Mrs. Fitzgerald's eyes, and Sinclair thought she was ready to give in.

"I just can't," she said.

"Can you at least put me in touch with Jane Arquette?" said Sinclair. "She deserves to know what's happening, and the numbers I have for her no longer work."

"I'm sorry. Jane's dead," she said. "She took her own life shortly after Samantha died."

Chapter 20

"No cigar today?" Braddock asked as they sat in the traffic crawling toward the Bay Bridge. They'd moved a half mile in the last twenty minutes yet still had another mile until the on-ramp.

"The chief showing up at our crime scene upset my routine," said Sinclair. "And it's not like I can light up a cigar just any place."

"I don't mind," she said. "I like the smell. Reminds me of my dad."

Sinclair leaned across Braddock, fished around in the glove box, and came out with a Rocky Patel, a five-inch cigar with a medium brown wrapper. He clipped the end and lit it with his Zippo. "I sometimes wish I was on OPD back in his day. Cops could kick ass and lock up bad guys without anyone second-guessing them. Your dad's one of the legends from that era."

"Police work was in his blood, just like you." She rolled down her window and the smoke wafted out.

"You, too. Your grandfather, your father, and now you."

Braddock laughed. "He tried to talk me out of it. Said that good cops give everything to the job and that leaves nothing left. He didn't want me to become like him."

"They never talked about how the job affected their personal lives back then."

"Families kept better secrets in those days. I try to remember the good stuff. He worked traffic most of his career, and all motor officers took their bikes home back then. He would walk out the door in the morning dressed in his leather jacket and boots and fire up his Harley. As a kid, I learned why motor cops were called leather gods. But I was deathly afraid of him—a weird mix of love and fear. After my mother remarried—"

"I didn't know your parents split up."

"I was thirteen when they divorced. Ryan and I have promised ourselves our kids won't grow up like I did."

Sinclair had never looked up to his father, but he remembered fearing him, not knowing what mood he'd be in when he got drunk. His father had been a heavy drinker as long as he could remember, but it got increasingly worse after Sinclair's little brother died. Unlike Braddock, Sinclair never wanted to be anything like his father—his father was mean, self-centered, bigoted. He worried that if he ever did have a family of his own, he might become just like him. But he wasn't his father, he continually reminded himself. He may have picked up the genetic disposition to alcoholism from his father, but unlike his father, he was doing something about it.

The traffic began moving. Sinclair took several puffs off his cigar and hung his arm out the window. "I'm still thinking about Jane Arquette's suicide, assuming that's what it actually was."

"I can't imagine the devastation I would feel if my daughter died," she said.

"Enough to take your own life?"

Braddock was quiet for a moment, and Sinclair knew she was thinking about how she would handle it. "I'd feel like it, but wouldn't do it. I can see some mothers doing it, though."

"Then she makes the fourth death linked to the bus bench," he said.

★

Everyone else had gone home except for Sinclair, Braddock, Jankowski, and Sanchez. Sinclair looked up from his desk to see Lieutenant Maloney drag himself into the office.

"Thought you already went home," bellowed Jankowski.

"I wish." Maloney's eyes were bloodshot and his sparse hair was plastered to his oily scalp. "The chief had me at the mayor's office with him watching the news and brainstorming about how to keep the media from creating panic."

"Did Sinclair get them all riled up like he usually does?" asked Jankowski.

"Actually—and this was a big shocker—the chief and mayor were pleased with the PIO and Matt. We watched the coverage on every channel and they thought Matt handled the questions very professionally."

"Sinclair? Professional? I never thought the chief would use those two words together," said Jankowski.

"I guess I haven't been canned yet," said Sinclair.

"Oh, they discussed it." Maloney paused, and Sinclair could tell the lieutenant was contemplating how much of the chief's conversation to divulge. "Nothing to worry about for now."

The *for now* part didn't leave Sinclair feeling all warm and fuzzy. Nevertheless, he ignored it and told Maloney about their strikeout with Mrs. Fitzgerald, Jane Arquette's suicide, and their action plan for the rest of the evening.

"I got more sleep than you two," Maloney said. "And I'm only running on two cylinders. There's nothing that can't wait until morning when you're fresh. Go home and get some sleep. If a break comes, I need you sharp."

Sinclair was too tired to argue. They cleared their desks and walked out the door together. The sun had dropped below the buildings along the waterfront and the sky was clear. The temperature still hovered in the high seventies, a warm evening for Oakland. Braddock pulled her gear from her Crown Vic. Sanchez would take over the car since he was now on standby. As the senior partner, Sinclair was authorized to take the team's car home even when not on standby, and although this allowed him to save on gas and wear and tear on his five-year-old Mustang, it carried with it the obligation to respond on fresh murders if another team needed help. He popped the trunk and Braddock threw her duffle bag inside.

Sinclair stood there. In all the years he worked with Phil, they ended every standby with a round of beers at the Warehouse, debriefing their cases and discussing their lives. No longer an option. He needed sleep, but he was too wound up.

Braddock's phone rang. "I'm leaving right now . . . Can't think of a better way to spend an evening. Love you too."

Sinclair grinned. "So how *are* you going to spend your evening?"

She laughed. "We're going to give the kids their bath."

Sinclair laughed.

"When you have kids, you'll understand. What about you—off to Liz's?"

"Not tonight. A few nights a week together is enough for both of us."

She started walking to the back of the lot where her personal car was parked. Over her shoulder, she said, "We did good today."

Sinclair began to pull out of the parking space but then put the shift lever back into park and sat there. He was mentally and physically spent, but his brain was spinning. He could see two of the victims lying on the stainless steel tables in the morgue, the girl lying on the hospital bed in a coma, the faces of Susan's husband and Zachary's parents.

No one cared about many of Sinclair's murder victims. Drug dealers and prostitutes, whose friends and families had given up on them years before. One of the first cases he and Phil had worked together was the murder of a young, black crack fiend who they suspected had been killed for stealing the corner stash. After two days, they hadn't found a single person willing to talk about the murder. Over drinks at the Warehouse that night, Phil said, "Sitting at this bar are the only two people in the world who care about finding out who killed this young man. In homicide, we speak for the dead. It's a lonely and thankless job and an awesome responsibility." But Sinclair knew it was about more than just the victim. A murderer could not be allowed to kill and walk the streets freely. When people can kill with impunity, society crumbles. He wanted to tell Phil how it often felt like they were the only ones standing between civilization and anarchy and how that lonely and thankless responsibility was even more awesome than merely speaking for the dead but was afraid that his partner wouldn't understand.

These three victims—maybe a fourth—had people who cared. Their families and friends, the police brass, and Oakland residents were counting on him. He wondered if he could live up to their expectations.

Sinclair did not just want a drink—he needed one. He put the car in drive and pulled off.

Chapter 21

Nestled into the business district of the upscale community high in the Oakland Hills, A Great Good Place for Books in Montclair Village was as much a neighborhood meeting place as a bookstore. Dr. Brooks's wife, Carol, had been inside for an hour, a long time to buy a book, the man thought. The last time he strolled by the window, he noticed a flyer announcing a book reading and signing tonight for some woman's debut novel. Pretending to read the flyer, he looked through the window and saw Carol rise from a folding chair where she had been sitting with a predominantly female audience listening to the author. She was dressed impeccably, as always, in a salmon-colored blouse, beige crop pants, and ivory linen blazer. She stepped into a line, waiting her turn for the author's signature.

He crossed La Salle Avenue and walked up the street, stopping near Montclair Pharmacy, where he had a clear view of the bookstore. When working, he often passed through a dozen Bay Area cities a day, but the diversity in Oakland's neighborhoods always amazed him. In the flatlands of West and East Oakland, poverty, gangs, and drugs flourished. Rap music thumped from cars, interrupted by gunshots or firecrackers in the distance. Steel bars covered windows and doors, and cars sat on cement blocks in front yards. Montclair, five miles away, was a different world. Small houses sold for millions of dollars, and Mercedes and BMWs lined the streets. Faces were mostly white, and of the few blacks, Asians, or Hispanics he saw, none wore baggy jeans halfway down their asses or catcalled the women who strolled along the sidewalk. It was no wonder that people who lived here referred to their residence as Montclair, as if it were a separate city and not merely a district of Oakland.

He dressed to blend in—khakis, a white polo shirt, and a navy blue sweater. No one gave him a second look, other than an occasional woman who gave him a quick up and down glance followed by a smile.

His target exited the bookstore, followed by a woman about her same age and as stylishly dressed. They turned right and walked side-by-side up the hill. He paralleled them on the opposite side of the street, ready to rush ahead and get in position before they reached the parking garage. Instead, they turned right on the next street and disappeared into Jamba Juice a few doors down from the corner. A light wind carried the aroma of grilled meat from the gourmet burger place down the street.

A few minutes later, the women exited the shop carrying plastic cups with straws poking from the top. They strolled back to La Salle and up the hill, sucking on their drinks. He waited thirty seconds after they entered the parking garage and followed. He expected the women would part ways once inside, but instead, they walked together to Carol's Mercedes. He stopped ten cars away and watched the women hug. His target opened her car door, and the friend turned and walked in his direction.

An SUV with a mother and a bunch of kids drove past him searching for a parking space.

Too risky to make his move here. Too many witnesses.

He spun around and hurried to his van. Halfway down the row, the Mercedes started and rolled toward the exit.

He twisted the key, pulled the shifter into drive, and followed. He trailed her onto Moraga Avenue and made the light with her onto Snake Road and up into the hills toward her house. Five minutes later, she pulled into the driveway of the sprawling house tucked among the pines and redwoods on Woodrow Drive. Could he do it? Rush into the driveway and grab her before she closed her garage door?

His heart raced.

The man stopped his van just before her driveway, prepared to jump out.

Her car pulled into the two-car garage. Now or never.

Chapter 22

A few miles from the freeway and business district, in between clusters of ranch-style houses on wide, tree-lined streets, the Lafayette Community Center stretched along a winding road that ran from Lafayette to Moraga. Several old wooden buildings, used for classes ranging from arts and crafts to mother-and-toddler aerobics, ringed the parking lot. Athletic fields for youth soccer and baseball sat behind the buildings, and beyond that rose a hillside covered with large oak trees and grasses dried to a golden brown. The smallest building, located on the far edge of the complex, was where the Alcoholics Anonymous groups met.

Unlike the church basements where AA groups traditionally gathered in their early days and still commonly did on the east coast, this room was light and airy. Ten people sat around a table in the center of the room and forty more sat in rows of chairs behind the table.

The meeting was ten minutes under way when Sinclair came in and took a seat in the back. He crossed his arms and tucked his hands into his armpits so no one would see them shaking. After leaving Oakland, he'd driven straight to the Lafayette Wine and Spirits Shop, just down the street from his apartment. He sat in the parking lot, staring at the displays in the window, unable to go inside yet unable to muster the courage to leave. He wanted to have a drink like any normal person. But he knew that was wishful thinking. Still, another part of him thought it was possible—that he wasn't really an alcoholic after all. And another part of him didn't give a shit—even if one drink would lead to a bottle. As he sat there, that "one day at a time" slogan running through his head, he decided to go to a meeting, and afterward, if he still wanted it, the liquor store would be open.

Tonight, the meeting format was speaker discussion. Walt sat at the head of the table speaking in his mellow baritone. He was a fixture at the community center meetings, where everyone knew his story. A Vietnam vet, Walt had gone to college on the GI Bill and eventually got a doctorate in clinical psychology. He grew a successful practice, specializing in post-traumatic stress disorder, and treated combat veterans and victims of childhood and sexual abuse. By the time he turned forty, his life appeared perfect: a charming wife and two preteen sons, a house in Lafayette, and a reputation as one of the most respected therapists in the state. However, he had begun combining his drinking with painkillers and sedatives prescribed by five different physicians, each without the knowledge of the others.

"My drinking and drug use allowed the dark side of my personality to take over," Walt said. "I felt entitled to do whatever I wanted. I was having an affair with three of my patients, women who came to me for help, when one of them made a complaint to the board. After the investigation, the courts took over. I was convicted of insurance fraud for billing patients' insurance for services I never performed, sexual offenses, and drug charges for my abuse of prescription drugs. I served sixteen months in prison, lost my license, my house, and every cent I had in the bank.

"I thought my life was over. Although I had preached it for years as a therapist to my patients, I secretly thought AA was for people like all of you. You know—skid row bums." He paused to let the laughter in the room of well-dressed people subside. "I attended my first AA meeting in prison and learned I wasn't unique. It didn't matter if you were a doctor, lawyer, or janitor. The disease affected us all the same way."

Walt took a sip of coffee from the ceramic mug in front of him and continued. "Amazingly, my wife stayed with me, and when I got out of prison, I moved into a small apartment with her and our two boys. I was on parole and had to register as a sex offender. The only job I knew was one I was no longer licensed to do. I hadn't worked with my hands in twenty years, but I found a job doing construction work as a carpenter's apprentice and driving a limo at night, mostly back and forth to the airport. We didn't have much in a material sense, but I had everything I needed."

A tear rolled down his cheek and he wiped it away. "You see, the success, the fancy house, and all the material things I had when drinking never brought me happiness. Today I'm grateful for what's truly important in my life: my family and friends and a sense of serenity I never dreamed possible. Both of my sons graduated from college, one from Berkeley and the other from Stanford, and started their own families. I work for a good man doing simple work. It's a far cry from listening to patients in a fancy office at two hundred dollars an hour, but it's honest work and keeps me humble. Most importantly, I haven't wanted to take a drink in twenty years. And for that, I am grateful."

When the meeting ended, members began milling about, talking and laughing. Sinclair made a beeline for the door.

"Matthew, hang on a minute."

Sinclair turned and saw Walt heading toward him. He was a short, wiry man, with snow-white hair and eyes the color of a calm, summer sky. His face and hands were brown and weathered. Although in his midsixties, he moved like a man years younger. He opened his arms to hug Sinclair, but Sinclair turned and extended his hand. He wished these AAers would just shake hands like normal people.

"I saw you on the news tonight. How're you holding up?"

"I wanted a drink. That's how I'm holding up."

"But you didn't. You came here instead."

"Yeah." Sinclair felt tears forming, but he blinked them away. The last time he nearly cried was at a police funeral, but he didn't feel sad now. He didn't know what he was feeling.

"It'll get easier."

"That's what you guys say, but it's getting harder."

Walt stood there with a warm smile on his face. Inviting him to speak—to open up.

"You wanna get a cup of coffee?" Walt asked.

"I haven't really slept in two days. I ought to get home."

Silence again with the same smile.

"Do you have a sponsor or anyone in the program you talk to?" Walt asked.

"I'm not sure I believe in that sponsor stuff."

"I understand." Walt took a card from his pocket and handed it to Sinclair. *Walt Cooper* and a phone number, nothing more.

"You don't have to do this alone," Walt said.

Sinclair nodded.

"If you feel like drinking, call me before you pick up," Walt said.

Sinclair extended his hand to avoid a hug. "I will."

"And Matthew," Walt said as Sinclair turned toward the door. "Things will get better. I promise."

Chapter 23

The man stood on the balcony of the twenty-second-floor apartment at 1200 Lakeshore, taking in the view of Oakland's downtown and Lake Merritt below him. A necklace of lights surrounded the three-mile shoreline, which included city parks, a jogging path, and high-rise apartments. Although expensive by Oakland standards, the $3,500 rent for the two-bedroom apartment would have been a bargain in Manhattan or even San Francisco. Gertrude Stein's famous quote about Oakland, "There is no there, there," seemed flippant and inaccurate from his vantage point high above the crime and despair the city was best known for.

He puffed on the Cohiba Maduro he'd picked up for ten dollars at a downtown cigar shop and reflected on the moment in front of Carol Brooks's house. Hand on the car door handle, ready to spring out, he had stopped. Caution prevailed. Too risky. Too many unknowns. He had watched as the garage door descended and Carol's Mercedes disappeared behind it.

When his watch read ten, he ground his cigar out in a crystal ashtray, went inside, and turned on the television.

After a few minutes of world events, the anchor introduced the top local news—the second murder victim in two days found on a bus bench near Children's Hospital. The man settled into the sofa as news reporter Liz Schueller filled the television screen, her golden hair and brilliant smile captivating every male viewer. Even her mannerisms and speech were perfect. She held a smile for just a few seconds, enough to give her audience a taste before turning serious. Murder was serious business after all.

She appeared so sincere, the ideal blend of sadness and professional detachment. A perfect actor in front of the camera—pretty, poised, yet human. Few people knew the real Liz.

He watched as she reported the names of the victims: Zachary Caldwell and Susan Hammond. Liz's cop boyfriend must have decided that making their names public would help solve the case.

Sinclair appeared on the television, dressed in a dark suit and a perfectly knotted tie. The man turned up the volume. Sinclair looked his normal, arrogant self as he stared straight ahead, exuding confidence meant to make Oakland residents feel safe and believe Sinclair could protect them and their families from the same fate.

After Sinclair's fifteen seconds, Liz appeared back on the screen and said the police still did not know the cause of death for either victim. It would require further tests by the coroner, but they had ruled out obvious trauma such as a gunshot, stabbing, or beating. The man knew they must have noticed the cuts on Susan's wrists. He doubted the coroner's office had figured out the drugs in both of them yet. Even if they had, the cops probably wouldn't tell reporters those details. Once Sinclair knew, he'd start connecting the dots.

The TV showed the entrance gate to Blackhawk, where Dr. Caldwell lived, and the front of the office building where Susan and her lawyer-husband worked. The shots panned out to capture the mood and then in for the detail—a little artistry. The male anchor's deep voice introduced the next story, and the man switched off the news and slipped in a DVD.

He had watched this one many times. It contained dozens of news broadcasts showing Sinclair talking about other murders during the last two years. Each with the same confidence and determination. He seemed to be on camera every time he handled a murder. The story about the hero cop's fall followed, when the highway patrol arrested Sinclair for drunk driving. Oakland PD suspended him from duty and booted him out of homicide. He watched the segments from the other networks as they uncovered the scandal: Sinclair turned out to be driving from Liz's apartment when he crashed the police car. At first, they only said he was visiting a "well-known television personality," but a day later, the other networks mentioned Liz Schueller by name.

The competition within the news business was vicious. The other stations loved trashing Channel 6 and showing the reporter as the seductress of a broken and troubled cop with a past littered with citizen complaints, lawsuits, and shootings. They pretended it was relevant news they couldn't ignore, but it was all about ratings and the important advertising money that fueled the business.

How it backfired on them was ironic. Channel 6's viewership actually increased 10 percent following the revelation. People in California had no problem with a cop having a romantic relationship that was rife with conflict of interest, especially when he was a handsome homicide detective with a bunch of medals for heroism and bravery on his chest. Viewers wanted to see more of the woman Sinclair was willing to risk his career and professional reputation for, and Channel 6 put Liz on camera more frequently. She acted her normal professional and poised self on the air, and the public loved her even more for not shrinking away.

Last Friday, Channel 6 had mentioned Sinclair for the first time in months. The man hit the fast-forward button and the DVD jumped to that broadcast. Liz was on the air in front of the Oakland Police Department, finishing a story about a major drug bust. The news anchor cut in. "Liz, we heard some rumors about Matt Sinclair coming back to work. What have you heard?"

In what was surely a perfectly rehearsed exchange, Liz replied, "An arbitrator announced a decision today that restores Sinclair's rank to sergeant, and effective Monday, he will be leaving crime analysis, where he has worked for the last six months, and return to homicide."

"Much has been reported about your relationship with Matt recently. Can you tell us how he's taking the news?" the anchor asked.

Liz glanced down for a beat, showing the perfect amount of rehearsed embarrassment, then smiled and said, "He's happy to be back, and I join the rest of our viewers in wishing him the best upon his return. The city needs detectives of his caliber and dedication to combat the terrible violence we see here nightly." One, two, three, the man counted to himself, as a close-up of a beaming Liz filled the entire television screen before it shifted back to the anchor sitting at the desk.

Liz deserved an Academy Award for that performance.

Chapter 24

Sinclair strained against the weight—two forty-five-pound plates on each side of the Olympic bar—and locked out his eighth rep. Arms aching, he was ready to lower it onto the bar rest when he heard a voice from across the department gym. "Not bad for a skinny white dude."

Sinclair dropped the bar on the metal rests with a loud clang and sat up on the bench as Officer Tokepka, one of a dozen or so Tongan and Samoan officers on the department, walked toward him.

"Your office said you'd be here," Tokepka said. "You got the one-eighty-sevens at Children's, right?"

"Yea, you know something?"

"I popped a white dude last night for six-forty-seven F. Had a couple of syringes on him. Said he was a nurse at Children's and that's why he had the needles, but I think he was trying to score some heroin."

Sinclair stood and stretched his back. "You got a name on him?"

"Lance Keller. I have a copy of the CAR in my locker with his DOB and stuff," Tokepka said, referring to a consolidated arrest report form.

"What time was this?"

"Beginning of shift—around midnight. I'm sure the jail already released him. They don't hold people for drunk in public longer than four or five hours. I just needed to get him off the street. White dude walking around West Oakland that time of night is looking to get robbed or killed."

Sinclair showered and changed and then stopped at the city jail admin office. Keller had been released two hours earlier, but Sinclair got a copy of his consolidated arrest report and walked into the homicide office a few minutes before eight.

Braddock, Jankowski, and Sanchez were already there. A copy of the *Oakland Tribune* lay in the middle of Sinclair's desk, the headline reading, *Bus Bench Killer Claims Second Victim.*

"Catchy, huh?" said Braddock, sipping on her morning coffee.

"You know we've rated when they give our killer a nickname," said Sinclair.

Braddock's phone rang, so Sinclair grabbed a cup of coffee and strolled to the back of the office. Sanchez was still sucking information from every electronic device at his disposal and entering it into his database but hadn't discovered any connections. Jankowski was reading the paper.

"Good news," said Braddock. "I had ACH look into Jenny Fitzgerald's hospital admission. We know her clothes were collected as evidence by the tech who took photos of her injuries at the hospital. ACH gets a bunch of bogus claims of missing property, so they take any valuables from critical patients and hold them for safekeeping. It seems that two purses came in with her in the ambulance."

The explanation was simple. Both girls' handbags were on the bus bench, so either the paramedics grabbed both along with their patient or the officers on the scene put them on the gurney with the patient—Jenny, in this case. Sinclair had done the same thing when he was a street cop. No officer wanted to get blamed for misplacing someone's personal property and surely didn't want to do a report and extra paperwork to recover and turn in personal items when it was easier to toss them in the ambulance with a patient.

"When Jenny was released, her mother signed for one purse, containing, quote, one cell phone, miscellaneous personal items and ID, and twenty-two dollars in cash. Guess whose name is on the ID in the other purse?"

"By any chance is there a cell phone in that purse?" asked Sinclair.

"Yep."

A few minutes later, Sinclair and Braddock were in their car surrounded by the morning downtown traffic. He told her about Lance Keller's arrest.

"Let's hit ACH first since they're waiting for us," Braddock said.

Sinclair agreed as his cell phone vibrated. The screen showed Liz.

"Did you see the interview?"

"No," he said. "I was still working during the early broadcast and sound asleep by ten. Did you make me look good?"

"You looked very professional and incredibly yummy. Are you coming over tonight?"

"Might be a long day."

"Any arrests imminent?"

"Not unless we get lucky."

Sinclair put his phone away.

"I get it—I really do," said Braddock. "She's beyond beautiful, but she doesn't seem like the settling-down type."

Sinclair had never had a female partner before. He should've expected it would be different. He had known Phil's favorite football teams, every car he ever owned, and what he paid for his house long before he knew his wife's name. Phil never asked how Sinclair's marriage was going, even when it was obviously falling apart, and never told him his opinion about his relationship with Liz.

"Who says I want to settle down?"

"At one time you did," she said. "When you and that pretty DA got married, everyone talked about your being the perfect couple."

Sinclair had thought a lot about his marriage over the last six months. He figured out that he had gotten married not because he was ready to settle down but because he thought marriage might make him settle down. He regretted that he ruined the life of a wonderful woman because he wasn't capable of a being a husband and knew she was one of a long list of people he'd have to eventually make amends to.

"We know how that worked out."

★

Highland Hospital, also known as Alameda County Hospital—ACH to cops—had one of the busiest trauma centers in the state. Its emergency room handled an average of two hundred patients per day, with two or more trauma activations every shift for life-threatening injuries—gunshots, stabbings, or major car accidents. After Vietnam and until Oak Knoll Naval Hospital closed in 1996, the Navy used to send its doctors to ACH to gain firsthand experience in treating gunshot wounds. Thanks to the Oakland criminals, the Navy doctors received plenty of training.

ACH's ER was quiet as Sinclair and Braddock made their way down the long hallway, past the treatment rooms that contained only one or two patients, unlike most Saturday nights when every trauma room bustled and beds with patients overflowed into the hallway. They slipped past the nurse's station, where three nurses sat behind stacks of medical charts, and into the break room.

A nurse dressed in green scrubs looked up from a chipped Formica-topped table where she was sitting. She was in her late forties, tall and thin, with a smoker's wrinkled face. She gave Braddock a quick smile.

"Claire, this is my partner, Matt Sinclair," said Braddock.

"Nice to see you again, Claire." Sinclair knew most of the ER nurses and doctors, since homicide cases brought him there a few times a month, but he also knew Claire was among many of the older nurses who had begun eyeing him with disdain when he began dating several of the younger, single nurses at the hospital after his divorce. She smiled slightly at Sinclair, then pulled a black clutch purse and a chain of custody form from a plastic hospital bag and handed it to Braddock. "It wasn't our screw up in ER," she said. "When no cop picked it up by the end of the shift, we handled it according to protocol."

"No problem. I'm just glad you found it." Braddock signed her name on the form and opened the purse. The phone was inside.

Braddock said to Sinclair, "We should probably get this printed before we handle it."

On their way back to the car, Sinclair said, "Jeez, if looks could kill."

"Before Liz, you did have quite a reputation among the nurses."

"Really, like what?"

"I overheard comments like slut and man-whore thrown around in the break room."

"You're messing with me."

"I am." She laughed. "But you're easy."

Fifteen minutes later, Sinclair and Braddock stood in a windowless room in the basement of Children's Hospital staring at a bank of twenty video monitors. A uniformed security officer sat at one of three consoles, and Bob Daly, a mustached man in his midfifties wearing a brown suit, hovered over another.

"We have a state-of-the-art system," said the hospital's director of security. "Over one hundred cameras throughout the hospital complex, all recorded digitally and retained for three years. We have the capability to monitor any camera, but obviously, we can't watch every camera simultaneously."

Sinclair told Daley what he was looking for.

"It's a long shot, since we only have a few external cameras. The incident from last August will be easier to locate because we have a precise time. I can check cameras, say . . . five minutes prior and five after for anything unusual. The other two incidents will take longer since we'll have to search through hours of video."

"If you make copies, I can get people at the department to view it."

"This isn't like looking at video of a liquor store holdup. You'd have to know how to navigate through a hundred camera views, and a desktop computer can't do that. Besides, what you're asking for is hundreds of hours of video." Daly glanced at the security officer sitting at the computer console. "The hospital's given me carte blanche on overtime for anything connected to these incidents. I can put a team on it around the clock and make you a copy of any incident the least bit suspicious."

Sinclair left his card and made his way to human resources. An obese sixty-year-old woman with ultrashort hair listened to their request, made three phone calls, and peered at the two detectives over reading glasses perched on her nose. "Lance Keller resigned last week in lieu of termination. He was caught stealing narcotics for his own use."

"Did he work around Doctor Caldwell by any chance?" asked Sinclair.

"Nurse Keller worked in emergency. It seems he had been shorting patients their painkillers and using it himself. The mother of a patient saw him inject half a syringe of Demerol into her child's IV and then drop the syringe in his pocket. She reported it to the ER physician who went into the nurse's break room and found Keller with the needle in his arm."

"Any idea where he's working now?" asked Braddock.

"He was escorted out that night. The nursing department sent a report to the state the next day to suspend his license. There's a long process including drug treatment and probation before he'll ever work as a nurse again."

The woman handed Braddock a stack of papers from her computer printer. "I've included his employment application, a print version of our electronic personnel file, and the report of the incident with the Demerol."

"Looks like Keller's got a reason to be pissed off at Children's Hospital," said Sinclair, as they walked down the corridor to the elevator. "But is it enough to kill for?"

Chapter 25

In the homicide office, a tech brushed silver powder on Samantha's phone. He shined a flashlight on it from several angles before announcing there were smudges but no usable latent prints.

Sanchez plugged the phone into a power cord. "Battery's long dead. Service has been disconnected for over a year."

Jankowski meanwhile spread several pages of printouts across Sinclair's desk and leaned over him. "Here's what I've found out about Lance Keller so far. No arrests anywhere before last night. One car, a two-year-old Volvo registered to him at the same address as on his driver's license. Two moving violations on his DMV history—stop sign in the Volvo and speeding in a Chrysler."

Sinclair paged through the papers Children's Hospital had given him. The home address in Keller's employment file matched the DMV records. He handed Jankowski the entire package.

"The paperwork shows he was working in ER the night Samantha came in," said Sinclair. "Run his references and see if anything jumps out. If you can be discreet, go to his house, shake some trees. See if anything falls out."

"Why don't we just drag his junkie ass in and squeeze him?"

Sinclair knew that a murder suspect was tough to crack under the best circumstances, but to conduct an interrogation with nothing to confront the suspect with and nothing to use as leverage was a recipe for failure.

"What have we got on him, besides being a nurse at Children's?"

"He stole drugs and was trying to score smack on the streets of Oaktown," said Jankowski. "And the boy died from an overdose."

Sinclair wished he could reveal what the coroner told him—that Zachary was injected with heroin—but he gave his word. "That's not much. We don't have any connection between Keller and the girls from last year or Susan Hammond.

"We need a hammer. Find something I can jam him up on when he denies. If you find something, then I might be willing to drop everything else and focus on Keller."

"Okay." Jankowski gathered up the papers and returned to his desk.

Sanchez handed Sinclair a sheet of paper with the last ten numbers from Samantha's call log. Sinclair shuffled through the case packet looking for a match with the numbers. The last call from Samantha's phone was to her mother's cell phone, which was consistent with what her mother had said about receiving a call from a man who used Samantha's phone. There were eight other calls, seven of them incoming missed calls. That made sense too. Her mother had said she called Samantha numerous times that night after Samantha failed to make it back to San Francisco. The remaining call, one that lasted four minutes, was at 8:04 p.m. to a 646 area code, the same area code as Samantha and her mother's phone.

"The complete call log covers the previous thirty days," Sanchez said. "There are also seventy-four contacts, mostly just first names and phone numbers. Anything else would be on the service provider's computers, and we need a search warrant to get that."

"Is there any way to expedite?"

"Not without telling them we have a hostage situation or something. Otherwise, expect five to ten days."

"Do it," he said to Sanchez and then turned to Braddock. "You ready to make a cold call?"

They both knew the advantage female officers had when blindly calling a phone number. If the person on the other end were a man, he'd more readily talk to a woman, out of curiosity, if for no other reason. If it were a woman, she wouldn't feel as threatened by a female caller. Furthermore, even crooks didn't immediately think "cop" when hearing a female voice.

Braddock pressed the speaker button on her desk phone and dialed the number.

"Hello." The voice was female and sounded young.

"Hi," said Braddock. "Are you a friend of Samantha?"

"Who's this?"

"My name's Cathy. I'm calling numbers from Samantha's phone, hoping to connect with some of her friends."

A long pause. "Sam's gone."

"I know. It's so sad. What's your name?"

"Madison."

"Hi, Madison. Were you and Sam friends?"

Hesitancy filled her voice. "Yeah, like best friends."

"Please don't hang up, but I'm a detective in California and we're working to find out what happened to Sam. You talked to her that night."

"You're from California . . . where the car hit her?"

"That's right, Oakland. What did you talk about that night?"

"She was worried her mom would be pissed because she was supposed to be home already. Well . . . not home, but, like, where she was staying with her mom's friend in Frisco. She was with an older girl. The girl's mom's house was where Sam was staying."

"Jenny?" suggested Braddock.

"Yeah, Jenny. Sam was really excited. She and Jenny hooked up with some boys at a frat party in Berkeley."

"Really?"

"I told Sam to be careful 'cause the boys were older."

"Did she mention any names?"

"She said the boy she was with was Adrian."

"How about the fraternity?"

"Alpha Kappa Lambda. I even Googled it and thought it would be cool to go to a fraternity party by the time I was sixteen," said Madison. "I don't want to anymore, you know, after what happened."

Chapter 26

Sinclair slid his car behind a marked Berkeley PD car parked in a yellow zone on Telegraph Avenue and strolled with Braddock toward the University of California campus three blocks north. The sun baked the sidewalk, the thermometer already above eighty. Sinclair could tell it was heading toward a record high. Two bicycle officers, both with beards and dressed in blue shorts, utility shirts, gun belts, and bicycle helmets, stood astride their bikes talking to a twentysomething woman with long, stringy hair, who was sitting on the sidewalk in the shade. Wearing an ankle-length, flowing dress, she had an old backpack beside her and a metal cup and a cardboard sign that read, *Food Laundry,* in front of her. A skinny white man in his thirties with dreadlocks and no shirt, baggy brown pants, and sandals stood nearby.

"That's a whole different kind of police work from Oakland," Sinclair said as they checked out the street vendors that lined the sidewalk. They passed carts with incense sticks, flowers, patches to sew on clothes, and crocheted hats in the green, black, and gold colors of the Jamaican flag. They stopped at a table with handmade jewelry. There were bead necklaces, a hundred different rings, and a dozen peace sign medallions. The vendor sported hair halfway down his back and John Lennon glasses.

"Wearing peace next to your heart allows you to feel it in your heart," he said.

"I'm looking for one more like this." Sinclair removed a photo from his pocket and showed it to the man.

The vendor looked at the cropped enlargement of the medallion. "Mine are handmade by local craftsmen."

"Yeah, but my niece likes this one," said Sinclair.

"Try Berzerkeley Boutique, just up the street."

Sinclair and Braddock continued up the sidewalk, past People's Park, and through the throngs of pedestrians, a mix of college kids, street people, homeless, and hippies who looked as if they were still living in 1968. Sweat broke out on Sinclair, sticking his shirt to his back. He wished he could ditch his coat in the car, but with a gun, handcuffs, spare ammo, and a badge on his belt, taking off his jacket while strolling in public wasn't an option.

A blast of air conditioning hit them when they pushed through the door into Berzerkeley Boutique. Racks of T-shirts, peasant blouses, and hippie dresses covered most of the store. Sinclair weaved through the clothes to a glass display counter, behind which sat a woman with dusty cornrows and piercings in her lip, eyebrows, and nose.

Braddock spotted it first. "May we see that?" she asked the clerk.

The woman removed a peace medallion from the case and handed it to Braddock. "These have become quite popular recently." A silver stud protruding from the tip of her tongue clicked against her teeth as she spoke.

Sinclair held the medallion alongside the photo. They were the same. "What do you mean?"

"All we have left is the display model, and it's not for sale. There were twelve underneath the counter for months, until some guy bought them all last week. We should be getting in more—"

"This man," Sinclair said, "can you describe him?"

"Are you *the* man?"

Sinclair showed his badge. "Oakland Homicide."

"Homicide?" she echoed. "I wasn't here that day. I normally work Thursdays and Fridays."

"Do you keep sales receipts?"

"Not that far back. The owner takes them home every few days. She does the books there."

"I'll need the owner's name and that of the employee who was working when that man came in."

"Skye—she's the owner—was the one who told me about the man buying them all."

"Skye?" said Sinclair. "Skye what?"

"Just Skye." She wrote on the back of a business card and handed it to Sinclair. "Here's her phone number, but she's not there."

"If she's not at that number, where is she?"

"She left Wednesday night for her spiritual commune, somewhere on the Russian River. She'll be back Monday to open the shop at ten."

"What if there's an emergency, how would you reach her?"

"What kind of emergency?"

"Like if you had a heart attack."

"I'd ask the paramedics to lock the door, and Skye would open up on Monday. If I'm not here, the store doesn't open. If I'm here, I handle whatever needs handling."

Sinclair left his card and returned to the heat outside. He pulled his sunglasses from his pocket and slid them on, dulling the blazing sun to a tolerable level. He dialed the number and listened to a recording, hitting the speaker button so Braddock could hear. *Hello, this is Skye. Have a beautiful day. You may leave a message if you'd like. Peace and love.*

"That's got to be our guy," said Braddock.

"I'm sure he paid cash. We'll probably only get a generic description out of Skye, if anything. But things are looking up."

Chapter 27

Thirty minutes later, Sinclair and Braddock were sitting at a long table in the dining room of the Alpha Kappa Lambda fraternity house. "The UC police told me you were in charge of fall recruitment last year," said Sinclair to the college senior seated across from them.

"Yeah, I was the chair of our Rush Week committee." With his short blond hair and blue eyes and wearing a loose tank top, shorts that fell below his knees, and flip-flops, Cameron looked like he'd stepped off a Southern California beach.

"And you were in charge of the party that Adrian showed up to with some young girls."

"We don't have anyone in the fraternity named Adrian, nor anyone by that name who rushed last year," he said.

A manila file folder lay on the table in front of him.

"What's in there?" asked Sinclair.

"Our roster of members and pledges from last year."

Sinclair reached across the table.

Cameron placed his hands on the folder. "Don't you need a search warrant or something?"

"You sure you want to mess with me?"

Cameron slid the folder across the table.

Sinclair scanned the names. No Adrian. "I'll need a copy of this."

"Take it," said Cameron. "I can print another one."

Sinclair slid two photos, snapshots of Samantha and Jenny, out of his portfolio and set them in front of Cameron. He glanced at them for a second and looked up at Sinclair and Braddock impassively.

"Recognize them?" After a few seconds of silence, Sinclair said, "My friends at the university tell me your fraternity's on probation. One call from me and they shut down your house."

"I recognize them."

"Tell me what happened," said Sinclair.

Cameron told them about the Saturday night before the first week of classes last year, the night when all fraternities had their first party of the school year. The active members screened guys at the door to keep nonstudents out but seldom checked student IDs on girls.

"A lot of girls at a frat house makes for great recruiting of new pledges," said Sinclair.

"You got that right," Cameron said and told them that a few hours after the party began, he spotted Brandon, a sophomore who had expressed interest in joining the fraternity. Brandon was drinking beer in one of the rooms with another kid and two girls. The girls definitely weren't college age.

Sinclair scrolled down the names on the roster. "Brandon Shaw, is that the Brandon you're talking about?"

"Yeah. He knew the rules. Absolutely no underage girls allowed, and no one under twenty-one is allowed to drink."

"The girls?" asked Sinclair.

"The ones in your photos," said Cameron. "They were totally wasted. I told Brandon to get them out of the house."

"Did he?"

"I didn't see them the rest of the night. He came by the house the next afternoon and apologized and said he still wanted to pledge, so we had a long talk."

"Did he become a member?"

"We let him in as a pledge the fall semester, but it didn't work out."

"What happened?"

"Fraternities aren't what they used to be. None of that *Animal House* stuff, but it's not like we inspect our fraternity brothers' rooms to make sure there's no booze or females. If they're not twenty-one and they drink, they have to be cool about it. Brandon wasn't. There was also talk that he was dealing, and if this house got caught with drugs, we'd be shut down."

"What kind of drugs?"

"Party stuff, mostly X, pot, pharmies."

"How about roofies or molly?"

"Maybe."

"Where's Brandon now?"

"Haven't seen him since the end of that semester—just before Christmas."

"What about the other boy?" Sinclair asked.

"Only time I saw him. Brandon was trying to get him to pledge, but the boy's father wouldn't let him live on campus or join a fraternity. I saw his student ID that night, so I know he was a Cal student."

"Remember his name?"

"No."

"Describe him."

"Middle Eastern, maybe Indian or Pakistani. Freshman age, small kid, maybe five-eight, black hair."

After Sinclair and Braddock took a taped statement from Cameron, they returned to their car on the shaded street three blocks from campus. Braddock called homicide to have someone run Shaw, while Sinclair called a detective at UCPD. The detective told him Brandon Shaw was a sophomore engineering major during fall semester last year when the party occurred. His grades dropped from As and Bs as a freshman to all Cs and Ds that semester. He was placed on academic probation and dropped out in March. The last address the university had for him was on Lee Street in Oakland.

"CORPUS shows a Brandon Shaw," said Braddock, referring to the county criminal history system, "age twenty, former address the same as the fraternity house, current address on Lee. Arrested in March for possession of methamphetamine and narcotics paraphernalia, probably a crystal meth pipe, and then last month for possession for sales of crack cocaine. FTAed on his last court date, so there's a warrant in the system."

"From engineering student to crack dealer," said Sinclair.

"And of course, he ends up in Oakland," said Braddock.

Chapter 28

Twenty minutes later, Sinclair and Braddock pulled up to a gray apartment building in the Adams Point district of Oakland, a few blocks from Lake Merritt. The patrol squad working that district had weekends off, so to draw that squad on day shift required at least twenty years of seniority. The tall, lean uniformed officer who stood in front of the building was at least ten years older than Sinclair.

"I talked to the apartment manager," the officer said. "Shaw lives in two-twelve, a two-bedroom unit with three other men. We ran them out. They've got a bunch of arrests for property crimes, drugs, and misdemeanors, but no violence or weapons. Sometimes they get loud, but otherwise, the manager says they're not bad tenants. He gave me a key so we don't kick down the door."

The officer radioed another officer who was watching the back in case someone jumped out the window and then led the way inside and up the stairs.

They stacked alongside the door and Sinclair rapped loudly. "Police. Arrest warrant. Open the door."

In most departments, an arrest for a possession-for-sales warrant would require a tactical entry. Crack sales and guns go hand-in-hand, and since most crack dealers are also users, they can be unpredictable. But in Oakland, such arrests were routine, and the average patrol officer had more experience making felony arrests than SWAT cops in other departments. Besides, Shaw didn't fit the profile of an armed crack dealer, and the apartment wasn't a fortified crack house. Nevertheless, each officer's hand rested on the butt of his pistol.

Sinclair was leaning across the door to knock again, when the door squeaked open. "Show me your hands," he ordered.

Two hands protruded into the hallway. Sinclair grabbed a wrist and pulled a young blond man dressed in baggy jeans and T-shirt out of the apartment and shoved him toward Braddock, who cuffed him. Sinclair continued watching the open door.

"What's your name?" asked Braddock.

"Brandon Shaw."

"Anyone else in the apartment?"

"No."

While Braddock handcuffed Shaw, Sinclair drew his gun and entered. The uniformed officer followed. Sinclair and the officer walked through the front room, a combination living room and kitchen, and started down the hallway. They swept through the bedrooms and bathrooms, checking closets, shower stalls, and under beds. Once satisfied there was no one else in the apartment, the officer radioed his partner to come around the front.

Braddock was waiting with Shaw in the living room. She patted him down and removed a wallet and cell phone from his pockets. Then she reached deep into a front pocket and pulled out a small glassine zip-lock baggie containing four small white rocks.

"Looks like you've got a new charge on top of the warrant," Braddock said to Shaw.

"That's not mine," Shaw said.

"I guess someone must've put those drugs in your pocket," said Braddock.

"Or maybe you're wearing someone else's pants," said Sinclair.

Shaw shrugged.

Sinclair pulled a sheet of paper from his coat pocket and unfolded it. "Brandon, this is a consent to search form. If you don't sign it, we'll get a search warrant. That'll piss these officers off, because they'll have to sit around for hours while we type it up and find a judge to sign it, and then when they search your place, they'll probably make a terrible mess. But if you give us your voluntary consent, we'll be real neat and out of here in a few minutes."

Shaw nodded. Braddock removed his right handcuff so Shaw could sign the form.

"Which bedroom's yours?"

"First one on the left."

Sinclair told one officer to transport Shaw downtown. Once Shaw was gone, Sinclair gave the other officer instructions on what to look for in the front room while he and Braddock went to the bedroom. Two mattresses, heaped with a tangle of sheets and blankets, lay on the floor, and a dresser with a broken leg leaned against a wall under the window. Piles of dirty clothes lay around the room, which smelled like the inside of a gym bag. Braddock took the closet and went through the pockets of all the clothes. Sinclair did the same with the clothes on the floor and then went through each drawer of the dresser. There were papers and photos in the top drawer. Although nothing appeared related to the murders, Sinclair stuck it all in a bag.

When they were finished, the officer was sitting at the kitchen table. "Found a few pipes in a box by the TV, but the kitchen and bathroom turned up nothing."

Sinclair pulled off his gloves and washed his hands in the kitchen sink. "Nothing in the bedroom but dirty clothes and cockroaches and some papers we'll look through downtown."

"Did you include his phone on the consent to search form?" asked Braddock.

"Electronic devices," he said. "Cell phones fall under that."

Braddock scrolled through the phone. "Looks like over a hundred contacts, his recent call history, and a bunch of texts. Maybe we should have Sanchez do a dump on the phone so he can sort it on the computer."

"Makes sense. There's too much data for us to sort through unless we know what we're looking for."

"The call history only goes back six months," said Braddock. "So there wouldn't be anything from when Samantha and Jenny were raped."

"What about photos?"

Braddock handed Sinclair the phone. He swiped through scores of photographs and then stopped. "Cathy," he said, holding up the phone so that she could see. Sprawled out on a large bed with burgundy sheets, her long, blonde hair splayed across a pillow, was Samantha Arquette. Her eyes were closed. Between her breasts rested a silver peace medallion on a shiny chain.

Chapter 29

Back at the office, Sinclair and Braddock gathered around Sanchez's computer after he had plugged the phone into his computer with a USB cord and, using a special program, dumped all the phone's data onto his hard drive.

Sinclair felt Braddock's fingers digging into his forearm. He turned to face her, expecting to see tears in her eyes. Instead, he saw rage. He placed his hand over hers, and she relaxed her grip.

"There's more," said Sanchez as he clicked to the next photo.

Bare-chested and grinning, Shaw sat in a bed next to a naked Jenny Fitzgerald. She was obviously older than Samantha, her body more developed. Her eyes were glassy and unfocused. The next photo showed a dark-haired boy in a similar pose, sitting in bed next to Samantha, who had a zombie-like stare fixed on her face.

"Looks like we have the lineup." said Sinclair. "Jenny with Shaw and Samantha with this boy, who might be Adrian, if Madison is right."

"That would be Adrian Nadeiri," said Sanchez. "He's the only Adrian I saw in Shaw's contact list."

Sinclair entered the name into CORPUS. No matches. He tried DMV. The computer spit out an Adrian Nadeiri, nineteen years old, with a Berkeley address. Sinclair brought up the record and looked at the photograph. A definite match with the picture in Shaw's phone.

"What's his address?" asked Jankowski. "I'll go snatch the little fucker out of his house."

"Let's do this right," said Sinclair. "I don't want some judge to throw out a confession because we acted without a warrant."

"I'll ask him to come voluntarily," said Jankowski. "They never refuse."

"And no judge would ever consider he was coerced," added Braddock.

Jankowski gave them a sly smile.

Sinclair called UC, Berkeley, and gave them Nadeiri's info. The UCPD detective said, "Junior, engineer major, same address as his DMV record. His class schedule puts him in calculus right now."

"We've got enough to arrest him on probable cause for rape, and as long as he's in a public place, we don't need a warrant," said Sinclair.

"I'll send a unit there pronto and head over myself."

"Call me if you get him," said Sinclair. "I'll send an OPD car to bring him back."

"Hell, we'll bring him to you. It's not like we get to work a murder every day."

"Don't tell him what he's wanted for. And take his phone. I don't want him tipping off someone at his house."

Sinclair asked Jankowski to type up an affidavit and search warrant for the house and told him how to interrupt the interview with Shaw and what to say. Sinclair pulled a DNA sample collection kit from the locker, opened the interview room door, and stepped inside. Braddock followed.

Room 201 was six feet by eight with a stained linoleum floor and blue painted wood panels four feet up the walls. Above that, acoustical tiles covered the walls and ceiling. A metal table sat against one wall surrounded by three chairs. Shaw stood in the back corner, shifting his weight from one foot to the other, apparently full of nervous energy.

"I thought I was arrested over drugs," said Shaw. "The sign on the door says homicide."

"We'll talk about that in a little bit, but first, we need to do this," said Sinclair as he ripped open the package and donned a pair of plastic gloves. He grasped the first cotton swab, which looked like a Q-tip with a long handle.

"Open your mouth," Sinclair ordered.

Sinclair rubbed the cotton tip against the inside of Shaw's cheek, rotating it as he moved it in and out several times. He placed the swab on the packaging to air dry.

"What's this for?"

"DNA sample."

"What for?"

"We'll talk about it in a little bit. Open again."

Sinclair took the second swab from its sterile package and swabbed the other cheek. Braddock stood by the door with her notebook in hand.

"Time of test?" asked Braddock.

Sinclair glanced at his watch. "Fourteen-thirty-eight."

"Shaw, Brandon," Braddock said as she filled out the form. "Date of birth?"

Shaw started to speak, but Sinclair interrupted. "I have all that in his file."

"You have a file on me?" asked Shaw.

Sinclair smiled as Jankowski rapped on the door and stuck his head inside. "The crime lab's on the phone. They pulled the DNA evidence on the two girls and are waiting on you."

"Tell 'em I'll be right up with the samples," said Sinclair.

"What girls? What's this all about?"

"We'll talk about it." Sinclair and Braddock gathered up the DNA kit and left the room.

Once outside, Sinclair grinned at Jankowski and Braddock. "You both should get academy awards for your acting."

"Did he buy it?" asked Jankowski.

"I'll bet Shaw's having visions of rows of test tubes and swirling lab machines getting ready to spit out a DNA match," said Braddock.

"I just hope he doesn't know that the lab has a backlog of over a thousand DNA cases, and even if they dropped everything, we couldn't see test results before Monday," said Sinclair.

"What now?" asked Braddock.

"We let him stew and grab a sandwich."

Ten minutes later, they were back at their desks, a turkey sandwich on whole wheat in front of Braddock and roast beef on a hard roll with chips and a diet coke in front of Sinclair. Connie told them the UC police called and were en route with Adrian Nadeiri.

Sinclair was three bites into his sandwich when Lieutenant Maloney stopped in front of his desk, his arms folded across this chest. "I feel like something's going on and everyone's in on it but me."

Sinclair brought Maloney up to date and added, "We need an admission from both to make a chargeable case on the rapes. If they don't talk, no DA will file on them without a DNA match."

"You think they're good for the murders too?" asked Maloney.

Sinclair had been asking himself that question ever since they learned Brandon Shaw's name at the fraternity house. The murders of Zachary and Susan felt bigger than Shaw and Nadeiri, but Sinclair had learned never to underestimate even the most normal person's capacity to kill.

"I'll know better once we talk with them," said Sinclair.

"I need to inform the chief."

"Can you hold off? We don't know where this'll lead, and if it leaks, evidence and other suspects might disappear."

"I'll mention the importance of confidentiality," said Maloney.

Sinclair and Braddock discussed their interview strategy as they finished their sandwiches. Then they entered the interview room for the next round. Shaw sat slumped in the chair farthest from the door.

"I'll trade you," said Sinclair, pulling out the chair in the middle of the table for him. "Can I get you some coffee, water, or a soda?"

"I'm good."

Sinclair took the chair Shaw had been sitting in. Braddock sat across the table from him. He opened his portfolio and slid out a yellow pad. He wrote the date, time, and room number in the upper corner.

"My name is Sergeant Sinclair and this is my partner Sergeant Braddock. We work homicide. Let's start by confirming some information. Your last name is Shaw?"

"Yeah."

"First name Brandon?"

"Yeah."

"Middle name?"

"James."

Sinclair continued asking him for information that would be required on a booking sheet, slowly writing his answers on his legal pad. Although he already knew most of Shaw's personal information, going through the process got Shaw used to answering whatever Sinclair asked. When finished, he placed his pen on the pad and locked his eyes onto Shaw.

"Brandon, I'm sure you're curious about why you're here. I'd like to tell you why, but under the law, before we talk, I'm required to read you your rights. Is that okay with you?"

"Yeah, I guess. I got nothing to hide."

Sinclair slid a form out of his notebook, and even though he knew it by heart, he read it verbatim. He kept his eyes on the form, avoiding eye contact, trying to make the Miranda waiver process seem like nothing more than a routine bureaucratic process.

"Do you understand each of these rights I have explained to you?"

Out of the corner of his eye, Sinclair could see Shaw nodding his head.

"I need an oral response," Sinclair said, pen poised above the paper.

"Yes."

"Having these rights in mind, do you wish to talk to us now?"

Chapter 30

Another reason Sinclair kept his eyes on the form was so that Shaw couldn't see the anticipation in his face. Everything hinged on Shaw waiving his rights. The longer Shaw thought about it, the more likely he'd realize how dumb it was to talk. Sinclair had to make it appear as if it were no big deal.

"Well?" he asked, still looking at the form.

"Okay."

Sinclair turned the form around and handed his pen to Shaw.

"I need your initials here, next to where I wrote *Yes* to you understanding your rights. And your initials here next to the *Okay* that you're willing to talk with us. And then your signature here."

After he initialed and signed, Sinclair slipped the form into his portfolio—out of sight, out of mind—wrote the time and *Waived/Signed* on his yellow pad, and then looked up at Shaw. "When I earlier asked your occupation and work address, you told me you're a student at UC Berkeley. What's your major?"

"Civil engineering."

"That's impressive. How are you doing?"

"It's tough, but I've got a three-five GPA."

"I guess you're just beginning your junior year, huh?"

"That's right."

Sinclair took notes of his answers to get him used to the process, even though Sinclair knew they were lies. "Why do you live way down by Lake Merritt? Isn't it easier if you live near campus?"

"I used to live there, but the rent is outrageous."

"Did you live on campus or at a fraternity?"

"I lived in the dorms freshman year and tried a fraternity, but it didn't work out."

"What happened?"

"Too many rules. Worse than the dorms."

"What fraternity was that?"

"Alpha Kappa Lambda."

"So was that last year, your sophomore year, when you rushed the fraternity?"

Shaw's eyes focused on Sinclair and then darted above and past him, finally settling on an imaginary spot on the wall. Sinclair could tell the gears were turning in his brain.

"That's right," Shaw finally said.

"So I guess you went to the party there during pledge week, like all new pledges."

"I guess."

"Did you or didn't you?"

"Yeah, I was there, but I didn't stay long."

"How come?"

"It was sort of boring, so we left to check out other parties."

"We? You and Adrian?"

"Who?"

"Adrian. Weren't you with him that night?"

"I don't know who you're talking about. That was a year ago. I don't remember who I was with."

"Were you with any girls?"

"No, not really."

"How about these two?" Sinclair slid two photos in front of him.

Shaw stared at them for at least ten seconds before he looked up and said, "I don't know them."

"Never saw them before?"

"Nope."

"Their names are Samantha and Jenny. Does that ring a bell?"

"I said I never saw them before."

"Okay. We'll be right back." Sinclair and Braddock gathered up their paperwork and notebooks and left the room.

"Is he stupid or what?" said Braddock as she settled into her desk.

"He's very bright. He thinks you and I are stupid."

"Adrian Nadeiri's in two-oh-two," said Jankowski.

Sinclair and Braddock entered the interview room next to Shaw's room and went through the same DNA collection process as they did earlier. After Jankowski said his line, Sinclair and Braddock began to leave. Sinclair stopped at the door. "We'll be a few minutes. You want the paper or something to read?"

"That would be nice," Nadeiri said.

"News? Sports?"

"Sports."

Sinclair tossed the sports section of the *San Francisco Chronicle* on the table and shut the door.

"In five minutes, take the paper from him," Sinclair said to Jankowski. "Tell him it's yours and he can have it when you're finished with it."

Braddock raised her eyebrows.

"To show him he's not in control here."

Sinclair and Braddock returned to Shaw's room. "We're gonna take your statement and then get you out of here."

He turned on the recorder, reread the Miranda warning, and had Shaw acknowledge that he was read his rights earlier and waived them. Oftentimes, a denial statement—a series of lies about a suspect's involvement in a crime—when combined with evidence to the contrary, can be even more damaging to the suspect at trial than a confession. It shows a callousness and lack of remorse that a jury and sentencing judge will remember. Sinclair repeated his earlier questions and Shaw repeated his lies. When finished, Sinclair switched off the recorder.

He pulled Shaw's chair toward him until their knees touched. He leaned in, his face inches from Shaw's. "Brandon, you lied to us."

Shaw looked away.

"Look at me," Sinclair said.

Shaw looked up. After a few beats, Sinclair released his stare and leaned back in his chair. "We spoke to Cameron at the fraternity. He told us that you and Adrian . . ." Sinclair pulled a photocopy of Adrian's driver's license photo from his notebook and set it on the table. "Adrian Nadeiri and you brought those two girls to the party. They were underage and drugged, so Cameron asked you to leave. You and Adrian had sex with them."

"No, we didn't—"

"You're still lying." Sinclair set photocopies of the naked girls from Shaw's cell phone on the table.

"Where'd you get those?"

"From your phone."

"I know my rights. You can't search my phone—"

"You signed the consent form back at your apartment. We have Adrian in the next room. He's talking already."

Shaw covered his face with his hands and rocked back and forth in his chair.

Sinclair peeled Shaw's hands from his tear-streaked face.

"I don't believe you're a rapist."

"I would never rape a girl."

"But that's how it looks."

Shaw wiped his eyes and nose and slowly nodded his head.

"I'll bet there's an explanation for what happened," said Sinclair. "But it can only come from you."

"Adrian's father said he took care of it." Shaw sat up straight in his chair. "That if we never said a word, we'd be okay."

"Adrian's father can't help you. Only you can do that."

Shaw looked at the floor for a couple of minutes. Sinclair said nothing. Shaw finally looked up.

"Are you ready to tell the truth?" asked Sinclair.

Chapter 31

Over the next hour, Shaw told them everything. He and Adrian looking for action. Spotting Samantha and Jenny on College Avenue. Smoking a joint in People's Park and then visiting a friend's apartment and drinking some beer. The girls said they wanted to party and each took Ecstasy. Although Sinclair didn't believe the girls took Ecstasy knowingly, he didn't challenge Shaw on the issue.

The girls got friendly and they started making out—Shaw with Jenny and Nadeiri with Samantha. The studio apartment was crowded with people, so Shaw suggested they go to the frat house, where they could find an unoccupied room. They were just getting comfortable in one of the rooms when Cameron came in and asked them to leave. They got in Nadeiri's car and drove to a rave concert in Richmond. The guards wouldn't let anyone in without ID proving they were eighteen.

Sinclair interrupted. "How old were the girls?"

"Jenny said she was eighteen and Sam sixteen,"

"Did you see their IDs?"

"No."

"Would it surprise you to know that Jenny was fifteen and Samantha was fourteen?"

Shaw shrugged but said nothing. Sinclair had him continue.

"We hung around outside the rave for a while, drank some beer, and smoked some more weed. Me and Adrian talked about going over to his place. His father would be asleep, and we could do whatever we wanted. He's got like an apartment over the garage behind the main house."

"So is that what you did?"

"Yeah, we drove over there. The lights were off in Adrian's father's house, so we knew he was asleep. The girls were feeling tired and wanted another Ecstasy pill."

"They asked for it?"

"I don't remember," Shaw said. "Maybe the beer and weed was getting to them, but they wanted to keep partying. Maybe Adrian suggested it . . . I don't remember, but I gave them another X. We had the music on, not real loud 'cause we didn't want to wake Adrian's parents. We were dancing and the girls were getting hot and took off their clothes."

Sinclair saw Braddock stop writing and bite her lower lip. Ecstasy caused users' body temperature to rise. When combined with other drugs and alcohol that lowered inhibition, it was common to see kids at raves stripped to their underwear. He was feeling the same disgust as Braddock, but he had faith that if a jury heard Shaw's self-justifying bullshit, they'd see right through it and feel the same way he and Braddock felt at this moment, so he didn't challenge Shaw's story.

"The photos of those girls on your cell phone don't look like two girls all hot and amped up on Ecstasy. What else did they take?" asked Sinclair.

"Just beer and weed."

Sinclair stared at him. "We found traces of Rohypnol in both girls."

"Roofies—no way. You're not gonna pin no date rape on me."

Sinclair sat silently, waiting.

"I picked up some Xanaxes at the rave."

"Why Xanax?"

"Did you ever try to go to sleep after taking X?" Shaw asked.

Sinclair looked at him.

"I guess not," Shaw said. "You can either stay awake half the next day until you crash or take something to come down. Xanax works."

"But not roofies?"

"They'll bring you down, but they can make you do weird shit."

"Like have sex with someone and not remember?"

"I didn't give anyone a roofie. Look, the girls were high on the X, sweating and clenching their teeth. I gave them a Xanax and they calmed down. Adrian took Sam into his room, and me and Jenny went into the guest room."

"And you fucked her?"

"You already know that. You got my DNA."

"Tell me about it."

"There's nothing to tell. We did it. She wanted to. It's not like I forced her. It was just regular sex, nothing kinky. Then Jenny started dozing. I took the pictures, you know, to remember the night, and next thing I know, Adrian's father's in the apartment. He calls some guy who works for him. We get the girls dressed, and the man takes them home."

Sinclair turned to Braddock. It was tough being the secondary during an interview—take notes, don't interrupt the primary, let him determine the strategy—basically keep your mouth shut and bite your tongue. "Sergeant Braddock, do you have any questions for Brandon before we go on tape?"

"Just a few," she smiled. "Did Jenny ever tell you to stop, either before you entered her or while you were having intercourse?"

"No."

"Was she participating, you know, moving with you, or was she just lying there?"

"I don't remember."

"You don't remember?" Braddock leaned toward Shaw and furrowed her eyebrows. "When I'm making love with someone, I fully participate. Could it be that she wasn't participating because she wasn't mentally present—because she was so drugged that she was comatose?"

Sinclair interrupted Braddock. "Let's turn on the recorder and finish this up."

The recorded statement took a half hour. When they returned to their desks, Braddock said, "I'm sorry. I lost it in there."

"Yeah, you did. We both know what happened in that bedroom, and any jury will know as well once they see the evidence and hear this tape. But we can't push him so hard that he shuts down. We got what we needed on the rape. Now we have to keep him talking until we can put a red line through the murders."

Sinclair turned to Jankowski. "How you coming with the warrant?"

"All done except for whatever Shaw told you."

Sinclair gave him a quick summary of Shaw's statement. "Add what's relevant to the affidavit, get the warrant signed, and serve it. I doubt you'll find any physical evidence of the rape after thirteen months, but be on the lookout for anything related to the murders."

Sinclair gave his notes to Sanchez and asked him to comb through them for any information that he could add to his database.

"The Internet has a bunch of stuff on Nadeiri's father," said Sanchez. "In 1979, Rashid Nadeiri was a twenty-four-year-old engineering doctoral student at UC, Berkeley, but had to return home due to the Iranian Revolution. He left two years later because of the ruling clergy's repression. He got a job at Microsoft then went to Oracle, where he worked his way to the top levels. Ten years ago, he and another man started their own company, and two years ago, his company, Nadgold, climbed into the top one hundred grossing companies in the Bay Area."

"I guess his engineering degree wasn't for building bridges," said Sinclair.

"Computer systems, programming, and software."

"Any record?"

"Clean as a whistle, but that kind of money could keep plenty of dirt hidden."

Sinclair and Braddock opened the door to Nadeiri's interview room and found him pacing back and forth. His hair was damp, his face covered in sweat.

Sinclair read him his rights and Nadeiri said he understood them. "Having these rights in mind, do you wish to talk to us now?" Sinclair asked.

"I'd like my father present," Nadeiri said.

Sinclair pulled Nadeiri's printout from his notebook. No CORPUS, so no arrests since he was eighteen. His JUVIS showed arrests for shoplifting, vandalism, and possession of marijuana at fourteen. Possession for sales of marijuana and joyriding at fifteen. No convictions. Nothing since.

"You're an adult now. Having a parent present is a right for kids."

Nadeiri wiped his eyes with shaky hands. "Okay, let's talk."

Just as with Shaw, Sinclair allowed Nadeiri to deny everything, took a taped denial statement, and then confronted him with his lies. Nadeiri's story was similar to Shaw's, but he claimed he didn't know what kind of drugs Shaw gave him and the girls. He said he was high and probably not thinking straight. When he took Samantha into his bedroom, she began crying. She said she didn't want to have sex, but she didn't resist. Although she said she was older, once he saw her naked, he realized she wasn't much older than fourteen.

Nadeiri began describing his father's entrance into the apartment when Sanchez cracked the door and handed Sinclair a note. *Jankowski encountering major problem with BPD and an Atty over the warrant. When you can break, he needs to talk to you.*

Sinclair got more out of Nadeiri than he had expected, and after four hours in the interview rooms, he and Braddock needed a breather anyway.

"We're going to take a short break. Can I get you anything? Coffee? Water?"

"Water would be nice."

Braddock grabbed two cups and headed to the water cooler, and Sinclair called Jankowski's cell.

"I hate to bother you with this shit. If it was my case, I'd just tell 'em all to fuck off, but since it's yours—"

"What's up?"

"First of all, this is a big ass house, so I brought O'Connor and Larsen with me. I called Berkeley since we're in their city. They sent two uniforms over. We knock and announce and your kid's father answers the door. I give him a copy of the warrant and he shows me the kid's apartment over the garage. Larsen's babysitting him back in the main house. It's on the warrant too, so we'll search it next."

"Sounds good so far," said Sinclair.

"Soon a Berkeley PD sergeant shows up, starts nosing around. Then Larsen buzzes me, says a lawyer showed up and talked to the father. Larsen orders the lawyer to stay with him so he can keep an eye on him along with the father. Lawyer ignores him and heads straight to my location. Guy walks right in on us. You ever heard of Robert Zimmerman?"

"Big time San Francisco defense attorney, right?"

"Yeah, major scumbag. Before your time, he defended a few of our Oakland assholes, but these days, he only represents big money clients. He walks in with a video camera and demands to observe our search, giving that line of shit about being an officer of the court, like I'm supposed to be impressed. Also says our warrant for the main house is invalid because the kid, Adrian, doesn't live there. He demands we postpone our search of the main house until he can litigate the warrant."

"I hope you told him to fuck off," said Sinclair.

"I did, but since he had his camera on, I didn't say fuck."

"Good. If Zimmerman won't stay where you tell him to, escort him off the property or arrest him for interfering. He has no right to be there."

"Except then, this Berkeley lieutenant arrives. She—I think she's a she, but it's Berkeley and their medical plan even pays for sex changes—anyway, this lieutenant says she doesn't see a problem with Zimmerman being here, that we should have nothing to hide and it would avoid conflict if we cooperated."

"Tell her I love conflict. If Berkeley won't control Zimmerman, tell her you'll call a bunch of OPD units up there to do it."

"That's what I wanted to hear. Oh yeah, Zimmerman knows you have the kid in custody."

"How'd he find out?"

"No idea, but he said he was giving me official notice that he's the kid's lawyer and we have to cease any questioning until he's present."

"Like that's gonna happen. Any chance of you being able to interview the father and see what he knows?"

"Not with Zimmerman here."

Sinclair hung up and thumbed through a pile of messages on his desk. One caught his eye. Daly from Children's Hospital called at 1617. Connie's neat handwriting read, *Might mean nothing, but 6 min before girl hit by car, a Cadi Esc, blk, partial plate 312 or 812 entered ER lot, stopped, and backed out. Will copy onto CD tomorrow.*

"Do you believe these kids' story about a mystery man who drove the girls away?" asked Braddock.

"It fits," said Sinclair. "A guy like Rashid Nadeiri would have someone on staff to fix problems like this. When we go back at these two, we'll start there."

Sanchez said, "I'll add Shaw and Nadeiri's information to the database and search for a link with the victims."

"How long will that take?" asked Sinclair.

"Gimme twenty minutes."

"While he's doing that, I'll find a clean photo of Zachary and Susan to show them," said Braddock. "Why don't you step outside and relax for a few?"

"I'll help you look for the photos."

Braddock reached into Sinclair's desk drawer, grabbed a cigar, and set it in front of him. "Go."

Chapter 32

Sinclair's brain was fried. A dull headache was settling in. He puffed on his cigar and leaned against the railing overlooking Washington Street. The sun had just dropped below the horizon and the sky to the west glowed blood red. The heat from the day was beginning to dissipate, but with the absence of the normal bay breeze, the night wouldn't cool much.

Sinclair called Maloney at home and brought him up to speed.

"Do you think these two will roll on the other murders?" asked Maloney.

"We'll go at them again, but I don't think they did them."

"The chief will want to make an announcement tomorrow."

"Announce what, that we arrested two kids who roofied some girls and had sex with them?"

"It's just . . ."

"I know, lieutenant, I want to find the killer, too."

"Call me if anything changes."

Sinclair hung up and listened to his voicemails while puffing on the cigar. Two from Liz. He erased them and called her.

"You coming over tonight?" asked Liz.

"Looks like a late night."

"Come over any time. If I'm asleep, wake me."

The thought of crawling into bed with a drowsy Liz was appealing. "I'll let you know," he said.

"Did you get a break on the bus bench killings?"

"Not yet."

"What about on the rape of the girls from last year? One turned into a homicide, right?"

Sinclair felt a lump form in his throat. "What are you talking about?"

"I'm a reporter. Your department crime stats show a homicide at the same location last year. I did some research. I also remembered you talking about it when we first started dating."

Sinclair took a few puffs on the cigar, drew some smoke into his lungs, and blew it out.

"You still there?" she asked.

"You can't report this."

"It's my job. If you can't give me something, I'll have to start digging on my own. If I figured this out, others will too."

"Can we talk tomorrow?"

"I'll wait until tomorrow. If you do make it over tonight, I promise not to ask about it, at least not until . . ."

Liz was right. Other reporters would figure it out, and he couldn't lie to them. His reputation—the trust that the media gave out sparingly—was based on being straightforward with them. When he couldn't tell them something during an active investigation, he told them so. However, if he stonewalled them on this, they'd begin snooping, which would create a shit storm as every paper and television station started speculating. Soon, every potential witness and suspect would go into hiding, and leads would disappear. It looked like keeping this quiet until tomorrow's evening news was the best he could hope for.

Sinclair walked up the sidewalk along the front of the PAB. Spotlights lit up the American flag flying from the flagpole in the center of the small plaza in front of the building. He needed to wrap up everyone involved in Samantha's case before the media reported it and people talked to each other and got their lies straight. He pulled out his phone and called Jankowski. "Is there a Cadillac Escalade parked at Nadeiri's house?"

"No Cadi," said Jankowski. "There's a Lexus SUV in the garage. It's registered to Rashid Nadeiri, and from the crap in the console and glove box, it looks like the wife drives it. There's a new Lexus LS sedan, the big luxury model, that's registered to Nadgold."

Sinclair thanked him and jogged up the back steps two at a time and into the office. He opened the DMV screen on his computer and ran vehicles registered to Rashid Nadeiri. Only the Lexus SUV showed up. He ran vehicles registered to Nadgold Corporation in Emeryville. There were two new Lexus LS sedans, a Ford van, and a 2013 Cadillac Escalade, license 6TRJ812.

He called the communications section on his desk phone and a dispatcher answered. The beeps on the line reminded him he was being recorded. "Can you call Emeryville PD and have them send an officer by Nadgold to see if there's a Cadi SUV parked there and if there's anyone still working there?" He gave the dispatcher the address and vehicle license numbers of the four cars registered to the company.

Sinclair turned back to his computer and did a Google search on Nadgold. Their company website didn't mention the names of any company officers, not even the CEO. "Hey, Lou," he yelled to Sanchez. "When you dug up the stuff on Nadeiri, did you find the names of anyone else who worked at Nadgold?"

"Only Peter Goldman, the guy that left Oracle with Nadeiri to start the company. Goldman was a marketing and finance man. An article in the *Chronicle* two years ago said Nadeiri and Goldman were the owners, but no one else was mentioned."

"I'll bet Goldman drives the other Lexus."

Sanchez looked at him, puzzled.

"Never mind," said Sinclair as his desk phone rang. "Homicide, Sinclair."

The patrol officer from Emeryville identified himself and launched right in, saying, "I was the one dispatched to go by Nadgold and check their parking lot for you."

"See anything?"

"The business is on my beat so I know it pretty well. The two Lexus sedans are driven by the two bosses. The van is the only vehicle that stays there overnight. They use it to shuttle people and run errands during the day. I sometimes see it crammed full of employees around lunch time."

"What about the Escalade?"

"The security director drives that and gets to take it home."

"Is it parked there now?"

"No, lot's empty except for the van, and the place is locked up for the night."

"What do you know about him?"

"Ted Griffin," the officer said. "Nice guy. Met him a year or so ago when an employee's car got broken into. Talked to him a couple of times since then for one thing or another."

"How would I find him after hours?"

"ADT Alarm monitors Nadgold's security system. Call them. I responded when the alarm went off one night. Broken window, so I needed the owner to arrange a board up. ADT called Griffin to respond."

"How long did it take him?"

"Not long. He said he lives halfway between the two locations of his work: the corporate headquarters and his boss's house in the Berkeley Hills."

Sinclair went back to his computer and found a Ted Griffin with a driver's license address on Lawton Avenue in Oakland's Rockridge District, ten minutes from Emeryville. A check of CORPUS and CII showed no arrest record at either the country or state level.

Sinclair and Braddock left Sanchez to babysit Brandon Shaw and Adrian Nadeiri and drove through the evening traffic to the freeway. He radioed dispatch for a unit to meet them down the street from the Lawton address and then said to Braddock, "We don't have enough PC to arrest him in his house, so we need to convince him to come downtown and talk to us."

"It's nice to hear you considering the little things like probable cause," she said. "What if he refuses?"

"Then we're screwed. If he is involved in more than just the girls, the last two murders must connect somehow to Nadgold or Nadeiri. We've got to get him in a room talking before Zimmerman or another lawyer tells him to shut up."

"Do you really think those two boys and Griffin are responsible for killing Zachary and Susan, too?"

Sinclair turned and looked at her for a second and then back at the road.

"I know." She smiled. "You'll have a better idea once we're finished talking to them."

Sinclair merged onto the 24 Freeway and took the upper Broadway exit. He turned onto Lawton Avenue, a wide, tree-lined street of large, restored craftsman-style houses. He crept down the street, looking for house numbers. A black SUV backed out of a driveway a half block away and drove the same direction they were headed.

Sinclair sped up to verify the license, and Braddock grabbed the radio handset. "Thirteen-Adam-Five, we're following a vehicle wanted for questioning on a one-eighty-seven westbound Lawton approaching College."

"Description and plate when you can," said the dispatcher.

"Black Cadillac SUV, license Six-Tom-Robert-John-eight-one-two," said Braddock.

"Copy. Six-Tom-Robert-John-eight-one-two shows clear on a twenty-thirteen Cadillac, registered to Nadgold Corporation in Emeryville. Two units to respond."

"Two-L-Twelve," said a male voice over the radio. "You dispatched me to meet the homicide unit. I'm a block away. Where do they want me?"

Sinclair said to Braddock, "Have him get in front of us and make the stop"

The Cadi slowed at the stop sign on College Avenue and made a right turn. Sinclair followed.

Braddock relayed the instructions over the radio and added, "Let's low-key this. He might just be a witness and we want him cooperative."

Sinclair knew the risk of failing to handle this as a felony car stop—racking a shell into shotguns, ordering the occupants out of the car at gunpoint and onto the ground prone. If Griffin was a serial killer and decided to fight to the end, handling the stop casually could get cops killed, but if they took him down at gunpoint, it would be hard to later convince a judge in a suppression hearing that Griffin came to their office and talked voluntarily.

The Cadi proceeded north on the street lined with trendy shops and restaurants. Both sides of the street were filled with parked cars and people strolling along the sidewalk. A half mile north was the border with Berkeley, and College Avenue ended at the UC campus another mile beyond that.

Sinclair saw headlights coming up behind him rapidly and then heard the roar of a V8 engine as a marked car shot around him, pulled behind the Cadi, and turned on its emergency lights. The SUV pulled to the right into a bus zone and stopped. Sinclair stopped behind the marked car and Braddock said into the handset, "The stop is at College and Keith."

The officer approached the driver's window, and Sinclair moved to the passenger side, his hand on his gun. The passenger-side window was down.

"Evening, sir," said the officer. "May I see your license and registration?"

The driver, a heavyset man wearing a dark suit and tie, turned to face the officer. Sinclair couldn't hear what he said.

The driver removed a wallet from his breast pocket, handed the officer his license, leaned across the console, and opened the glove box. Sinclair readied himself, knowing a gun could appear in a flash.

The driver removed an envelope, shuffled through some papers, and handed the registration to the officer.

"Wait here," the officer said and backpedaled to the rear of the SUV. The officer handed Sinclair the driver's license. It read Ted Griffin and showed him six feet tall, 230 pounds, with a date of birth that made him forty-five.

"Have him step out," Sinclair said to the officer.

Griffin's expensive suit coat stretched tight over his considerable middle as he ambled onto the sidewalk in front of a Mexican restaurant advertising half-price margaritas on its window. He pushed his silver-framed glasses back up his nose.

"Where are you headed, Mr. Griffin?" asked Sinclair.

He looked toward Braddock, now standing beside the marked unit's passenger door, and then back at Sinclair. "What's this about?"

"We'd like you to come downtown with us so we can talk."

"You're detectives, right?"

Sinclair nodded.

"Homicide?"

"That's right."

"That's where I was headed," Griffin said. "My boss asked me to find out where his son was and ascertain his situation."

"Would that be Adrian Nadeiri?"

"Yes, is he in your custody?"

"If you accompany us downtown, we can talk about it," said Sinclair.

"I can follow you in my car."

"We'd prefer you ride with us," said Sinclair.

Chapter 33

Room 203 was what homicide called a soft interview room. The same size as the lieutenant's office, the room contained a metal table and three chairs against one wall, just as in the other interview rooms. A green vinyl couch sat against the opposite wall, and a row of metal file cabinets took up the back wall. Nothing fancy, but it was the most comfortable and nonthreatening interview room on the floor and the preferred place to interview cooperative witnesses and family members. Sinclair decided to interview Griffin here so that he could later testify in court that Griffin was not under arrest, and he therefore didn't have to read him his Miranda rights. Reading a possible suspect his rights was always the safest route to take legally, but if he did so, Griffin would figure out that Sinclair suspected his involvement and ask for a lawyer. Since Sinclair's goal was to get the truth, telling someone they didn't have to talk was counterproductive.

Griffin was slouched in the center of the couch when they entered, his head craned upward so he could peer through the bottom of his glasses as he pecked away on his Blackberry.

"This is Sergeant Braddock, my partner," said Sinclair. "And I suspect you already know my name's Sinclair."

Griffin nodded and slipped his phone into his pants pocket. Sinclair and Braddock took their customary chairs at opposite sides of the table, leaving the middle one for Griffin.

"Ted, I want to make it clear that you're not under arrest. You're free to leave at any time."

Once Sinclair asked the necessary questions to get Griffin's personal information, he asked, "What do you do at Nadgold?"

"I'm the director of security." He pulled himself up straighter in the chair.

Sinclair raised his eyebrows. "Sounds like we're in the same business."

"To a degree, although private security is different in many ways."

"How long have you been there?"

"Mr. Nadeiri and Goldman brought me over from Oracle when they decided to start their own company."

"What did you do at Oracle?"

"I started as a uniformed security officer. I had always wanted to be a police officer—like you both—but security paid the bills while I sent out applications."

"What happened—you change your mind?"

"I applied at over twenty departments. Even though I had a college degree, half never let me test. I failed the physical agility course at a few. I worked out like a maniac but still had trouble scaling the six-foot wall. I didn't make it through the medical exam, the oral board, or the psychological at the others. I applied and tested for five years before giving up."

Griffin's story was common for many who ended up as security guards. Out of a hundred applicants for OPD, two made it through the selection process, and only one of those made it through the six-month academy and the four-month field-training program. Observing Griffin, Sinclair could tell that Griffin didn't have what it took to be a cop—even when he was fifteen years younger.

"Too bad. I'll bet you would have made a good cop," said Sinclair.

"I made the best of it. I worked hard at Oracle and they made me a supervisor in the main complex where enterprise software was developed. Mr. Nadeiri was a division chief there. He recruited—or maybe stole is a better word—everyone for his new company from that building."

Sinclair looked Griffin over. His suit surely cost more than a thousand dollars, his European wingtips close to that. His shirt, with French cuffs and gold cufflinks, was Egyptian cotton and cost over a hundred.

"Looks like you're doing well now."

"In eight years, Nadgold went from fifteen employees to three hundred. Last year, the company did four hundred million in revenues. I do alright."

"That brings us to why you're sitting here tonight." Sinclair set his pen down and pushed himself away from the table. "I'm sure you know we've been speaking to Adrian, your boss's son. We also have Brandon Shaw and he's given a statement as well. We know you took the two girls from Nadeiri's house that night. You drove them to the bus bench in the Escalade that's parked out front. From there, a man called the mother of Samantha Arquette—she was the girl hit by the car that night, the girl who never regained consciousness, the girl who later died. I suspect it was you who made the call."

"Do you intend to arrest me?"

"I can't say what the DA will charge you with. You have some responsibility for what happened. Only you can explain your intent—those mitigating factors the DA will evaluate. I will promise you that if you lie to me or don't tell me the whole truth, you might walk out of here tonight, but I'll make it my mission to see you prosecuted for manslaughter and as an accessory to rape."

Griffin looked at Sinclair, but his eyes were focused on the wall behind him. Sinclair knew that he was wondering how much the police knew and how little he could get away with saying.

"Why did you say manslaughter?" asked Griffin. "Do you think the girl being hit by the car was something other than an accident?"

"You're the only one who can tell me that."

"You said accessory to rape. Did Adrian and his friend say I had something to do with what they did with the girls or procured the girls for them or something?"

"I want to hear your side of the story. How did you get involved in this?"

Griffin pursed his lips, took a deep breath, and blew it out. "Mr. Nadeiri called me to his house that night and asked me to clean up a mess."

"What happened when you got there?"

"I told him the girls needed medical attention and we should call an ambulance."

"That's not what happened, was it?"

"I agreed to take them to the hospital, but if it ever came back on us, I wouldn't cover for his kid or anyone else. I would tell the truth and testify if necessary."

"This must have been tearing you up, knowing what eventually happened and all."

"Not a day goes by that I don't regret what I did that night. I saw the car hit the girl. I followed it in the papers. I heard when the girl died." Griffin pulled a monogrammed silk handkerchief from his suit coat pocket and wiped the tears from his eyes. "In a way, I'm glad it's over."

"Let's start from the beginning." Sinclair picked up his pen and began writing as Griffin spoke.

"Mr. Nadeiri called me at home that night and asked me to come to his house—to the apartment where Adrian stays. I'd been there before and bailed Adrian out on minor stuff previously. He's a bright kid but spoiled. Adrian was sitting on his bed, wearing only boxers. His pupils were huge, so I knew he was high on something. A girl was in his bed. I tried to wake her, but she didn't move. I pulled the blankets down and . . ."

"What did you see?" asked Sinclair.

"She was so young . . . so helpless. I have a daughter who was just thirteen at the time. I pictured her in that bed. I was so angry I wanted to kick Adrian across the room. Then I saw the blood. I had Adrian get me a washcloth and I wiped between her legs. I didn't see any cuts on her, but the blood was coming from her vagina. I first thought she was bleeding from rough sex, but Adrian said she *was* a virgin. As if it was a source of pride."

"How did that make you feel?"

"I was sickened. From there, I went to the guest room. The other boy, Brandon—he's a real piece of work—was sitting in a chair with a shit-eating grin on his face. Jenny—she looked to be a few years older than Samantha but still too young to be in that kind of situation—was passed out in the bed, a tangle of blond hair covering the pillow. I couldn't even see her face. I was able to wake her, but she was incoherent."

"I have to ask here," said Sinclair, "why didn't you call nine-one-one for an ambulance?"

"I owed Mr. Nadeiri everything. I knew what this would do to his reputation and that of the company."

"I understand your conflict," said Sinclair.

"My first priority was to the girls. They needed medical attention. We got them dressed. I still remember my anger when dressing Samantha. She was just a girl." His voice cracked. "I carried her in my arms to the car, and Mr. Nadeiri walked Jenny down the stairs to steady her."

Sinclair wasn't sure he believed Griffin's motives, but the sequence of events matched the evidence he'd seen and what the two boys said. They'd had plenty of time to get their story straight, however, and Griffin had thirteen months to rationalize and justify what he did that night.

"What happened next?"

"I drove to Children's Hospital. I'd taken my own daughter there, once when she broke her arm and once when she was running a high fever. But as soon as I pulled into the ER, I noticed their security cameras and got scared—scared that I'd be identified, that I was already covering up a crime—so I panicked and drove back out. I took the first right and stopped when I saw the bus shelter. I was going to leave them there and call nine-one-one, but I knew that there'd be a recording of my voice. I used Samantha's phone, found a number under *Mom*, and called. I thought they'd just sit there on the bus bench. If I had any idea . . ."

"I believe you."

"I drove up the street and pulled over, waiting to make sure someone came for them, and then one of the girls—I later read in the paper it was Samantha—walked into the street and a car came."

"Did you consider returning to render aid?"

"I was getting ready to, but I saw nurses and doctors running from the hospital, so I knew there was nothing more I could do. I drove back to Mr. Nadeiri's house."

"What happened there?"

"Mr. Nadeiri's attorney was there."

"Zimmerman?"

"No, his personal attorney. Zimmerman arrived later."

"What did you discuss?"

"Maybe I should take the advice of my attorney and not say any more."

Sinclair caught Braddock's eye.

Sinclair asked, "Are you saying that you have an attorney and now don't want to talk with us any longer or that you just don't want to talk to us about what you and the attorneys discussed?"

"The latter. Zimmerman told all of us that if the police questioned us, we should say nothing and call him. Obviously, I'm not taking that advice, but I don't think it right to mention what we discussed or implicate anyone else."

"Such as Mr. Nadeiri?"

"Can I ask you something?" Griffin asked.

"Sure."

"I've been expecting this for over a year. What took so long?"

Because I was drunk when I was assigned this case, Sinclair thought.

Braddock jumped in. "When this happened, there wasn't much more to go on. Recently, there were further developments that caused us to reexamine this file."

"You mean the two bus bench murders this week?"

Sinclair focused on Griffin's face, trying to read him.

Then he gathered up his papers and stood. "We'll be back in a few moments."

Chapter 34

Woodrow Drive was the kind of neighborhood where residents noticed strange vehicles. Two cars could barely pass each other when meeting on the narrow road, and residents parked their cars in their driveways and garages.

The man parked his van in a dirt lot on Shepherd Canyon Road, jogged across the road, and continued along the Montclair Railroad Trail, a hiking and bicycling path built on what was once a passenger train route between San Francisco and Sacramento. Dressed in brown hiking boots, tan cargo pants, and a forest-green, long-sleeve shirt, he looked like any other nature lover out for a little evening exercise.

It was just past eight o'clock. The moon lit up the paved trail, but once he stepped off the path under the thick canopy of trees, he could barely see his feet. He had scouted this route in daylight enough times that he could find his way even on a moonless night. He moved slowly and quietly through the forest of redwoods, eucalyptus, and oak. He skirted a massive redwood deck off the rear of one house, staying well back in the woods, and climbed a low knoll to the backyard of Dr. and Carol Brooks. He settled beneath a Monterey Pine.

Large windows on the rear of the house provided an unobstructed view into the kitchen and family room. No other houses were visible through the thick forest, and the curtains were open in every window of the house. Carol was sitting at the kitchen table, a laptop computer in front of her and a telephone to her ear. Her husband was working tonight, so she was home alone.

When she hung up the phone, the man crept into the backyard, along a stone path through a flower garden, and onto a brick patio. The pistol tucked in his belt under his shirt dug into his back. Invisible to anyone inside the brightly lit kitchen, he crept toward the sliding glass door. He pulled the handle, but it was locked.

He stepped back, pointed the semiautomatic pistol at the center of Carol's chest, thumbed off the safety, and pulled the trigger. The patio door shattered as the explosion reverberated inside his head. An alarm shrieked and Carol collapsed to the floor screaming.

He stepped through the aluminum frame and stood over her. She looked up at him, her eyes pleading. He pointed the gun at the middle of the expanding circle of blood on her purple blouse and pulled the trigger three more times.

He crunched through the shards of glass into the dining room. A half-dozen framed photographs were arranged on the wall above an oak sideboard, one of a smiling couple dressed in Hawaiian shirts with palm trees and a white-sand beach in the background. Removing a medallion from his pants pocket, he slid the chain around the picture frame. He slipped back outside, avoiding the jagged pieces of glass still hanging from the aluminum frame, and scurried across the patio and into the woods. By the time he reached the trail, the alarm had stopped and the only sound he heard was the ringing in his ears. He hurried down the trail, staying in the shadows. When there were no cars in sight, he sprinted across Shepherd Canyon Road to his van.

He was more than a mile away when he heard a siren and saw a police car screaming past him up the hill.

Chapter 35

Sinclair and Braddock came out of room 203 to find the office empty. A handwritten note lay on Sinclair's chair. *We got a call out. Headed to a house in the hills where a female was shot. Finished serving the search warrant, found nothing that relates to other murders. Jankowski.*

"Wouldn't you know it—Jankowski and Sanchez probably have a mom-and-pop homicide in a nice clean house," said Braddock. "Should we get another team to help us while we finish up these interviews?"

"If we solve these murders, it'll happen in those rooms," said Sinclair. "More investigators sitting in the office won't help."

Braddock picked up her cup, grabbed Sinclair's from his desk, and headed to the coffee pot. "Are you really going to let Griffin walk out of here tonight?"

"We got him for accessory after the fact on the rapes. The DA will charge him if I ask him to, but when was the last time you saw anyone do the statutory three years for accessory?"

"Not in Oakland," she said. "But we can hang that over his head to convince him to testify against the kids and tell us what he knows about the other murders."

"You think he knows something?" Sinclair asked.

"One of those three has to know something. We can tell Griffin we can make a case against him for involuntary manslaughter."

Griffin's actions met the elements of section 192(b) of the penal code. Facing up to four years in prison, on top of the three for the accessory charge, would convince most anyone to cooperate. But the DA's office wouldn't take it to trial, as convincing twelve members of a jury that leaving the girls at the bus stop might result in one's death would be difficult. Sure, it was stupid, but a few jurors would likely view it as little more than a tragic accident. He was trying to help after all, Griffin would argue.

"I don't plan to waste my time on an accessory charge and a bullshit manslaughter," said Sinclair. "We can't ignore the rapes the kids committed. They're going down for that, but as long as Griffin tells us everything he knows, I'll let the DA sort it out later."

"Do you believe him?"

"Yeah, but I've been duped before, and he's holding back on what old man Nadeiri said to him."

"Because that would make Nadeiri an accessory as well."

"I'm only concerned with what he might know about the murders."

"What now? Go in and confront them with the two murders?"

"First we try to find their connection to Caldwell and Hammond."

Braddock shrugged. "Maybe there isn't one."

"The bus bench and medallion connects them. Zachary's father works at Children's. The girls and Zachary are around the same age."

"But one girl's from New York, the other San Francisco, and Zachary's from Danville. Sanchez couldn't find any connection between them."

"Which means we missed it. It could be anything. What if Griffin's wife and Susan got their hair done at the same place? What if Zachary met the girls at that rave?"

"According to his parents, Zachary didn't party at all," said Braddock.

"The point is we just don't know everything about them."

"What's our interview strategy?"

"We go back at them—one at a time—pin them down during the time frame when Zachary and Susan were killed. Verify their alibis. If they lie, we hammer them. Show them photos of those vics, see their reaction, press them, see how they react."

"Looks like it'll be a long night."

"You got a better place to be?"

"Are you kidding?" said Braddock. "I live for this stuff."

Sinclair's desk phone rang. Caller ID said it was the patrol desk. "I got this lawyer in the lobby raising hell. Says you're holding his clients without cause, and he demands to see them."

"His name Zimmerman?"

"Right. He ordered me to formally record his demand to see his clients and that they're not be questioned without him."

"Tell him I'm busy."

"He insisted I call the watch commander when no one answered in homicide."

"Tell me you didn't."

"Sarge, I had to. I can't afford another complaint. The lieutenant said to tell you to come down and at least talk to the guy."

As Sinclair made his way down the stairs into the PAB lobby, the desk officer pointed to a man dressed in a black double-breasted suit that was several times more expensive than Griffin's. He appeared to be in his fifties, his jet-black hair certainly dyed to keep it that way. He stopped talking on his cell phone and glared at Sinclair.

"Mr. Zimmerman, my name is—"

"I know who you are," the lawyer interrupted. "I demand to see my clients, Mr. Nadeiri and Griffin. You have violated their rights by preventing their consultation with counsel prior to questioning. The court will hear about this, and I'm putting you on notice that anything they might have said to you is inadmissible."

Sinclair smiled.

"Do you find this amusing, Detective?"

"Actually I do," said Sinclair. "Both the US and California Supreme Courts have ruled that the right to counsel belongs to the arrestee. A lawyer has no legal right to invoke Miranda for a suspect."

"You mean an accused or a defendant?"

"You use your language, I'll use mine. I read Nadeiri his rights, and he agreed to speak without an attorney. Griffin is here voluntarily and not in custody, so I don't need to advise him of his rights."

"Did you advise them of my presence?" Zimmerman asked.

"I didn't know you were here until a minute ago."

"I advised your associate of my presence at Mr. Nadeiri's house an hour ago and this officer thirty minutes ago. Why are you obstructing me from meeting with my clients?"

"You'd tell them to not talk with me."

"To protect their rights."

"To prevent me from getting the truth."

"Are you intending to charge them?"

"I intend to charge Adrian with rape and several enhancements related to drugs and the victim's age. I'll talk to the DA before deciding about homicide charges."

"Homicide?"

"A fourteen-year-old girl died."

"Adrian had nothing to do with that."

"If the DA decides to charge him with murder, you can argue that in front of a jury. By the way, who's your real client? Who's paying your bill?"

"That's privileged information."

"Seems to me, representing two potential codefendants would be a conflict of interest."

"Should more than one person be charged, additional counsel will be arranged," said Zimmerman.

"Please tell Adrian's father, Rashid Nadeiri, who I'm sure is the one paying your bill, that I'd like to talk to him."

"Do you intend to arrest him?"

Sinclair thought for a moment. "If his involvement is only as an accessory after the fact, I'll take his statement and release him. I'll let the DA decide what to do. If he's truthful and didn't kill anyone, he's not my concern."

"We may be able to work something out. What will happen to my clients tonight?"

"I still have a few things to discuss with them and then I'll take Adrian to the jail for booking."

"Those few things—might you mean the two recent murders that have been all over the news?" Zimmerman asked.

Sinclair met his gaze, saying nothing.

"My clients had nothing to do with those."

"And I'm supposed to take your word for this?"

"I just left Mr. Nadeiri's house. Since the incident with the young ladies last year, he and his wife have kept a very short leash on their son, and I'm sure we can prove he was elsewhere during the time of the murders."

"Parents have been known to lie for their kids."

Zimmerman thought for a moment. "I'll make them available to speak with you. I think you'll find them both quite honest."

"I'll need to determine that myself," said Sinclair.

"I should hope so. Concerning the other matter, my clients truly regret what happened."

"Is that why they kept quiet about it for over a year?"

"Youthful indiscretions, for which Adrian may now be held accountable. Mr. Nadeiri is guilty of protecting his son. What father wouldn't? And Mr. Griffin of loyalty to his superior and an obligation to protect his company."

Sinclair nodded. He wasn't about to point out that just about every criminal he ever met was able to rationalize the crimes he committed. The only difference was that the wealthy ones had high-priced lawyers to articulate it for them.

"Why are you doing this—I mean cooperating at this stage instead of waiting until trial to spring it on the DA?"

"I'd prefer you and the DA don't overcharge my clients to hold them because of the public pressure for the police to take action on the two recent homicides. I'm helping you to see their innocence, so that you can focus on finding the actual perpetrator."

"Assuming this checks out, I appreciate it."

Braddock was just hanging up the phone when Sinclair walked back into the office.

"That was Jankowski. He's on Woodrow Drive. Call came in as gunshots less than an hour ago. Female victim's DOA. Her husband's a doctor, and hanging on the wall next to the body was a peace sign medallion."

Chapter 36

Sinclair examined the pool of blood on the kitchen floor. On his way out of the office, Sinclair had told Braddock to coordinate with Jankowski and split their teams, send Sanchez back to help her finish the interviews, and leave Jankowski at the scene to assist him. That way, Sinclair would take charge of the fresh murder while Braddock cleaned up the old one, and the detectives with the most knowledge of the investigation would lead both tasks.

"What've you got?" asked Sinclair.

"Two residents called it in," said Jankowski. "Patrol talked to them. One heard two shots, the other four. Neither saw anything. A few minutes later, Bay Alarm reported an intrusion alarm at this address. Two units were dispatched. The front was secure, so they went around the back and saw the patio door shattered and the victim, a Carol Brooks. They called for medical, checked for a pulse, but found none. Fire department arrived first, started CPR. Ambulance arrived, scooped, and transported. They pronounced her upon arrival at ACH"

Sinclair stepped closer to the glass door and looked outside to the brick patio where two technicians were taking measurements for the scene diagram.

"Tech recovered one shell casing outside, nine millimeter, ten feet to the right of the door. Consistent with the shooter firing the first shot outside. Three more casings inside the kitchen. The tech already photographed and recovered them."

Sinclair followed Jankowski into the dining room. A heavy oak table with six chairs took up the center of the room, with a matching sideboard against the wall. Above the sideboard, several photographs hung on the wall, one of them showing a couple on a Hawaiian vacation. A peace medallion was draped over the picture.

"I called you when I saw this," said Jankowski.

Sinclair knew a serial killer didn't normally change his MO. They were creatures of habit, and once they found a method of killing that worked, they stuck with it. But the smarter ones adapted to fit the circumstances. When that occurred, the police seldom linked the cases. Although Sinclair had suspected it when he noticed the medallion on Susan Hammond's body, there was now no doubt in his mind that the killer was leaving it for the police.

"Looks like he's escalating," said Jankowski.

"Could be he's just changing to a more efficient method of killing."

"Why'd he stop using the bus bench?"

"Too risky," said Sinclair. "A department with more manpower would have staked the place out. Besides, I think he only used the bus bench to get our attention and send a message."

"That this was the work of one man, which he can now do with less risk by leaving a medallion."

"That's my guess," said Sinclair.

"The rest of the house was undisturbed. No signs of forced entry. All lights in the house were off except for the kitchen. One car in the garage, empty space for another."

"Husband?"

"Dale Brooks. Works the night shift in the ER at Children's. We sent a marked unit there to take him downtown, but he'd left by the time the unit arrived. The officer that followed the ambulance to ACH found him there. We got him in a car outside."

"How'd he find out about the shooting?"

"Says Bay Alarm called his cell after the alarm activation and told him OPD was en route to a report of gunfire. Children's ER is tapped into the emergency medical response system, so when he found out an ambulance was dispatched for a female victim, he drove to ACH."

Sinclair made a note to verify this later so they could eliminate the husband as a suspect, although nothing so far indicated this was the work of Dale Brooks. Sinclair noticed dirt and debris on the hardwood floor alongside the sideboard. Crouching down, he saw two brown pine needles and a piece of gravel.

"How many people tramped through the scene before it was secured?"

Jankowski looked at his notes. "Four patrol officers. Two of them went upstairs and searched to make sure the suspect was gone and there were no additional victims. Plus two paramedics and three firemen for the medical response."

Sinclair noted bloody footprints and smears consistent with the huge boots firefighters wore. Compromising a crime scene was never their concern, especially on medical runs. He went out the back door and walked back and forth along the brick patio scanning every inch. He pulled his Surefire flashlight from his pocket and followed its beam down the cement walkway and around the side of the house to the driveway. No gravel or pine needles on the walkway. Four uniforms milled about at the front of the house. He returned to the back and walked to the edge of the patio where a stone path led toward the woods. He bent down and picked up a piece of gravel, rolling it between his fingers, and followed the path to a decorative bench at the edge of the yard. Pine trees towered above him, and a carpet of pine needles extended into the forest where the grass ended.

Sinclair yelled down the hill. "Has anyone been up here?"

The evidence technician looked up from his work. "Not that I know of."

"Any idea what's back here?"

The tech pulled a battered Thomas Street Guide from his briefcase. "The rear yards of houses on Shepherd Canyon Road, then the walking trail that parallels it."

"That explains why none of the neighbors saw our suspect or a car."

"I don't follow you."

"Our suspect came in and left through the woods. He left pine needles and gravel in the house."

"You want us to search back here for footprints and any evidence he might have dropped?"

"You won't find any footprints on this ground. Probably a waste of time in the dark anyway. Tell the patrol sergeant to have someone canvass the houses on Shepherd Canyon. Maybe a resident saw something."

Sinclair found Jankowski sitting in his car. A clean-cut man with a stoic look on his face sat in the backseat.

Wearing navy blue scrubs and with styled hair and brilliant white teeth, Dr. Brooks was a young-looking forty. Jankowski briefed Sinclair on what they had covered thus far: personal information about Brooks and his wife and a timeline of their activities throughout the day.

Sinclair asked the standard questions about enemies, problems with anyone, and anyone who might want to hurt his wife, but as he expected, nothing materialized. Brooks's voice remained steady, emotionless, like when a doctor tells a mother her son didn't make it through surgery.

"Did your wife know Zachary Caldwell?" Sinclair asked.

"Doctor Caldwell's son? Not that I'm aware of."

"Can you think of any connection between them, anywhere their lives might have crossed?"

"The only connection was Doctor Caldwell and me."

"How well do you know him?"

"We work together. We're in different departments but have operated on trauma patients together a number of times."

"What about Susan Hammond?"

"Who's that?"

"Russell Hammond?"

"If you're asking about patients, I might see twenty patients a day in the ER. I don't focus on names in charts."

"Samantha Arquette?"

"Accident August last year. Car hit her right in front of the hospital. I was in the ER that night."

"You remember her?"

"She wasn't your typical sore throat or broken arm. Besides, I received constant reminders about her."

"What do you mean?"

"Her family sued the hospital—wrongful death and medical malpractice. The hospital and my insurance carrier both interviewed me and I was deposed by lawyers."

"What happened?"

"Getting sued is part of a physician's life these days, especially in emergency medicine. Like most, it settled. The hospital and my insurance paid something."

"You were sued individually?"

"That's standard. Lawyers name every doctor who touched the patient. Sometimes those who did nothing more than consult."

"Was Doctor Caldwell named in the suit?"

"Probably. He was on-call from neurology that night. After we stabilized the internal injuries, the head trauma was the primary medical concern."

"Excuse me." Sinclair pushed out of the car seat and jogged down the street to his car. He paged through his notes and dialed Russell Hammond's home phone.

"Hello." Hammond's speech was thick and slurred.

"This is Sergeant Sinclair, are you able to talk?"

"Yeah."

Sinclair couldn't blame him for being drunk; if his wife had been murdered, he'd stay drunk for a week.

"You told me that you do medical malpractice as well as personal injury. Were you involved in the lawsuit involving Samantha Arquette?"

"Why?"

"I'm investigating your wife's murder."

"I was the plaintiff's attorney."

"Were Doctors Brooks and Caldwell named in the suit?"

"Yes, along with four other defendants and the hospital."

"Who was your client?"

"Jane Arquette, the girl's mother."

"You know she's dead, right?"

"What?"

"She committed suicide. You didn't know?"

"She was alive when the case settled. That was a while ago. Most of my communication was with her family attorney."

"I'll need his name and number."

"I don't have it at home."

"How much did Mrs. Arquette get?" Sinclair asked.

"There's a nondisclosure agreement between the parties."

"I don't give a shit."

"I really can't say without permission from the other parties and my client."

"Your client's dead."

"I'll need permission from her estate."

"I'll need to see your files."

"They're in my office. It's after hours and I'm in no condition to go out right now."

No shit, thought Sinclair. "Let's do this first thing in the morning—eight o'clock, my office, bring your files, and we'll go from there."

"Can we make it nine?"

"Eight," said Sinclair, followed by the words others had used with him. "Hammond, I need your head clear, so put a plug in the jug and get some sleep."

When Sinclair hung up, he saw Lieutenant Maloney standing alongside his car. After Sinclair filled him in, Maloney asked, "If your theory's correct, why the year break between the girl's death and now?"

Sinclair knew that the normal reason for a lull in a crime spree was because the suspect was sitting in jail somewhere, often on an unrelated crime, and once he got out, the killings resumed; however, that didn't feel right to him. Samantha's death and the last three murders were different.

Before he could talk it through with Maloney, he saw two men coming toward them, the unmistakable shaved head of Chief Brown bobbing a foot above the PIO, George Thomas. Sinclair stood by quietly while Maloney briefed him.

"I don't get it," said Brown. "How are these three murders connected to the lawsuit over the girl's death a year ago?"

"I don't know yet," said Sinclair. "But we now have a direction."

"What if it's the wrong direction?"

"Then we look elsewhere. That's the nature of investigations."

"I don't need a lecture on the nature of investigations," Brown said to Maloney, as if Sinclair wasn't there. "I need results."

Maloney said nothing.

"I'll support this hunch for now," said Brown. "The hospital administrator offered whatever we need, so I'll call him and get someone from legal to meet with you in the morning."

"Thanks, Chief," said Sinclair.

"I'm not doing it for you. I don't want to be accused of ignoring a possible avenue, even if I think it's a tangent. But if this doesn't lead to the killer, we're going to reassess the direction of the investigation and who's running it."

Brown turned and walked away. Thomas scurried to catch up.

Maloney gazed at his shoes for a moment. "I sure hope you're right."

Sinclair wandered the scene. Jankowski was still talking to Brooks. Two officers sat in their cars typing on computers. Another stood at the top of the driveway controlling access to the house. Around the back, two officers and the patrol sergeant stood on the patio. Both techs were inside the kitchen with latent print brushes in their hands. Sinclair sat on the bench at the edge of the forest and pulled out his cell. The phone showed it was 11:19 p.m. He had two missed calls.

He lit a cigar, called Braddock, and briefed her on the latest murder. She and Sanchez had pressed Griffin and both boys, but they denied any knowledge of the recent murders. Sinclair knew her heart wasn't in it, and he couldn't blame her. It was tough to push someone to confess to a crime when you didn't believe they committed it, and with the three of them sitting in homicide when Brooks was killed, it was hard to fathom they were involved. Braddock said they'd have one more go at them before taking final taped statements.

Sinclair puffed on his cigar. The smoke hung above him in the still air. The murders hadn't previously made sense because he was looking for a connection between the victims: Samantha, Zachary, Susan, and now Carol. However, he now knew the connection was between Samantha and the victims' family members: Dr. Caldwell, Attorney Hammond, and Dr. Brooks. Samantha's death was different from the last three. She was an accident of sorts. Whenever a dope dealer was gunned down in Oakland, one of

Sinclair's first steps was determining which gang the victim belonged to. The murder often stemmed from a precipitating event, such as one dealer selling on another gang's turf. A series of retaliations, sometimes developing into a major turf war, often followed.

He'd been looking at this all wrong. The same person didn't kill all four victims. Samantha's rape and death was the precipitating event. The others were killed because of what happened to her. However, if that were true, then why weren't Nadeiri, Shaw, and Griffin targeted? Why the wives and children of the lawyer and doctors? As was common in an investigation, he had more questions than answers. He wondered how deeply NYPD had looked into Jane Arquette's suicide and whether her death might be a murder as well.

Chapter 37

Sinclair grabbed the first suit in the front of his closet, a navy blue pinstripe he'd bought on sale two years ago. Not nearly as nice as the suits Griffin and Zimmerman wore last night, but better than what most other detectives wore. When he started in homicide, he had established a system of hanging the suit he wore that day in the back of the closet. That routine was invaluable on days such as this, when his brain was on autopilot and didn't need to make any more decisions than absolutely necessary.

He had set his alarm for six and rolled out of bed with barely two hours of sleep in hopes of catching some NYPD detectives still at their desks with their morning coffee. He ground black French roast beans, made a pot of strong coffee, and called the precinct detective squad that handled the case when Samantha died in the hospital. The detective who worked the case had transferred out, but a clerk summarized the report for him. There was little in it that Sinclair hadn't heard before and no mention of any relatives of Samantha's besides her mother, Jane. The detective had met with Jane several times, but only to coordinate between her, the hospital, the medical examiner, and the funeral home. Sinclair had performed investigative assistance before for other departments. The detective's focus was to facilitate the chain of custody of evidence and information to the requesting agency for their murder prosecution. The NYPD clerk suggested Sinclair call the Nineteenth Precinct, which handled Jane Arquette's suicide. Sinclair called, but the detectives were out on a robbery that had occurred overnight, so he left a message.

Sinclair stepped to his dresser and wove the plainclothes leather gear onto his black dress belt: ammo pouch that held an extra magazine with eight hollow-point .45 rounds, handcuff case with stainless steel handcuffs, and matching custom holster. He clipped his badge on the belt in front of his ammo pouch and his phone on the other side in front of his holster. He worked the push-button combination to the small safe on the closet shelf, removed his Sig Sauer, and slid it into the holster.

Sinclair had finished checking his voicemail and e-mail by the time Braddock pushed open the office door juggling two boxes, a briefcase, and a large handbag. Jankowski rushed across the room to help.

"You sure move fast for a big man," said Greg Larsen, a ten-year veteran of the unit.

"Like a cat," said Jankowski.

"Like a lion moving in for the kill," said Jerry O'Connor, Larsen's partner.

Jankowski ripped open a box and plucked out a donut. A gob of red jelly squirted out as he bit into it. He caught it in his hand and licked it off.

"Looks like you killed it," said Larsen.

Sinclair grabbed an apricot Danish with a paper towel and returned to his desk.

"I'll never understand you youngsters with your fancy pastries," said Jankowski. "When I came on, Friday morning donuts consisted of donuts—period."

Braddock filled her coffee cup and sat down.

"You're not having one?" said Sinclair.

"Of course not. Pure saturated fat," she said. "You got an early start."

Sinclair briefed her on his morning phone calls.

"Timesheets are due," shouted Connie.

Investigators returned to their desks and the office quieted. Sinclair filled out last night's overtime slip—eleven hours from when his normal shift ended at 4:00 p.m. until he left at 3:00 a.m. Larsen stood over his shoulder as he filled in the boxes on the form.

"Only thirty hours," said Larsen. "Embarrassing standby performance."

"Give him a break," said O'Connor. "He only got back on the rotation Monday."

"And we didn't get our first case until Tuesday," said Sinclair.

"Thirty hours of OT in three days ain't bad," said O'Connor.

"Three numbers on the board—high profile ones at that—you should be able to milk them for big bucks," said Larsen.

"As long as he doesn't solve them too quick." O'Connor grabbed Larsen's wrist, sporting a gold Rolex, and shoved it in front of Sinclair. "See this?"

"Nice," said Sinclair.

"I got it when you were gone," said Larsen. "I paid for it with the overtime from three homicides."

"It was awful nice," said Sinclair, "for those three men to give up their lives so you could wear that watch."

It was never about the money to Sinclair. Phil used to say money was just another way of keeping score. Most homicide investigators made more in a year than captains and deputy chiefs, who were on straight salary, but the brass didn't need to climb out of bed whenever one gangbanger decided to shoot another.

Sinclair and Braddock took the elevator to the eighth floor and walked into the police chief's outer office. Russell Hammond was talking with a fiftyish woman dressed in a professional gray skirt suit and white blouse. Hammond wore a black suit. Sinclair wondered if it was to show he was mourning. The woman introduced herself to Sinclair and Braddock as Phyllis Mathis and handed them business cards that said she was vice president and general counsel at Children's Hospital.

Sinclair hated talking with people in the chief's conference room. Successful interviews often relied on power. A conference room with views of the Oakland skyline was more Mathis's environment than Sinclair's. He got better results when people were on his turf and at least slightly uncomfortable.

They sat at the far end of the twenty-person table. Sinclair said, "As I'm sure the chief told you—"

"No opening statement is necessary," said Mathis. "We're all family at Children's Hospital, and we're mourning the loss of two family members. I'll answer any questions except for details of the settlement."

"Why is that off limits?"

"In today's litigious society, hospitals are sued frequently. If our settlement pattern were to become common knowledge, it would hamper negotiations in future cases. A nondisclosure clause is standard."

"Was the amount a nuisance fee?" Sinclair had learned that whenever someone tried to withhold something from him, it was the information he most needed.

"I had a strong case," said Hammond.

Mathis smiled. "Our exposure was minimal. Nevertheless, one cannot predict what a jury might do. We made an early offer and the plaintiff accepted it."

"What prompted the lawsuit?" asked Sinclair.

Hammond said, "Dr. Brooks was the first physician to see Samantha. He made an initial assessment that her head injury was secondary."

"Which was reasonable with the extent of blood loss and visible trauma in the patient's chest and pelvic region," said Mathis.

"However, he should have had neurology present in the OR to evaluate the traumatic brain injury and initiate surgery immediately."

"Dr. Brooks conferred with Dr. Caldwell, who was standing by—"

"At home," Hammond interjected. "He didn't come into the hospital and personally examine Samantha until four hours later."

"There was no need to. Standard protocol for that type of injury is watchful waiting for the first twenty-four hours."

"However—"

"Enough," Sinclair said. "I get it."

"As sad as it is," said Mathis, "there was nothing anyone could have done with the extent of her injury."

"There's always something," said Hammond.

Sinclair held up his hands as if he were a parent trying to silence two bickering children. "Why'd Mrs. Arquette settle?"

Hammond said, "When I initially spoke to her and described the process, I thought she was prepared. As it turned out, other people were more interested in pursuing this than she was. When I presented her with the hospital's offer, she was ready for it to be done."

"What other people?" asked Sinclair.

Hammond glanced at Mathis before looking at Sinclair. "I think it was Jane's father and other family members."

"What led you to believe that?"

Hammond shifted in his chair. "I only spoke to Jane once and that was my impression. Most of my dealings were through the family attorney in New York."

"Is that normal?"

"I normally work directly with a client—the plaintiff. But she was out of state and her family attorney handled her personal legal affairs. At that level, a family attorney is accustomed to coordinating a number of legal specialists who handle issues outside his expertise. I'm sure he was not well versed in medical malpractice or licensed to practice in California."

"Who is this family of hers you're referring to?"

"Her father, Bernard Arquette, is a commercial real estate developer in Manhattan," said Hammond. "He comes from old New York money. Jane ran the family foundation, an assortment of charities they supported and a few they directed."

"Was she married?"

"I don't think so. There was no mention of a husband or of Samantha's father."

"Did you ask?"

"Sure," said Hammond. "I had to make sure another aggrieved party, such as another parent, wasn't filing another claim that would muddy the waters. When I spoke with Mr. Horowitz, he assured me there was no father figure in the picture, none listed on Samantha's birth certificate, and no other person who might have standing in a claim or lawsuit over Samantha's death."

"He's the family attorney?"

"Yes, Harold Horowitz."

"I'll need his contact information."

Hammond copied information from his file and handed it to Sinclair. "I don't know if he'll speak to you. These kinds of families are very private. It's the family attorney's job to protect that privacy."

"Any other family members that you know of?"

"That's it. Like I said, most of my dealings were with Mr. Horowitz."

Sinclair turned to Mathis. "Have you paid the settlement?"

"We sent a check the day Jane Arquette signed the agreement," said Mathis.

"I FedExed a check to my client for the full amount, minus my commission, a few days later," said Hammond. "That was more than six months ago."

"Just prior to Jane Arquette committing suicide," said Sinclair.

"Are you suggesting the money from the settlement is the motive?" said Hammond. "The Arquette family fortune is massive. Jane's trust is well into the millions."

"What trust?"

"It's common for people with significant assets to hold them in a family trust. There can be tax advantages and it makes transfer easier upon death."

Hammond slid some papers from his briefcase. "We made the check out to the J. Arquette Family Trust. It was endorsed by . . . the signature looks like Harold Horowitz."

"Is that normal?"

"A large family trust is more involved than balancing a checkbook and managing a few mutual funds," said Hammond. "Attorneys, accountants, and financial advisors are all involved."

Sinclair stared out the window. Penetrating the Arquette family and getting answers wouldn't be easy.

Mathis asked, "Should I be worried about other hospital employees?"

"Who else was listed in the lawsuit?" asked Sinclair.

"The president and CEO, the VP for medical affairs, and two other surgeons."

"Two people named in this lawsuit are already dead." Sinclair thought for a moment. "I don't think this guy is finished killing."

Chapter 38

Sinclair walked through the door and saw Maloney sitting in the front of the homicide office surrounded by Sergeants Braddock, Jankowski, Sanchez, and Larsen. "What did the autopsy reveal?" Maloney asked.

"Cause of death due to shock and hemorrhage as a result of multiple gunshot wounds," said Sinclair. "It didn't take a medical degree to figure that out. The doc dug out four slugs. All look intact."

Maloney said, "I talked to Mary in the lab. She'll do a rush on your casings and slugs and enter them in the system today if you get them there by two."

"I'll do the lab request and walk it up," said Braddock.

"You and Matt will be busy."

Jankowski said, "I'll handle it."

Maloney turned to Larsen. "How's it going with Children's?"

"I want to thank you, boss, for this shit detail." Larsen sat on a desk belonging to one of the homicide suppression team officers. "We met with the security guy, the hospital CEO, and a bunch of other bigwigs. They're going to send the surgeons and their families out of town. The hospital's springing for the hotel. They're arranging body-guards through a private security company for the CEO and medical affairs chief and their families. O'Connor's still there coordinating the details."

"How long will they protect them?" asked Sinclair.

"Through the weekend at least," said Larsen. "They'll reassess Monday morning."

"I want you and O'Connor to stay on this," said Malo-ney. "We can't afford to have one of these people killed."

"Don't tell me you're forcing us to work overtime."

Maloney grinned. "Split it up, twelve on and twelve off through Monday morning."

"Ka-ching. I take back what I said about this being a shit assignment."

Sanchez said, "I just got phone records and some finan-cials on Brooks, so I'll get that into the database."

"NYPD's Nineteenth Precinct called when you were out," Connie said, handing Sinclair a message. "The detective who handled the case was on vacation, but his partner said there was nothing suspicious about Arquette's suicide. She ODed on prescribed Valium. Everyone said she was distraught over her daughter's death. She left a note."

"Did you think to request a copy of their report?" asked Sinclair.

"I'm sorry—"

Maloney glared at Sinclair. Then he said to Connie, "It's okay. You didn't know."

She smiled, and Sinclair felt like an asshole for jumping on her.

"From now on, I want someone available to field calls like this," said Maloney. "Sanchez and Jankowski, you two work it out."

"I'll call NYPD back and try to get that report as soon as we're done here," said Sinclair.

"I know you think you can do everything yourself, but Jankowski can do that. The DC had vice narcotics look into Keller's hospital drug incident," said Maloney, referring to the deputy chief of the bureau of investigations. "It was Doctor Brooks—the husband of your latest victim—who caught him. When interviewing folks at the hospital, narcotics learned that Keller worked extra shifts in surgical ICU. He could have had contact with Doctor Caldwell there."

Sinclair felt the case slipping away from him. He hadn't gotten around to reading the paperwork the hospital gave him yesterday. If he had, he would have seen Dr. Brooks's name on the incident report and would have looked into Keller last night. He hated having other people tell him details about his case that he should know. But there was too much happening and not enough time. He'd been reacting—racing from one homicide to the next. No time to think or plan. Things were falling through the cracks.

Maloney continued, "Narcotics took the case to the DA and got a warrant for Keller's arrest. Theft of pharmaceuticals."

"Isn't it unusual to go criminal on something like this?" asked Braddock.

"The DC wants him off the street in case he's the one," said Maloney.

"If he is, we just shot our wad," said Sinclair. "There's nothing to prove he killed anyone, and he'll either bail on that bullshit charge or the judge will OR him come Monday."

"Narcotics got a search warrant for his place to look for any further evidence," said Maloney.

"Of what, pharmaceutical drugs?" asked Sinclair.

"You should be there," said Maloney "Coordinate with narcotics. Have a look-see for anything else."

"And if there's nothing that links him to the murders?"

"Then you interview him."

"And say what: even though we ain't got shit to prove you did it, we'd really appreciate you confessing to three murders?"

"This isn't my doing, Matt."

"Whose fucking case is this anyway, mine or the deputy chief's?"

Maloney stared at him for a few counts. Braddock looked at the notebook in her lap. Jankowski looked at the floor. Larsen and Sanchez stared into space.

"We all have bosses," Maloney said. "You're the lead investigator. Don't give one of your bosses a reason to change that." Maloney scanned the faces in the room, walked to his office, and shut the door.

"Takes a lot to piss off the LT," said Jankowski.

"I'm sure the eighth floor is putting a lot of pressure on him. Stuff we don't see," said Braddock.

"All I did was ask a question," said Sinclair.

"Don't you think he questioned the deputy chief when he involved himself in our homicides?" she said. "The lieutenant isn't the bad guy."

Jankowski and the others slinked back to their desks. Sinclair felt embarrassed, first getting slammed by the boss and then getting a verbal spanking from his rookie partner.

"I guess we go see the narcs" Sinclair headed for the door. "Since obviously they've solved our murders for us."

Chapter 39

Sinclair and Braddock pulled into the Casper's Hotdogs lot on MacArthur Boulevard in East Oakland. He could smell raw onions and hotdogs from the far corner of the parking lot. A burly man with a messy beard and unkempt, shoulder-length hair stepped out of a gray Camaro. Sergeant Ian Powell looked more like a Hells Angel than a cop.

"I got two of my guys spotting the subject's apartment. He's been loading stuff into his car for the last half hour. Looks like he's getting ready to rabbit."

"Does he know you're watching him?" asked Sinclair.

"Who knows. We narcs live in a constant state of paranoia about being made. Since two guys are all I could spare, we're set up closer than I'd prefer."

"I'd like to follow him, see where he goes."

"A mobile surveillance would take my whole squad. I broke these guys off a multikilo coke deal."

Powell held up his finger, pulled a radio from his belt, and yanked out the earbud jack so the external speaker took over. "Target's starting the engine," said the voice on the radio.

Powell said to Sinclair, "Let him go or call in patrol to grab him?"

"Arrest him."

Powell spoke into the radio, "Stay with him if he rolls, direct patrol in for the arrest. Don't forget, you're under, so stay out of it. Switch to main freq."

Trying to keep cops from involving themselves in an arrest, even when they're undercover, was like stopping dogs from chasing cats, but Sinclair understood the reason Powell was a hard-ass about this. Sinclair and Powell had worked together as narcotics officers in the same squad nine years ago. One night, a new narc assigned to the unit broke from his undercover drug-buying role to arrest a car thief. Two uniformed officers arrived on the scene to see a gangster-looking man pointing a gun at a teenager. Both shot. The narc died, and the two patrol officers who shot eventually decided to change careers.

Powell advised the dispatcher of the location and description of the suspect and car and requested marked units for the arrest. She dispatched two units, and two others announced they'd also respond when the dispatcher mentioned murder suspect.

"He's starting to roll," one of the narcs said over the radio. "Southbound toward MacArthur. Black Chrysler Three Hundred."

"Southbound toward MacArthur," echoed the dispatcher.

Sinclair and Braddock jumped in their car, started the engine, and nudged to the edge of the lot.

"Stopped at the stop sign on Mac, preparing to make a right turn," said the narc.

Sinclair heard a loud screeching of tires to his right and then the narc's voice, a half octave higher, on the radio. "He's made us. We're in pursuit westbound MacArthur."

The Chrysler shot past Sinclair, a white Toyota Camry on its tail. Sinclair flipped two switches under the dash, and the flashing lights in the grill came to life followed by the scream of the siren. He swung the steering wheel to the left and floored the accelerator.

Powell's voice came over the radio. "Undercover cars are not authorized to pursue. All narcotics units terminate."

Sinclair swung the Crown Vic into the left lane and passed a line of cars that had pulled to the right.

Braddock picked up the handset, "Thirteen-Adam-Five, we're in pursuit of the one-eighty-seven vehicle. Unmarked vehicle with operational emergency equipment. Traffic is moderate. Speed is fifty-five in a thirty-five."

Sinclair's speedometer read seventy, but if they admitted going that fast in an unmarked car, some command officer who was more concerned with liability than catching criminals might order the pursuit terminated.

Some cars pulled to the right, while others—probably with windows up and stereos blaring—were oblivious. Sinclair pulled into oncoming traffic to weave around a car that stopped in the fast lane. What part of *pull to the right and stop* didn't these people understand?

They were still a block behind and not gaining as they approached Fruitvale Avenue, a main north-south thoroughfare. The Chrysler slowed.

Braddock's voice was slow and calm. "Southbound on Fruitvale."

The Chrysler entered the corner too fast and drifted wide, plowing into a car parked against the curb. The narc in the Toyota braked hard and pulled to the right, finally deciding to get out of the chase.

Sinclair planted his foot on the brake, slowing to thirty. The Chrysler's tires smoked, and Sinclair heard the roar of its engine over his siren.

"Nine-oh-one into a parked car at Fruitvale," Braddock said on the radio. "Suspect vehicle continuing southbound."

Sinclair gave the big Ford more gas, bringing the front end out of the braking dive and settling the suspension. Its back end hunkered down and pushed the car out of the corner. Sinclair cut the distance to five car lengths as he powered out of the turn, but now on a straightaway, the Chrysler pulled away. The way it accelerated told Sinclair the 300 contained one of the optional V8 engines with at least a hundred more horsepower than the police interceptor package in the antiquated Crown Vic.

"Crossing School Street, still southbound," said Braddock.

Traffic ahead was moving at the thirty-mile-per-hour limit on the two-lane road. The Chrysler swung into the oncoming traffic lane to get around it. Now a half-block back, Sinclair did the same but had to cut back into his lane to avoid a head-on with a delivery truck. A few blocks ahead, Sinclair saw traffic stopped. The Chrysler's brake lights flashed and the back end swung out to the left.

"Turning right, westbound on East Twenty-Seventh Street," said Braddock.

Once again, the Chrysler took the turn too fast and tried to brake in the corner. The voice of his academy driving instructor sounded in Sinclair's head: *smooth is fast, complete all braking before the corner, accelerate out of the turn.*

The Chrysler fishtailed and slid into a car stopped at the intersection, glancing off its side with a screech of metal against metal before accelerating again. Sinclair braked before the corner, gave the Ford enough gas to transfer the weight to the rear wheels, and took the sharp corner at thirty. He was right on the tail of the Chrysler before its bigger engine began pulling away again on the straightaway. He smelled burning rubber and overheated brake pads.

Small stucco houses, many with cars parked in front, lined East Twenty-Seventh Street. A car backed out of a driveway. The Chrysler clipped the rear of it, tearing the bumper off and sending it careening across the road. As they flashed past Twenty-Fifth Avenue at sixty miles an hour, Sinclair saw a marked car out of the corner of his eye pull in behind him.

"Two-L-Eighteen, I'm number two behind the homicide unit," a voice said over the radio.

The marked unit closed the gap until its light bar, lit up like a Christmas tree, filled Sinclair's rearview mirror. At Inyo Avenue, the street zigged to the left and dropped downhill to the light at Twenty-Third Avenue. The signal shone red and Sinclair let up on the gas. The Chrysler rocketed down the hill at sixty. A few car lengths from the intersection, the Chrysler's brake lights lit up as a car crossed in front of it through the intersection.

The Chrysler swerved right, then left, finally spinning 360 degrees through the intersection and slamming into a retaining wall on the far side of the intersection. Sinclair pulled his car behind the Chrysler and flipped off the siren.

An airbag bulged out the Chrysler's window. The front end sat crumpled into the engine bay. Steam hissed from the hood.

The marked patrol car pulled alongside. Another patrol car pulled in at a right angle. Two uniformed officers jumped out of their units and approached the driver's door with guns drawn. Sinclair and Braddock drew their handguns and crouched behind their open doors.

Both officers holstered their pistols, and one spoke into his lapel mike. "Driver's trapped in the vehicle. We need an ambulance, Code Three, and fire with jaws of life."

Chapter 40

"The chief won't like hearing that," said Officer George Thomas, the PIO, as he twisted his chair to face Sinclair.

Sinclair stood in Maloney's doorway. "Then tell him what he wants to hear—Keller's the killer and the city's now safe."

"We're not lying to the chief," said Maloney.

"Help me out here," pleaded Thomas. "We can't continue to say we haven't a clue who's massacring families of doctors and lawyers in our city."

"It could be Keller," said Maloney. "We're also looking in other directions."

Maloney was being diplomatic. Sinclair and Braddock had searched Keller's Chrysler at the crash scene. Clothes and other personal belongings filled the trunk. The GPS was set to the address of an alcohol and drug treatment facility in Napa. They searched his apartment, where they found plenty of empty liquor and wine bottles. Powell called a few numbers from Keller's cell phone call log. Keller was dialing while drunk last night at the time of the murder, telling friends and ex-girlfriends how sorry he was and how he was changing his life.

"There's nothing that connects him to the murders," said Sinclair.

"When will you be able to interrogate him?" asked Thomas.

"There won't be any interrogation." Keller's left leg and arm were fractured, and the airbag broke his nose and caused other facial injuries when it smacked him in the face. The hospital pumped him full of morphine for the pain, and even if the nurses allowed Sinclair to talk to him, he'd be wasting his time. If Keller gave a statement, a judge would throw it out because he was incapable of understanding his rights in his condition.

"Every news station heard the chase on their scanners, so we have to say something about his arrest," said Thomas.

"Why don't you tell the truth? He was arrested for a warrant on an unrelated charge, and he was someone we wanted to talk to because he had worked with the doctors."

"Can I say he's a person of interest?"

"What the fuck is a person of interest?" said Sinclair.

"It means—"

"It's a term your media friends made up to force cops to label someone who isn't a suspect. Then when we do, they beat us up for information to justify why we called him that."

"Come on, Matt, I'm—"

"Last I recalled, you're an officer," said Sinclair. "And we're not on a first-name basis."

"Sorry, Sergeant." Thomas turned to Maloney. "After the chief reads his prepared statement and I brief this arrest, maybe Sergeant Sinclair can talk about the kind of person he's looking for."

"You mean like a profile?" asked Maloney.

"Yeah, something that might tell the public these aren't just random killings."

Sinclair hated when police claimed killings were random. Serial killers rarely selected their victims at random. Police administrators claimed killings were random when they didn't have the courage to admit they hadn't yet found a common factor that connected the murders or didn't know enough about the killer to understand his motivation. To Sinclair, random killings meant the homicide detectives had more work to do.

Even many cops misunderstood the limitations of criminal profiling. It wasn't a panacea that magically led detectives to a killer as portrayed on TV, and Sinclair didn't have much faith in the psychological profiles the FBI had been touting for decades as the means to solve serial killings. There were only a handful of times when an FBI profile led to the killer. Usually, detectives would spend days filling out forms and copying mounds of paperwork for the FBI, and months later, they'd receive a profile telling them their killer was likely a white male in his thirties who worked in a menial job and wet his bed as an adolescent. Sinclair relied on his gut, and after seeing this killer's work three times, he was getting a good idea of the kind of person he was looking for.

"I can offer up a generic profile that might ease the public's fear," said Sinclair.

Thomas slipped out the door, and Sinclair dropped into the chair he vacated.

"When the DC heard about the car chase and collision, he had me standing tall in front of his desk," said Maloney.

"What did he expect?" said Sinclair. "He devises a plan without consulting us and then doesn't like the outcome.

I would've told him that next time he should leave police work to real cops."

"Maybe that's why I'm a lieutenant and you're not."

On the way to his desk, Sinclair poured himself a cup of coffee, hoping the caffeine would change his mood. Jankowski told him the lab found no matches on the slugs and casings from the Brooks case. The rifling characteristics were consistent with a number of nine-millimeter pistols, the most common being Berettas. But there were thousands of Beretta 9mm pistols registered in Oakland alone, and it would be impossible to track them all down.

"I spoke to a legal secretary at Horowitz's law office," said Jankowski. "Horowitz rewrote Jane Arquette's family trust and will at her request after Samantha died."

"Did she tell you who the beneficiary is?"

"She told me she probably said more than she should have already and cut me off."

"Anything else?"

"Not much. I did get her former home address. Three-bedroom apartment sold for four point two million two months ago. A woman from the realtor company that listed it said the check was made out to the family trust and mailed to a law office."

"Probably Horowitz. If money is the motive, it seems like he holds the key to who is benefiting."

"The lady will try to get the paperwork from the transaction, but it was already after five in New York when I talked to her, so the soonest she could get it to me is Monday morning."

"Anything from NYPD?"

"Nothing from the nineteenth detective squad. I just put a call in to the precinct watch commander—the regular nine-to-five people are gone. I hate snitching off my brother detectives to the brass, but these guys need a fire lit under their asses."

★

At four o'clock, Sinclair and Braddock made their way to the auditorium. With seating for three hundred, a thirty-foot ceiling, and a raised stage, it reminded Sinclair of his high school auditorium, where he had sat through hundreds of boring assemblies, plays, and concerts. His memories of this auditorium were no better. Chief Brown stood behind the podium in the middle of the stage, the four stars on each collar shining just a shade brighter than his shaved head. Two deputy chiefs and three captains, wearing ties and long-sleeve uniform shirts with glistening gold brass on the collars, flanked him.

Sinclair and Braddock stood in the back and watched the sea of cameras and microphones jockey for position near the stage. Their numbers swelled to double what it was at the press conference two days ago. The press briefing was open to the public and a hundred people without cameras, recorders, or steno pads filled seats in the back.

Brown spoke about how violent crime in Oakland was down 3 percent from a year ago and how, even with these recent murders, homicides were showing a downward trend this year. The journalists listened politely but looked bored. They didn't come here for a PR spiel. He then discussed the rape and murder of Samantha Arquette, praising the hardworking members of *his* department for never giving up even though the leads had grown cold. Once finished, Brown abruptly left the stage without taking questions. His entourage followed.

232 | Brian Thiem

Thomas recited the details about the last murder and the arrest of Keller. He parried reporters' questions without revealing anything about the ongoing investigation or saying anything substantial. Once no additional hands rose, he introduced Sinclair.

Sinclair climbed the steps to the stage and moved behind the podium. "I'm going to tell you what is surely obvious by now. These four homicides are related." The room fell silent as Sinclair laid out each murder. "As the chief told you, we've identified and arrested those responsible for Samantha Arquette's death. They didn't kill the latest three victims. We don't yet know who did."

Sinclair took a deep breath and looked around the room. Liz winked at him. Sinclair saw a rotund cameraman with greasy hair next to her instead of Eric, which wasn't unusual since reporters and cameramen worked different schedules. "We've identified others who might be targeted by this killer and have coordinated security plans for them. These aren't random killings. I can't discuss the motive at this time, but I can tell you that no rational person would kill innocent women and children like this. These murders only make sense inside the twisted, sick mind of a savage killer."

Someone yelled, "Are you saying the bus bench killer is insane?"

"He knows exactly what he's doing. Once we catch him, his lawyers will try the insanity route to keep him off death row, but it won't work."

"A psychotic serial killer?" another reporter yelled.

"Although he fits the serial killer definition, he's not psychotic. There are no little voices in his head telling him to do this. He falls into the mission-oriented killer subcategory. He's a sociopath, and to him, the killings are justified."

"Why *would* someone do this?" asked a journalist in a corduroy blazer.

"When we arrest him, all of this will come out. These are irrational acts by a vicious and ruthless man."

The room erupted with more questions. Once it quieted, Sinclair leaned toward the microphone. "I wish I could stay longer, but I've got a lot to do."

As he turned to the rear of the stage, he caught a look of disbelief on Thomas's face. Sinclair almost felt bad leaving him with the crowd.

Braddock met him at the back door. "I hope you know what you're doing," she said.

"What do you mean? The lieutenant and Thomas asked me to profile him."

"How's that tough-cop line go? *I'll bullshit my friends and you can bullshit yours, but let's not bullshit each other.*"

"I had to do something to upset his routine."

"You think this will stop him?"

"It might cause him to . . . reassess."

"I hope you're right."

Chapter 41

Sinclair sat at his desk and played his voicemails. The fifth one perked his interest. *Sergeant, this is your confidential source, the one who cannot reveal his identity. As previously, please keep this to yourself. Preliminary tox screening revealed a therapeutic level of Valium in the blood and tissue samples of Hammond. The levels would be sufficient for deep relaxation or sleep, but not so high as to cause death. I think she would have felt no pain as her wrists were cut.*

Half the medicine cabinets in the country contained Valium. It was an ideal drug to knock out victims and make them easier to handle. It could be a coincidence that Valium was what Jane Arquette had ODed on, but it might be another connection, similar to the bus bench and peace medallions.

Sinclair's cell phone buzzed.

"That's why every journalist loves Matt Sinclair," Liz said. "Ruthless, vicious, sociopath, irrational, twisted, sick, savage: any one of your words could make a headline or teaser. Homicide detective says bus bench killer's mind is *twisted*—more at ten."

"Did I sound okay?"

"You're a rock star. I wish you could have tipped me earlier about the connection between the murders. I'm now competing with everyone else when I should be out ahead."

"Sorry, I've been going nonstop all day."

"I understand," she said, but from her tone, Sinclair sensed disappointment. "I'm getting off right after the six o'clock broadcast. Do you want to do dinner?"

"I don't know when I'll punch out, and I only got two hours sleep last night."

"We can order in then go straight to bed. No reporter questions. I'm sure that's why you didn't come over last night."

"Liz, I was interviewing suspects until I got called to the Brooks murder scene and worked that most of the night."

The phone went silent. Sinclair didn't know whether he should wait or build onto his excuse.

Finally, she said, "Well I hope you can come over tonight."

"I'll give you a call in a few hours and let you know."

"Good. I love you, Matt."

Sinclair put his phone back on his belt and stared at the ceiling.

"Everything okay?" asked Braddock.

"It's complicated."

"All relationships are," she said.

"Including you and Ryan?"

"We work to keep it simple."

Sinclair returned his attention to the reports on his desk.

"I didn't mean to eavesdrop, but are we working through the night or cutting out in a few hours?" Braddock asked.

"Unless a hot lead materializes in this pile of paper, we should get a good night's sleep and come in fresh tomorrow. Why?"

"Friday night's movie night at my place. Tonight it's *Toy Story.*"

Although Sinclair and his ex-wife had talked about having kids when they first married, their careers and then Sinclair's drinking eventually consumed their lives. The closest he remembered to a movie night from his childhood was watching TV with his two younger brothers while his father, passed out from two or more six-packs of beer, snored in the Barcalounger. The image he pictured at Braddock's house was different, the way he and his ex had once envisioned their future. But that was the past. His childhood was over, and he had screwed up his marriage.

They went back to their paperwork, and at six o'clock, Braddock, Jankowski, and Sanchez left, agreeing to meet in the office at seven the following morning. An hour later, Sinclair realized he had reviewed a two-page supplemental report and couldn't recall a word he'd read. He called Liz and told her he was on his way, turned off the lights, and walked out the door.

He rolled down the car window and let in the cool night air as he drove down Broadway. Friday night in Jack London Square, all the restaurants were buzzing and cars were stacked up waiting for valets. Couples walking arm-in-arm, not a care in the world. He called Walt, got his voicemail, and left a message that he was sober another day and would try to get to a meeting tomorrow.

Liz was scooping Chinese food from cardboard containers into bowls when he got there. She wore loose-fitting fleece pants and a tank top without a bra. She pressed herself against him, pulled him tight, and kissed him.

"What's the matter?" she asked.

"Thinking about the case."

"Let's eat, and then I'll do my magic to take your mind off it."

She carried the food to the coffee table and then returned to the kitchen for plates and silverware.

"What would you like to drink?"

"Water's fine."

Sinclair spooned rice and Mongolian beef onto his plate. Liz set a glass of water in front of him and a half-full bottle of Pinot Grigio and a wine glass on her side of the glass table. When Sinclair had quit drinking, he knew he had no right to expect the rest of the world to do the same. He had two choices: to socialize only with the small percentage of people who didn't drink or accept alcohol and drinkers even though he couldn't imbibe. Although he stopped hanging out at bars and frequenting events that centered on drinking, drinking in moderation by others didn't normally bother him. Right now, he could smell the aroma and almost taste the crispness as she took her first sip.

"I'm still wired from the five o'clock broadcast," she said. "The news director asked me to sit at the anchor desk and narrate the cuts of you from the press conference. The questions and my responses were all prepared beforehand, but when I invited the bus bench killer to tell us his motivation so the viewing public could understand, it was surreal—like I was talking directly to him."

"You did what?"

"You said all those negative things about him and how no one could possibly understand his reasons for doing what he did. I offered to listen and tell his side."

Sinclair put his fork down. "You were addressing him, as if he were listening? What could he or anyone say to justify killing innocent people?"

"It's for ratings, silly. Besides, every story has more than one side."

"In this case, one side is deranged and sick."

"People have the right to hear divergent views."

"Are you telling me you'd really put some narcissistic killer's rationalization on TV?"

"Not that I could ever pull it off, but if I could get an interview with him, sure. It's news. In college, we watched Stone Phillips's interview with Jeffrey Dahmer. It was one of the most highly rated specials that year, a major coup for NBC."

"That was after they caught him."

"It wouldn't be sensationalizing it—just reporting the facts."

"This guy is probably out there right now planning his next killing, and I don't know enough to stop him. Meanwhile, you're—"

"I thought—"

"You thought we were withholding this guy's identity. That we're hiding how close we are to catching him. This isn't some kind of game about whether your station or CBS or ABC gets the highest ratings or the best scoop on the bus bench murders. This is about four people dead so far and probably more to come."

Sinclair got up, walked to the sliding glass door, and peered into the darkness.

Liz came up from behind and wrapped her arms around him. He felt her breasts pressing into his back, her warm breath and soft lips on his neck. Her hands rubbed his chest.

"I'm sorry, Matt. I thought you'd be excited for me. I didn't realize how much this case has affected you."

Her fingertips danced along his abdomen and slid under his belt.

"Come in the bedroom and I'll take your mind off this and everything else troubling you."

Sinclair's phone vibrated. He removed it from the case on his belt and looked at the screen. "I've got to take this." He stepped onto the patio and closed the door behind him.

Chapter 42

Sinclair took the freeway exit at Grand Avenue and lowered both front windows. The air blowing through the car dried the slick coating of sweat on his face. He didn't know what overcame him at Liz's apartment and worried he was having some kind of panic attack. He remembered the counselors at rehab warning them about becoming hungry, angry, lonely, and tired—the acronym HALT—and how that could set them up for relapse. All but hungry applied to him at that moment.

Walt's phone call had snapped him back to reality. Standing on Liz's balcony, Sinclair unleashed his jumbled thoughts over the phone. When he finished, Walt said, "You need to get out of there . . . now." Sinclair left Liz standing there with a bewildered look on her face as he hurried out the door.

Sinclair turned onto Sea View Avenue, looking for Walt's house number. A tiny city of less than two square miles, Piedmont was surrounded by Oakland yet was an independent city with its own police and fire departments and other services. When incorporated in 1923, it was known as the City of Millionaires, with the most millionaires per square mile of any city in the country. Compared to Oakland, Piedmont had no real crime, and Sinclair rarely had a reason to drive into the residential community nestled in the Oakland Hills.

It was obvious to Sinclair that many of those millionaires must have built their mansions on Sea View Avenue as he passed one massive old house after another. He spotted the number on a brass plate attached to one of the stone pillars guarding the driveway and pulled his car up to the ornate metal gate. Before he could figure out the keypad and speaker box alongside his window, he noticed a security camera pointed at him, and the gate clicked and rolled open on a motorized track. An immense Beaux Arts–style mansion was set well back across a lawn the width of a football field. It reminded Sinclair more of a nineteenth-century library or courthouse than a residence. He parked his car in the circular driveway and went up the granite steps to the two-story portico supported by four columns. Walt smiled and held the door open for Sinclair.

"I had no idea you lived—"

"My wife and I are just the caretakers. The house belongs to Frederick Towers." Walt led Sinclair across the marble floor of the foyer and past a sweeping stairway.

Sinclair recognized the name. Towers was the CEO of one of the largest corporations headquartered in Oakland and one of the city's most influential businessmen.

"Frederick Towers of PRM?" asked Sinclair, as he followed Walt through a dining room and around a long table surrounded by sixteen chairs.

"The older gentleman who often rides with me to meetings at the rec center."

"That Fred is Mr. Towers?"

"He's in Japan on business but asked me to give you his regards."

Walt pushed through a swinging door and stepped into a kitchen that looked like it belonged in an upscale restaurant: giant Wolf gas range, a Sub-Zero refrigerator/freezer bank the size of four normal refrigerators, two dual ovens, and what looked like acres of stainless steel countertops.

"Last week I was at a meeting," said Walt. "On my right sat Fred, who lives in this ten-thousand-square-foot home. Jerry, who sleeps under a freeway overpass, sat on my left. At the meeting, Fred spoke about his struggles dealing with his wife's death on what would have been his fortieth wedding anniversary. Jerry came up to him after the meeting and shared a similar experience and how he got through it. It was exactly what Fred needed to hear."

Walt pulled two mugs from the cabinet. "Decaf or regular?"

Over three cups of coffee, Sinclair told Walt about his relationship with Liz, his divorce, his work stress, and finally about his statement to the press.

"Back when I was practicing, I did a number of court-appointed examinations of criminal defendants."

"I thought you specialized in PTSD," said Sinclair.

"I was one of several psychologists on the court list."

"How many did you get off?"

Walt grinned. "None. I diagnosed some with PTSD based on their symptoms and case histories, but in no instance did the disorder negate their ability to exercise free choice. They all decided to commit their crimes."

"My killer makes deliberate and calculating choices too."

"You don't need a degree in psychology to understand the criminal mind. I suspect you've spent many more hours talking with criminals than most forensic psychologists. You understand this killer better than anyone. You know what makes him tick. Trust your intuition."

"It's just a hunch."

"It's telling you something that the rational part of your brain can't substantiate."

"I'm pretty sure the motive for the three murders this week has something to do with what happened to the girl a year ago."

"What are the most common motives for murder?"

"Love, lust, greed, revenge," said Sinclair. "Quite often the reasons overlap."

"What did the murder victims do or fail to do to make someone want to kill them?"

"The victims didn't do anything. The victims are the loved ones—a son and two wives—of men who failed Samantha in some way. Two doctors who didn't save her life and an attorney who didn't win a huge settlement."

"It sounds as if you've zeroed in on revenge as the motive."

"There's a lot of money involved in the family estate," said Sinclair. "But from what I know right now, I don't see money as the motive."

"Revenge is a powerful motivator."

"I know that understanding people's motivation is really important to psychologists, but it's only real value to me is if it points me to the identity of the killer."

"Understood," said Walt. "So, who would want to hurt doctors who didn't save Samantha and a lawyer who settled a lawsuit over her death?"

"Someone who cared about Samantha. Obviously her family, but her mother's dead and I don't know of any other family members other than a very wealthy grandfather who appears to be the patriarch of the family. Then there's Jenny's family. She was the other girl raped and left on the bus bench that night. Her mother's pretty unhappy about how this affected Jenny and was a good friend of Samantha's mother, who committed suicide, presumably over the death of Samantha."

"Could a woman have committed these murders?"

"The killer, assuming he acted alone, had to be someone strong enough to carry bodies from where he killed them to the bus bench. Jenny's mother couldn't do that. Besides, she doesn't strike me as a killer. Both families are really well off, so I can't rule out the possibility they hired someone to do this."

As he said that, he didn't believe it. The killings didn't feel like murders for hire. They felt personal.

"I'll bet if you were to sit down with those close to the girl and her mother, you'd recognize the killer among them."

"I think the key to this lies with the Arquette family, and they're all in New York and well connected."

"More coffee?"

A clock chimed in another room. Sinclair looked at his watch—ten o'clock. "I better get home."

Walt carried their mugs to the sink. "I saw the five o'clock news. When you poke a hornet's nest, you must remember they can be unpredictable little buggers."

*

At home, Sinclair grabbed a diet Sprite and sunk into his recliner. He needed to shut off his brain before sleep was possible. The day had stirred up feelings, but Walt helped him redirect his thoughts to the case. He kicked off his shoes and grabbed a pen and pad off the end table. When hundreds of pieces of information and random thoughts swirled around his head during an investigation, he found putting them on paper brought focus to the clutter. He listed the people he needed to conduct a full background on and interview: Donna Fitzgerald and her husband; Bernard Arquette, his wife, and any other family he could dig up; and the attorney, Harold Horowitz. Maybe he'd watched too many mafia movies, but something about Horowitz didn't feel right. Satisfied, Sinclair started writing a list of steps he could take tomorrow to learn more about Jenny and Samantha's family.

Chapter 43

The man switched on the TV and DVR, scrolled through the recorded programs to the five o'clock news, and hit play.

The news anchor introduced the bus bench murders as the top story. Standing in front of Dr. Brooks's house, Liz reported the latest murder. After a few sound bites from the chief and public affairs officer, Sinclair approached the microphone.

"Asshole," he whispered to the television when Sinclair left the podium. He hit rewind and watched it again.

Once the detective left the screen for a second time, the anchor returned, "It sounds as if the police have a good idea who is responsible for these heinous crimes, is that right, Liz?"

Elizabeth Schueller sat in the chair normally reserved for the coanchor. "They won't say they have a suspect in mind, so it may be they've only identified the motive thus far."

"Sergeant Sinclair says the reasons behind these gruesome acts, once revealed, will be incomprehensible. What do you think, Liz?"

"Possibly so. However, I'd love to talk with the killer and hear what happened to make him want to do these terrible things." She stared directly into the camera, a look of determination and sincerity in her eyes.

He hit the rewind button and heard her say it again. She seemed genuine. He shuffled through the file folders on the dining table to the one titled Melissa. His original plan had scheduled her for last night, but bypassing Carol in Montclair pushed his schedule back a day. He studied his notes in the folder and verified Melissa would be working tonight and nothing else in the plan would change by pushing it back a day.

The next folder was for Liz. It contained the extensive notes he took when he tailed her and printouts from the Internet. He spent thirty minutes drafting a new plan. To make it work, he'd need to prepare a few things, which would push his schedule back another day. Nevertheless, by Sunday, it would all be over.

He took a blank folder and wrote a new name on it. A few hours ago, he had gotten off work and drove by the police parking lot. He saw Braddock's Toyota minivan parked just inside the chain-link fence and waited. An hour passed before the minivan drove out the gate with Braddock behind the wheel. He followed her onto the freeway and settled in a few car lengths behind her. After getting off the freeway, she drove into a quiet neighborhood of suburban homes with decent-sized yards and swung into a driveway. He stopped a half block back and watched her walk into an open two-car garage crammed full of bicycles, toys, tools, and gardening equipment. At least Braddock would be easy.

But first, he needed to slow Sinclair down. He brewed a pot of coffee, and over a large cup, he worked out a plan to do just that.

★

Later that night, he walked along the sidewalk of the quiet residential neighborhood. Interspaced among small bungalows and cottages were a few duplexes and fourplex apartment buildings. Cars were parked on both sides of the street, leaving barely enough room for two cars to pass each other. Sinclair's police car sat against the curb in front of a teal single-story apartment building. Four cars filled a small parking lot behind the building. He crept toward a metallic blue Mustang. Its chrome GT trunk decal shined under an overhead light.

He clicked his lock-blade knife open and stabbed the convertible top, then cut a slit down the center. He removed one of the plastic bottles from his cargo pants pocket, unscrewed the top, and dropped it through the slit.

He slipped around the side of the building to the bedroom window of Sinclair's apartment. The room was dark, the apartment quiet. He removed the three remaining bottles from his pocket, set them on the ground under the window, and unscrewed the tops. The vapors burned his eyes as he crouched over them.

He drew his Berretta and fired a shot through the bedroom window.

Then he pulled the trigger twice more in rapid succession and threw the three bottles through the shattered window. He took a road flare from his pocket, removed the cap, and struck it against the igniter. Fire erupted from the top with a hiss. The smell of sulfur filled the air.

He lobbed the flare through the window and heard a loud whoosh as it ignited the gasoline vapors. He hurried to the Mustang, lit another flare, and dropped it through the slit in the top. A fireball filled the interior as he jogged down the road to his van.

Chapter 44

Sinclair was in a deep sleep, and when he heard the first shot, he thought he was dreaming. The second shot and the sound of breaking glass, however, jolted him awake. He slid out of the recliner onto the living room floor and drew his gun. Another shot rang out as he crawled toward the sofa. Even though it wouldn't stop bullets, he felt safer behind it.

More breaking glass from his bedroom. A whiff of gasoline.

He knew what would come next.

He had two options: stay where he was and wait for the fire or rush out the door and possibly meet a hail of bullets.

He low-crawled toward the kitchen, keeping his body as deep into the carpet as possible. A loud whoosh came from his bedroom. Flames filled the doorway, climbing toward the ceiling. He slithered across the tile floor to the back door, reached up, turned the doorknob, and flattened his belly back to the floor. He cracked the kitchen door open. Listened and peered into the darkness.

An explosion sounded and a burst of light flashed outside the door. He pulled his head back inside and pressed his face to the cold tile, covering his head with his arms. He peeked through the doorway. Saw a large fire raging in the parking lot. Felt the heat.

Fire or bullets—he had to choose.

He scrambled across the living room on his hands and knees, flung open the front door, and leaped through the doorway. He landed in a crouch, scanning rapidly from left to right with his Sig Sauer following his eyes.

Porch lights flicked on down the street. The door of the apartment next to him swung open. To his left, nearly two hundred feet away, a man dressed in dark clothing trotted down the street.

Sinclair bellowed, "Police—freeze!" as he assumed a two-handed shooting stance.

The man looked over his shoulder, reached in his waistband, and turned with a gun in his hand.

Sinclair had fired many thousands of rounds with a pistol in his career, and hitting a target at even a hundred feet in daylight on a shooting range was difficult with a handgun. To hit a moving target that was shooting back at night at twice that distance required more luck than skill. He also knew that in gunfights, bad guys seemed to make lucky shots far more often than good guys.

He dove behind a parked car as three shots rang out and a bullet pinged off a car fender.

He quick-peeked around the parked car. The man was running. Sinclair got up and sprinted after him. He was starting to close the distance when the man suddenly stopped and turned. Sinclair dropped to the street and slid alongside a parked car as two more gunshots rang out.

Sinclair poked his head up and saw the man open the door of a dark van and jump inside. He got to his feet and dashed toward it. The engine roared to life and the van took off down the street.

Too far away to read a license plate, Sinclair stopped, took careful aim, and fired one, then a second, and then a third shot at the vehicle. As he was aiming for a fourth shot, it turned left at the corner and disappeared from sight.

Breathing hard, Sinclair holstered his handgun and looked down at his feet and legs. His knees were bloody from crawling through broken glass and sliding on the street, and his thin dress socks were torn from running on the asphalt road. He limped back toward his apartment, leaving a trail of bloody footprints.

Chapter 45

Sinclair stood on a disposable paper blanket outside the back door of an ambulance. A circle of cops and firefighters surrounded him to block the gawkers that had formed outside the police tape. His torn pants and shredded socks lay at his feet. A young brunette paramedic brushed the final bits of gravel from his knees with gauze and squeezed the remains of a bottle of saline solution over the road rash. He shivered as the cold water ran down his bare legs.

Braddock slipped through the circle of people surrounding him, draped a blue coat with Lafayette PD shoulder patches on it over his shoulders, and handed him a Styrofoam cup of steaming coffee. "You look like you're in shock."

"I'm fine." He forced a smile. The coffee warmed him up. While the female paramedic applied bandages to his knees, her partner pulled a shard of glass from his thigh with forceps. Sinclair winced.

"I still recommend you go to the ER. This could use a few stitches," said the male paramedic.

"How many times do I need to tell you—"

"I got it." The paramedic pulled the incision apart, inserted a large syringe needle into the wound, and squirted the saline inside to irrigate it. It burned like rubbing alcohol. Sinclair clenched his teeth but didn't utter a sound. The paramedic dried the area and applied a butterfly bandage. Braddock handed Sinclair a pair of jeans, provided by a cop several inches shorter than him.

"I like the high waters." Braddock chuckled.

The paramedics had him sit on the back of the rig and each one examined a foot. He felt warmer now that he was dry and wearing pants. He sipped the coffee as the paramedics washed and scrubbed the soles of his feet, discarding pieces of bloody gauze in a plastic bag. They pulled another piece of glass and several sharp stones from his feet with forceps, applied butterfly bandages, and covered the raw skin with several layers of adhesive pads. Sinclair pulled on a pair of thick athletic socks and tried to put on a pair of black sneakers he had grabbed from a pile of clothes that officers and firefighters from Lafayette brought when they noticed his ripped pants and bare feet. They wouldn't fit, so he selected another pair and put them on. He stood gingerly and shifted his weight from foot to foot.

"Nice shoes." He raised each purple running shoe in turn. "With all the bandages the fuckin' paramedics stuck on my feet, I'm glad the cop who donated them wears size sixteen."

"They're elevens, Matt," said Braddock. "I'm glad your sense of humor, such as it was, is still intact."

Three hours had passed since the shooting, and only one fire truck remained, but scores of uniformed and plainclothes cops still filled the street in front of his apartment.

Outside the yellow tape, a hundred people and dozens of reporters milled about. With the abduction of Hammond a few days ago and then a running gun battle through its quiet streets, Lafayette had seen more violent crime in the last few days than it normally saw in months.

Sergeant Edwards, a stocky man with silver hair and bushy moustache, had worked homicide for the Contra Costa County Sheriff's Department as long as Sinclair had been a cop. Lafayette contracted with the sheriff for police services, and when a major crime occurred, their full resources were available. Edwards walked toward Sinclair's Crown Vic, followed by a handful of investigators and an older woman in fire turnout gear. Maloney, Braddock, and Jankowski joined the group.

"Your lieutenant and I talked," said Edwards. "This'll be a mix of OPD's protocol and ours. The walk-through's purpose is only to catch this asshole and collect the evidence to put him away, not to decide whether your shooting was justified or not, although I don't think there's any question about it. Sometime next week, once this settles down, we'll do a formal interview."

"I know the routine," said Sinclair.

"Let's start with you falling asleep in your chair."

Sinclair's feet squished on the wet carpet as he stepped into the apartment behind Edwards. Water dripped from the ceiling and soot covered the walls. Sinclair slogged across the living room carpet and stood in the doorway of his bedroom. All that remained of his bed were springs and pieces of charred fabric that was once a mattress. Huge chunks of dry wall, ripped out by firefighters, lay on the floor, and pieces of furniture and clothes from his dresser lay in soggy piles.

"I'll ask you not to touch anything," said Edwards. "The fire marshal, arson investigators, and our crime lab will go through this over the next few days. If there's any belongings you need right away, let me know and we'll see if we can locate them."

His clothes lay in water-saturated piles in the closet. The smell of burnt, wet wool reminded Sinclair of a wet dog—more like an entire kennel of them. He thought about his photo albums and the boxes of papers on the closet shelf and the keepsakes he stored in his top dresser drawer. His past—his memories.

"I can't think of anything important," said Sinclair.

"Have your insurance agent call me. We can let him in, but I'm sure he'll declare it a total loss," said Edwards.

Sinclair walked through the apartment, stopping occasionally to tell Edwards what he did, heard, or saw at each location. Then he led him outside, past the burnt hulk that used to be his Mustang, to the spot where he fired the shots at the escaping van.

When they finished, Sinclair asked, "What about the expended casings?"

"I think we got them all. The three shots you heard outside the bedroom window, five more on the street, plus your three."

Jankowski added, "Nine millimeter—same head stamp as from the Brooks scene."

"We found two of his slugs in a house down the street," said Edwards. "We expect to find the other three in your apartment walls once we sift through everything."

"Neighbors?" asked Sinclair.

Edwards studied his notes. "A few saw the gunman running. Descriptions ranged from six foot to six-four, and one-eighty to two-forty. Your estimate was right in the middle of that. You said average or muscular build. That's consistent with other witnesses. No one saw his face, so race and age would only be a guess."

"Too dark and he was too far away," said Sinclair. "No one could tell you his hair color because he was wearing a black beanie hat, low on his head."

"One neighbor said he was wearing military-type pants with large pockets on the side," said Edwards. "Does that mean anything?"

"Not camo ones, but maybe a civilian version of BDUs," said Sinclair, referring to the Army's battle dress uniform. "Dark, but not black. And now that you mention it, he was wearing a vest."

"Kevlar—a bulletproof vest?"

"No, like a fishing or photography vest, one of those with a million pockets."

"We'll add that to the comm order," said Edwards. "Anything else on the van?"

"Dark color, but with the lighting, that could be anything. Two windows in the back."

"We found broken glass down the street, so at least one of your rounds hit its mark."

"That'll make it easier to recognize," said Sinclair.

"Every cop in the state is looking for that van," said Edwards. "How about hanging around a little longer in case we have any more questions?"

Once the sheriff's investigators wandered off, Sinclair reached into his Crown Vic and took a cigar out of the glove box. "Do you mind?" he asked Maloney.

"Matt, if I went through what you just did, I'd be taking a snort of whiskey."

Maloney apologized for his reference to booze. Sinclair brushed it off. When he'd killed Alonzo Moore a year ago, all he could think about was getting drunk. He didn't feel that urge tonight. He wasn't sure what to make of it—whether the compulsion to drink had been lifted or it was lying low for the moment, waiting to spring back with a vengeance once he lowered his guard.

Sinclair sparked his Zippo and held it with both hands to keep it steady. He noticed Maloney and Braddock watching.

"Once they're done with you here, you need to get some rest," said Maloney.

"I plan to take him over to my place," said Braddock. "He can use our guest room for as long as he needs."

"I already told you, I'm not putting you and your family in danger. This guy's still after me."

"Ryan and I both carry guns for a living. Let him come."

"You've got kids," said Sinclair.

"He's right, Cathy," said Maloney. "Let me make some calls."

Chapter 46

The man pulled to the curb on a quiet street in San Francisco's Potrero Hill District. He gathered up what he would need, stuffed it into his pockets, and then crawled into the back. He had bought the van for cash on the streets from a Mexican who admitted he didn't register it and had bought it with cash himself. There were probably a line of unregistered owners that preceded him. He poured the remaining gas from the gallon can around the inside and climbed out. He lit a flare, tossed it on the front seat, and slammed the door.

He was three blocks away when he heard the fire engines.

After three more blocks, he reached the parking garage of San Francisco General Hospital and walked the line of cars in the physician parking section. The red Mini Cooper was parked by the stairwell. Melissa was working the ER tonight as part of her residence rotation, and with it being a Friday night, she'd probably work late.

He looked around for a concealed place to wait. Above the stairwell door, a security camera stared down at him, its red light flashing every few seconds. He had anticipated that and shifted to plan B.

He flagged down a cab and gave the Vietnamese driver a street corner in Noe Valley, an upscale neighborhood nicknamed Stroller Valley. When he had scouted the area last weekend, its sidewalks were jammed with young professional couples pushing baby strollers in front of its overpriced shops and restaurants. He paid the fare and walked two blocks to Melissa's flat. Along the way, he saw a poster for a lost cat stapled to a telephone pole. He ripped it off and stuffed it in his pocket.

The residential street of remodeled row houses was quiet. He found a dark walkway between two houses, crept into the shadows, and waited.

Normally, fog would blanket the city by this time of night, and the average nighttime temperature in the midfifties would feel like a bone-chilling forty. However, as often occurred in September, hot, dry winds from the central valley blew westward, blocking the natural air conditioning of the ocean winds. That kept this night's temperature in the midsixties, a bit cool to be without a jacket but not unbearable.

When the red car pulled into the driveway, he crept out of his hiding place and strolled up the sidewalk. Melissa turned off the engine and swung open the door.

"Excuse me," he said. "My cat ran off and I was wondering if you've seen her."

He held out the flyer. Melissa smiled and took it from him. She was twenty-five, heavyset, and wore dark blue scrubs. "I haven't seen any cats—"

He shoved the stun gun against her side and pressed the trigger. When she went limp, he dragged her to the other side of the Mini and folded her into the passenger seat. He zip-tied her ankles together and her wrists behind her back. He slipped a peace medallion over her head, fastened the seatbelt around her, pulled it tight, and shut the door.

As he zigzagged through the residential streets, Melissa came to and shouted, "What the hell is going on?"

He took the stun gun from his pocket and gave her a three-second jolt. Her muscles tensed and her eyes bugged out, but it wasn't enough to knock her unconscious.

"Sit there quietly, or I'll zap you again."

The on-ramp to the 101 Freeway lay less than two miles down Cesar Chavez Street. He shifted through the gears, winding the small four-cylinder engine near redline, and merged into the freeway traffic. He slid the shifter into sixth gear and settled in with the flow of traffic at sixty-five.

"You must have me confused with someone else," said Melissa.

"No mistake." He moved into the right lanes and merged onto Interstate 80, following the signs to the Bay Bridge. The bars had closed an hour ago, and the freeway was packed with cars leaving the city.

"I can get money, if that's what you want."

"Money won't right this wrong." He steered the car into the middle lane of the Bay Bridge's five-lane lower deck.

"Did I do something to harm you?"

They passed Treasure Island and the lights of Oakland came into view. "You did nothing. This isn't personal."

"I don't know what happened to you, but hurting me won't change it."

They were approaching the MacArthur maze, the short stretch of freeway where four interstates merged in less than a mile.

He leaned across her and unlatched the door.

She yelled over the wind noise. "What are you doing?"

He downshifted and accelerated toward a group of cars stacked together. He sped to the front of the pack and looked in his rearview mirror to see the cars switching lanes and jockeying positions for the right freeway.

He clicked her seatbelt undone and shoved her against the door, but she twisted her shoulder against the door-jamb. He pushed her harder, and the Mini Cooper swerved out of its lane. A car blew its horn.

He jammed the stun gun against her leg and pulled the trigger. She tensed and went limp. He pushed her out the door.

Horns blew and tires screeched behind him. In his mirror, he saw the body bounce and tumble. A compact car struck her on the right side of its bumper, knocking her into the next lane where a truck hit her full on. Cars skidded and crashed into other cars in a chain reaction pile-up.

He yanked the door shut and followed the signs to the 580 Freeway.

Chapter 47

Sinclair was sitting in the front seat of his unmarked car trying to doze. He opened his eyes and saw Maloney standing there.

"They found the van in San Francisco," he said.

Sinclair jumped out of the car. "Where?"

Maloney held out a cup of coffee and waited for Sinclair to take it. "It was torched, and you're not going."

"It's my case, and—"

"You want me to go?" asked Braddock.

"It's your job to babysit your partner," said Maloney. "I sent one of our guys with a sheriff's detective. They'll do what they can there and have it towed back to OPD for full processing."

"How do you know it's the right one?" asked Braddock.

"The SFPD officer who responded to take the arson report had heard the BOLO for the van and right away noticed two bullet holes in the rear doors," said Maloney, referring to the be-on-the-lookout radio broadcast.

"You mean my partner missed one round?" said Braddock.

Maloney grinned. "The other one took out the window, remember?"

"Any blood?" asked Sinclair.

"Too badly burned to tell. The crime lab will have to determine that, but two rounds exited through the windshield. Who knows where the third one ended up. SFPD notified all the local hospitals. SF General's just down the street, but no gunshot walk-ins so far."

"Let me know if you hear anything else."

Maloney nodded. "The chief will be here in about an hour. The sheriff called him personally. Said it would look bad if he didn't show up—one of his officers being shot at and all."

Sinclair relit his cigar. "So he's coming just to check on me. How sweet."

"Be respectful," Maloney said. "By the way, Liz Schueller's waiting outside the tape to see you. She says she's not working."

"Any idea when they'll be done with me here?"

"I'll check after the chief leaves." Maloney waded back into the crowd of investigators.

"You know the procedure," said Braddock. "You're both a victim and the subject of this investigation. You can't be involved or privy to the details."

"I'm wasting time sitting here."

"Why don't you visit with Liz for a while?"

Sinclair knew that cops don't visit with their girlfriends at the scene of officer-involved shootings. They take care of business stoically until their commander releases them and then go home and release whatever emotions necessary in the privacy of their homes. Girlfriends bring emotions to a scene where the cop involved in a shooting is fighting to control his. Sinclair didn't want Liz there. He didn't want other cops seeing Liz trying to comfort him, and he didn't want other cops seeing him having to comfort her.

"I'm already accused of giving her special treatment. How would it look, me walking out there just to say hi?"

"Her boyfriend was almost killed," said Braddock. "I'll escort her in."

A few minutes later, Liz slid into Sinclair's car and buried her face in his neck. He felt her hot tears on his skin. "I was so worried." She choked out the words between sobs.

Sinclair held her until she quieted. She pulled away and wiped her eyes with a tissue. "How are you?"

Sinclair stared out the windshield. "Okay."

She smiled and dabbed her eyes again. "I hate how we parted last night."

"I had a lot going on inside my head."

"About the case?" she asked. "Or about us?"

Their relationship and how she used it in her career was the last thing he wanted to discuss. "Have your media friends out there been told what happened?"

"Nothing formal, but it's obvious you were the intended target and the bus bench killer is responsible."

"I've been warned not to comment."

"I'm not asking you to." She turned in her seat to face Sinclair, but he continued to look straight ahead. "We knew when we started seeing each other that our careers might clash."

Sinclair puffed on his cigar and blew the smoke out the open window. "I can't wrap my head around this conversation right now."

Liz reached out and took his right hand in both of hers. "Where will you stay?"

"The lieutenant's working on something."

"Stay with me while you get through this."

"This guy's still after me. It wouldn't be safe."

"I'm not worried. I've always felt safe when sleeping with the toughest cop in Oakland."

Liz kissed him deeply and exited the car. Braddock walked her to the other side of the crime scene tape, the eyes of every cop following her as she walked by.

Sinclair had finished another cup of coffee and smoked his cigar to the nub by the time Chief Brown walked his way, followed by two deputy chiefs, the captain of the personnel and training division, and Maloney.

"I'm glad you're okay," said Brown, looking at the scorched apartment building behind Sinclair. "The press would have had a field day if this killer claimed the life of one of our officers."

"I appreciate your concern, Chief."

Brown didn't recognize his sarcasm or decided to ignore it. He turned to Maloney and his staff. "What do we do about the murder investigations?"

"As I briefed you," said Maloney, "we're following up on—"

"I mean about Sinclair. We can't leave him on the case."

"That's exactly what this prick wants," said Sinclair. "I'm getting close and that's why he did this."

"Or maybe it's because you insulted him like some kid in a schoolyard pissing match."

Maloney cleared his throat. "Sergeant Sinclair could have chosen his words more carefully at the press conference, but we'd be sending the wrong message by pulling him. The rank and file look up to Sinclair. You'd lose a lot of support, Chief, if you replaced him."

"We'll tell the troops it's for Sinclair's safety," said Brown.

"The department would look weak," said Maloney. "Besides, Matt's our best chance for stopping this killer."

The chief glared at Maloney. "If this man comes after him again and there's collateral damage, the mayor will hang me out to dry."

"Then we need to find him first," said Sinclair.

Brown turned to Maloney. "We'll leave him as the lead investigator, but he's restricted to the building. You've got plenty of other people to do the field work."

Sinclair was preparing to object when Maloney put a hand on his shoulder. "We'll make it work."

Chapter 48

After a long shower, Sinclair changed into the jeans and polo shirt he kept in his locker and made his way upstairs. The homicide office was buzzing with activity and noise. Every member of the homicide section was there, along with a cluster of uniformed officers and a dozen officers and supervisors in plainclothes. SWAT officers dressed in their black BDUs, pistols hanging at fingertip level in thigh holsters, flexed their arms and legs like a football team getting ready for a big game.

The room fell silent as Sinclair stepped inside. Beginning with a senior SWAT sergeant, they converged on him to shake his hand, slap his back, and offer encouragement: "We'll get this fucker," "Tell us how we can help," "He'll regret the day he was born."

Everyone in the room was there because the bus bench killer had violated the code of the streets—you don't mess with a cop's family or home.

Years before Sinclair even considered becoming a cop, the Oakland narcotics unit had initiated a long-term investigation into the Hells Angels' methamphetamine trade. After months of work, the narcs had picked off several underlings in the outlaw gang and were starting to disrupt their drug trade. One morning, an officer on loan from the traffic division for the investigation received a large envelope in the mail. Inside were photographs of the officer's home, his wife, and his children on their way to school and playing in the front yard, with a note reading, *Nice family. Best regards, Sonny.*

Whether Sonny Barger, the president of the Oakland chapter, had personally ordered the threat was never determined. Nor did it matter to the members of the department. The Hells Angels had declared war. Officers swept through every house and business associated with the motorcycle gang, stopped every car or motorcycle they owned, and dragged every hang-around, associate, prospect, and full-patch member they could find to jail, many requiring a detour through the emergency room. Although the DA threw out most of the arrests, since the cops mostly ignored the legalities of probable cause, search warrants, and due process, the code was reestablished.

The officer who had received the threat was Jack Braddock, and Cathy was one of the children in the photographs.

Sinclair knew the difference with the current situation. The department had no target on which to unleash its wrath. Nevertheless, everyone in the room looked to Sinclair for direction. He gathered the SWAT and uniformed officers and told them that he'd received a tip about the killer buying heroin somewhere in Oakland—a necessary lie to protect Dr. Gorman—and sent them out to scour the streets for anyone who might have seen a man fitting the broad description of the killer or van. It was a long shot, but it gave the street cops something to focus on. Sinclair assigned a group of investigators, mostly from the robbery and assault units, to run out every van listed in crime reports, field contacts, and traffic tickets. Every investigator dreaded the monumental task of sorting through thousands of computer hits with little chance of success, but none complained. Braddock meanwhile briefed a group of property crimes investigators about the recovery of the torched van and sent them to San Francisco to knock on doors in the area, with the hope that someone saw something or the killer had a connection to that area.

Once the crowd thinned in the office, Sinclair spotted Heather Kim sitting on a desk in the corner, swinging her legs to an imaginary beat. Kim was a veteran street cop who had been working the downtown walking patrol for several years. She was also on the board of directors for the police officer's association.

"My turn?" she asked with a big smile.

Sinclair waved her over to his desk.

"I'm here wearing my OPOA hat," she said. "Your lieutenant said the department will come up with funds to get you a hotel room. With OPD's wonderful efficiency, that might take days, so in the meantime, the association will get you a room at the Marriott."

"I don't need anything that fancy," said Sinclair.

"They have a state-of-the-art security system and professional staff, and they gave me a suite for the price of a regular room. We'll list you under a fake name and have two plainclothes officers outside your room."

"I don't need protection."

"The chief ordered it and the watch commander already has a list of twenty volunteers."

"I'd feel stupid having fellow cops standing outside my room while I sleep."

"The department's paying overtime, but every officer on the department would do it for free on the off chance the asshole shows up and they get to take him out."

Braddock, who had been sitting quietly at her desk, said, "He'll do it, Heather. And we appreciate the help."

"If we can catch this asshole, none of this'll be necessary," said Sinclair.

"In the meantime, you need a safe place to sleep," said Kim. "I'll also work with your insurance company. They'll probably provide money for emergency housing and other expenses. What else?"

"He needs to go shopping," said Braddock. "He won't feel like a homicide dick again until he's wearing a suit."

"This'll be fun," said Kim. "Me and you taking a studly man shopping. We'll be the envy of all the girls."

"Great," said Sinclair. "A chick outing."

Kim turned serious. "My cousin's boyfriend works at Macys. He can set it up so we're in and out in no time."

Jankowski came through the door just as Kim was leaving. "I just finished speaking to a detective from NYPD Nineteenth Precinct."

"About time," said Sinclair.

"He wasn't much help. Except for the initial scene and preliminary interviews, his partner did the follow-up alone, and because of who the family was, he kept it all hush-hush."

"Why won't his partner talk to us?"

"He's super evasive about that. He says he's trying to find his partner, as if he's a parolee-at-large or something."

"Something weird's going on there." Sinclair felt the intolerable twist in his gut that always meant one thing—he was being played. What were they hiding? Why was NYPD stonewalling them?

"He says they're positive the Arquette family had nothing to do with Jane's suicide."

"Pardon me for not trusting NYPD, but I want the facts so I can form my own conclusion."

"After I told the detective what happened to you, his tone changed."

"Does that mean he'll get off his ass and help?"

"He said he'll call his boss at home for authorization to work it from his end."

"If another agency asked us for help on a case like this, we'd drop everything and do whatever they needed."

"We complain about politics here in Oakland," said Jankowski. "It's nothing compared to a place like New York. Cops make detective based on politics and they only keep their gold shields if they play politics."

Sinclair was about to suggest they talk to Lieutenant Maloney to see if he'd use his rank and call the NYPD brass when he heard Lieutenant Maloney yell from across the room. "Sinclair, Braddock, my office."

Chapter 49

Sinclair staggered into Maloney's office. He hadn't moved from his computer in two hours, and every muscle in his body ached. His knees burned and his feet throbbed. A tall, slim man dressed in the tan uniform of the California Highway Patrol sat in Maloney's guest chair.

"This is Officer Clark with the MAIT team," said Maloney, referring to the CHP's Multidisciplinary Accident Investigation Team. "He was observing an autopsy on what they assumed was a fatal accident when the coroner noticed something."

Clark told them about responding to a multicar collision around three in the morning. A woman had fallen or had been pushed from a red Mini Cooper, which caused a six-car pile-up. Ambulances transported five people to ACH for a variety of injuries, the woman code blue and pronounced upon arrival.

"When I got to the coroner's office," said Clark, "they showed me two flex-cuffs that were transported with the body. The paramedics said her ankles and wrists were bound with them. They cut them to render treatment. The coroner pointed out a peace sign medallion around her neck and told me that is a signature of your killer."

Sinclair felt lightheaded. The killer was to some extent replicating what had happened to Samantha and Jane. Samantha was hit by a car just like this victim. Samantha was drugged, as was Zachary. Jane committed suicide, and Susan's death by cutting her wrists was a classic suicide method. He grabbed the back of the chair alongside the one Clark was sitting at. "You got an ID on her?"

"No ID. She was wearing blue scrubs, so we're guessing she works in the medical field."

"Description?" asked Sinclair, feeling better and letting go of the chair.

"Female white, late twenties, five-six, one-fifty, brown, and brown."

"That doesn't fit any of the people we're protecting, but I'll check with O'Connor to make sure," said Sinclair. "Did you recover the Mini Cooper?"

"It fled the scene. Male white driver, no further description. We've got a comm order out for it."

"Wearing scrubs," said Sinclair, thinking aloud. "The van dumped near San Francisco General. Maybe he needed transportation and snatched a nurse or someone driving by."

"Then why the flex cuffs and medallion?" asked Braddock.

"You're right." Sinclair shook his head. His brain was operating at half speed. "We need to get her photo to SF General, see if anyone can ID her."

"The body's pretty mangled," said Clark, "but the face is identifiable."

Sinclair moved toward the door. "Let's go."

"Matt, you need to stay here," said Maloney.

"This is a homicide. It's my case. I need to identify the victim, visit the crime scene—"

"The scene's gone, Sergeant," said Clark. "We opened the freeway hours ago."

Braddock said, "I'll take a photo of the victim at the coroner's office, send it to the team working the area of the van, have them show it around the hospital."

"I need to interview the witnesses," said Sinclair. "Someone saw enough to ID the driver as a white male. They must know more."

"Our officers asked the right questions," said Clark. "If there was more, we'd have gotten it."

"It's my case, damn it. I'm the one who needs to do the asking."

"Matt," Maloney said.

Sinclair looked at the lieutenant. Maloney met his gaze but said nothing more. Sinclair felt the eyes of everyone on him.

Maloney turned to Clark. "We'll assume jurisdiction of the investigation. How soon can you get us copies of your reports, photos, and scene work?"

A phone in Clark's pocket chirped. He listened for a minute. "That was dispatch. A unit spotted a red Mini Cooper on the Nimitz Freeway in Hayward and lit him up. The car took off, but we caught him on the city streets after a minor accident. Driver's a nineteen-year-old African American male."

"The driver's black?" said Sinclair.

"Yeah, the driver told our arresting officer he found the car with the key fob in it on East Eighteen Street in Oakland. There was a purse in the car with hospital ID and a driver's license in the name of Melissa Mathis, age twenty-seven, address in San Francisco."

"Mathis?" asked Sinclair.

"Yeah, why?"

"Shit."

"What?" asked Maloney.

"The lawyer from Children's that I talked to yesterday—Phyllis Mathis. I'll bet she's got a daughter named Melissa."

Chapter 50

Sinclair propped his leg on the toilet seat in the Marriott Hotel suite and applied a fresh bandage over the deepest cut. It had started bleeding a few hours ago when he stretched at his desk. Now it throbbed. His knees were scabbed over. He replaced the bandages on his feet. Although they were still tender, they didn't hurt as much as earlier. He popped two Tylenol and walked to the dressing area. The plush carpet felt good on his bare feet.

Sinclair removed two white shirts from their packaging and hung them in the closet so that the wrinkles would fall out enough by morning and he wouldn't need to iron them. Ironing was a skill he never acquired. He looked at the light gray pants and jacket—"suit separates," the personal shopper at Macy's called them. He had bought a regular suit as well, but the alterations wouldn't be complete until Monday.

He was pulling on the new, overpriced Levis and polo shirt when a knock sounded at the door. Sinclair peered through the peephole and opened the door. Officer Tokepka stood alongside a hotel employee with a room service cart. Tokepka wore a sport coat and tie, his dress shirt stretched tight over a ballistic vest. Sinclair was pleased when he learned Tokepka volunteered for the duty and was assigned the first shift. He couldn't think of a better person in the department to guard his door.

"I thought you were going to shower and go to bed, Sarge. You haven't had more than a few hours of shut-eye in days."

"I'm bushed, but I knew if I didn't eat first, I'd regret it halfway through the night," said Sinclair. "Why don't you come in—I can have them bring something up for you."

"We're fine. Besides, our place is outside."

"This feels weird. All my life I've been the one doing the protecting."

"We're proud to be doing this." Tokepka stood to the side and the employee pushed the cart inside.

The attendant placed a tray on the coffee table in the living room and arranged an assortment of plates, glasses, and utensils. "New York strip, medium rare, baked potato, and steamed broccoli. The food service manager wanted you to have this—on the house—as his thanks for all you've done." He pulled a bottle of Robert Mondavi Cabernet Sauvignon from the cart and a corkscrew from his pocket.

"No thanks."

He set the bottle and a wine glass on the table. "I'll just leave it in case you change your mind." He placed the corkscrew on the table beside the wine.

Sinclair didn't argue as the man pushed his cart out of the room.

He devoured the salad and roll and then cut into his steak as he reviewed the day's activities. After Phyllis

Mathis made a positive ID of her daughter, he had spoken to her on the phone. She held it together, but just barely. Meanwhile, the investigators in San Francisco interviewed the hospital parking lot attendant who noticed Melissa leaving the garage alone in her car. Techs recovered clear latents from the Mini Cooper's interior, and the crime lab compared them with elimination prints from Melissa and the doper that CHP had arrested driving her car. Three unidentified prints remained, which the lab ran through ALPS, the California Automated Latent Print System. They got no matches, which meant whoever left the prints had never been arrested for anything serious.

CHP had brought the driver of the Mini Cooper to homicide so Sinclair and Braddock could interview him. The man said he had found the car unattended outside a housing project at six in the morning with the doors unlocked. It started when he pressed the ignition button. When the highway patrol tried to stop him, he panicked and fled. After two hours in room 201, Sinclair was convinced the man was telling the truth and didn't know anything else. CHP took custody of him and booked him for auto theft and an assortment of traffic violations. When Sinclair returned from his Macy's shopping jaunt with Braddock and Kim, he sat at his desk and read a hundred pages of reports that had been written by five different police agencies about the shooting and arson at his apartment, the arson of the van, Mathis's murder, and the recovery of her car. Sinclair had still not received a call from NYPD by the time Braddock, looking as exhausted as he felt, dropped him off at his hotel room.

Sinclair chewed another bite of the steak and looked at the bottle of wine. With everything he'd been through in the last twenty-four hours, and the many family members he'd broken death news to over the last few days, he was feeling the strain. Mrs. Mathis never expected she'd be a target, but he should've figured it out. He was tired—mentally and emotionally exhausted. Thoughts swirled around his head: finding the killer before he took another life, his relationship with Liz, Chief Brown's scrutiny, his failure to solve Samantha's case when he should have—the cause of all that had happened.

Along with everything else he'd done, the killer stole one of the few moments of joy homicide investigators get to experience—the celebration of solving a case. Sinclair didn't get to feel elation from solving Samantha's case. He didn't get to high-five his partners. He didn't get to pull the paper with Samantha's number from the case packet, draw a thick red line through it, and pin it on the board for all to see. He didn't get to go to the Warehouse and drink beers others bought for him. Instead, he was in the midst of the next killing. One of Sinclair's favorite moments was calling a victim's mother and telling her he arrested her son or daughter's killer. Over the phone, he would hear tears of relief and gratitude along with words of thanks and praise.

With Samantha, there was no mother to tell. Even if Jane were alive, Sinclair doubted he could feel much joy from telling her he solved a case he should have put a red line through many months ago.

He did feel good about surviving the killer's attack. That in itself deserved a celebration. He deserved a reward after all he'd been through. He uncorked the bottle and held it under his nose, breathing in the oaky aroma. One glass wouldn't hurt. It would help him sleep. And he desperately needed a good night's sleep. He poured a half glass of wine, stared at it for several minutes, and poured the glass and then the bottle out in the sink.

Chapter 51

At six sharp, Sinclair heard a knock at the door.

Officer Randy Norris stood in the doorway. Norris had joined the department five years before Sinclair, and they served together as officers on the SWAT team. He now worked in the training division as a firearms instructor and range master, but last night he took an overtime shift guarding Sinclair's door.

"Looks like you have a visitor and breakfast," said Norris.

Norris ushered Walt and the hotel worker into the room and stood by as the room service attendant arranged food and coffee on the table in the living room and then escorted him back out.

Norris said, "When my relief comes on at eight, I'm heading to the range to run qualifying shoots for day shift."

"On a Sunday?" asked Sinclair.

"No shortage of overtime these days. I'll do your gun inspection if you stop by. That'll satisfy the officer-involved shooting protocol, and you won't have to leave it and carry a loaner gun."

Sinclair told Norris he'd try, and Norris returned to his post in the hallway.

Sinclair poured coffee for Walt and him. "I'm sorry I bothered you last night."

"You almost picked up a drink," said Walt. "You can call me anytime for that."

Sinclair picked at a bowl of melon and strawberries. "I don't know why I poured that glass of wine."

"You're an alcoholic. That's what alcoholics do."

"That simple, huh?"

"Yeah, but you didn't drink. That's the biggest step toward the solution."

Sinclair finished the fruit and started on the scrambled eggs. He wondered if a different job was the solution—one without the emotional upheavals of homicide.

"How long will you stay here?" asked Walt.

"At least until we get this guy. It'll take months to repair my apartment, but I can't go back there. My neighbors used to feel safe having a cop next door. Not now."

"I spoke to Fred. He'd like you to stay with us," said Walt. "The guest house in the back has been empty since his daughter died. I think you'd find it more comfortable than a hotel room."

"As long as the killer's out there, anyone near me's in danger."

"The estate is very secure. You're welcome to stay as long as you'd like."

"Right now, I'm just focusing on getting through today."

Walt grinned. "One day at a time."

"I just need to catch this asshole and . . ." Sinclair stared at a landscape print on the wall.

"What are you thinking?"

Failure. That was the crux of the thoughts swarming around his head. How his failures caused people around him to die. After his brother's death, he thought he had escaped it. He had become a police officer. He thought he had made good. Then he got called back into the Army. He was part of a small team of soldiers sent to capture an Iraqi insurgent who had planted an IED that took out part of an army convoy. He knew the mission required a platoon of forty, but he didn't challenge the order to do it with a squad of ten. He ignored the other signs: the deserted outdoor market, the absence of kids in the street, the doors of houses closing when they rolled into position. The people in the neighborhood knew the insurgents were there and that there would be a fight. He should've pulled them back, but he didn't. Five men died because of his failures that day and more died in the months to come because the bomber they failed to capture buried even more IEDs.

Sinclair shook his head. "This was the same way I felt when I was going after a different killer. That's when my alcoholism started."

"Events don't cause alcoholism. Sometimes we stop caring and then stop controlling our drinking because of tragedies in our life, but many people get through them without drinking."

"Before that point in my life—before I shot that killer—I controlled it . . . well most of the time. I know I started drinking a lot more after Iraq, but I was keeping it together. Just barely at times, but I was doing okay. At least I thought so at the time."

"Not that shooting someone under any circumstances isn't traumatic, but what was different about this?"

"I sort of went off like the lone ranger. Alonzo Moore had killed at least three people. All young black men. One was a competitor—dealing crack on Moore's turf. Another was one of Moore's underlings who smoked up the crack he was supposed to sell. The third also worked for Moore and let a tossup steal the money he made from selling Moore's dope."

"What's a tossup?"

"A slut, in street slang. Or in this case, a woman who exchanges sexual favors for a few hits off a crack pipe."

"I wonder what I might have been willing to do for a drink or drug if I hadn't stopped," said Walt.

"I flipped someone in Moore's organization who witnessed all three murders. The case was going to trial when my witness was killed. Everyone on the streets knew Moore did it. He wanted everyone to know—you deal on my turf, you lose my drugs or money, you testify against me, you die. There went the case."

"That must have been hard to swallow."

"Everyone else in the unit told me to let it go—that I'd done all I could do—but even though the victims weren't exactly pillars of society, no one had the right to take their lives. My first partner in homicide said it was our responsibility to speak for the dead. That the lives of every victim mattered, no matter who or what he was. He was right about that, and I couldn't allow Moore to kill without consequence."

Walt's face tightened. "What did you do?"

"I didn't go out and whack him, if that's what you're thinking," said Sinclair, seeing the concern in Walt's face. "I started following him, waiting for him to screw up. I did it on my own time because the lieutenant wouldn't allow it. Since I was technically off-duty, I couldn't use a department undercover car, and my unmarked car would have been made a mile away in that part of town. So, when

286 | Brian Thiem

I got off shift, I took off my suit coat and tie, pulled on a windbreaker, and cruised West Oakland in a rental to see what Moore was up to and who he was associating with. I figured that, eventually, one of his associates would get arrested for something and I could turn him, or Moore would make a mistake himself and I'd be there when it happened."

"Sounds like you were determined."

"Obsessed is more like it."

Chapter 52

Sinclair filled their coffee cups and settled into the uphol-
stered chair. He took a deep breath and began to tell Walt
the parts of the story he'd never told anyone, the parts of the
story that still woke him at 3:00 a.m. like a gunshot through
his bedroom window.

A year ago, after following Moore for two weeks, Sinclair had spotted his car one evening on a trash-strewn
residential street behind a rusted pick-up truck with four
flat tires. Sinclair parked his rental down the street and
slouched into the driver's seat to observe. Alonzo Moore
appeared in the doorway of an old, brown stucco house
and pranced down the steps, through the chain link
gate, and onto the street. Sinclair watched as Moore got
into his banana-yellow Cadillac and crept down the street,
his stereo blaring. Sinclair knew his routine. Moore would
stop off at each of his spots, chat with his crew, and accept a
roll of money. Sinclair followed, staying well back to avoid
being spotted. According to the narcotics officers Sinclair
had spoken to, someone else made the drug deliveries to
Moore's spots, and Moore never touched the drugs himself,
so Sinclair knew he wouldn't catch him holding. Moore

stopped at Thirty-Second Street, and Sinclair pulled his car to the curb a block away.

The sun had set an hour earlier, and the street lights cast a sickly, yellow glow over two rail-thin teenagers who Moore approached. Moore yelled something at them, but Sinclair was too far away to make out the words. Moore got into the face of one of them, still yelling, then grabbed him by his jacket with his left hand, stepped forward, and landed a powerful roundhouse to the side of his head. The young man slumped to the pavement as Moore pulled up the waistband of his black jacket and came out with a gun.

The adrenaline shot into Sinclair's system. He simultaneously pulled the gear shift lever into drive as he keyed the handset of his portable radio and yelled into it. "Thirteen-L-Five, Code Thirty-Three."

The dispatcher, hearing Sinclair's excited voice, immediately responded. "Thirteen-L-Five, you have the air. What's your nine-two-six?"

"Thirty-Second and Linden. Man with a gun. Two-forty-five in progress," said Sinclair, using the code for assault with a deadly weapon, as he mashed the accelerator to the floor, rocketing directly toward Moore.

"Any units, two-forty-five in progress, Thirty-Second and Linden. Thirteen-L-Five on the scene," the dispatcher relayed to all patrol officers in the sector.

By the time the first kid hit the ground from Moore's blow, the other was several steps into a full sprint. Moore fired two shots at him before he disappeared from Sinclair's view and then swung the gun back toward the one on the ground. Sinclair saw him lining up the barrel on the motionless form on the ground as his car roared toward them.

Sinclair was bracing for the gunshot, when Moore suddenly turned toward the sound of the rental's engine racing toward him. Sinclair knew that Moore only saw two headlights coming at him—the car and Sinclair invisible behind his high beams.

Moore swung the chrome handgun toward Sinclair's car, and Sinclair jabbed the brake pedal and swung the steering wheel to the left. The tires fought against the ABS and the asphalt, and the car screeched and skidded sideways down the street. Sinclair ducked just as Moore's gun spat out a fireball into the darkness, and the passenger window and windshield exploded, showering Sinclair with glass. The car jerked to a stop, and Sinclair rolled out of the driver's door while smoothly drawing his Sig Sauer .45 from the leather holster under his windbreaker.

Sinclair poked his head over the hood. He was greeted with a bright muzzle flash and loud pop from less than fifty feet away. He ducked down, crawled to the front of his car, and peeked around the front bumper.

Moore was running. He crossed the sidewalk and onto the front yard of a house as Sinclair fired two quick shots toward him.

Sinclair jumped up and gave chase.

Moore was in full stride, crossing the small strip of crabgrass and weeds that pretended to be a front yard, and disappeared between two houses. As Sinclair sprinted across the sidewalk, he brought his portable radio to his mouth and yelled in short bursts through his heavy breathing. "Shots fired. At me. Suspect westbound through the yards.

Male black, twenty-two. Six-foot, one-sixty. Black jacket, blue jeans. Name—Alonzo Moore."

The two houses were no more than fifteen feet apart. As Sinclair rounded the front corner of the first house, he saw a flash of movement disappearing over the fence. Two seconds later, he hit the fence with his left foot and catapulted himself over. He landed hard on both feet and scanned the backyard, seeing a dark form sprinting toward the far fence. Moore vaulted the six-foot wood fence without hardly slowing.

Sinclair sprinted across the yard, dodged an old Weber grill, and nearly tripped over a rusted tricycle in the dark. He grabbed the top of the fence and was ready to throw his right leg over but then stopped. There was no noise from the next yard.

He peeked over the decaying wood fence into another backyard, and a gunshot exploded in front of him. The bullet whizzed inches from his face.

He dropped back down, crouching behind the fence. His breathing came hard, his heart pounded.

A moment later, he heard the sound of splintering wood on the far side of the yard and peered over again. Overgrown weeds and junk covered the backyard. At the front of the lot sat an abandoned house. The back door swung on a broken hinge. "Thirteen-L-Five," he whispered into his radio.

"Go ahead Thirteen-L-Five."

"He made the first yard and turned north. I think he went into the rear door of a nine-oh-five house on Thirty-Second, between Linden and Filbert."

"Copy. All units, suspect possibly entered abandoned house on Thirty-Second Street between Linden and Filbert.

First unit on the scene, advise," the calm voice of the female dispatcher relayed.

Sinclair threw his right foot onto the top of the fence and gracefully swung himself over. He dropped softly to the ground in a crouch and listened. He heard the police sirens in the distance and a dog barking several houses away. An interior door banged against a wall inside the house.

He crossed the yard in a half crouch and stopped at the rear door. Fear and common sense told him to remain there and wait for the responding units. If Moore was smart—and no one survived on the streets of Oakland by being stupid—he would make his way out the front door and across the street before the patrol units got into position. However, if Sinclair moved to the front of the house, Moore could slip out the back and disappear before the units set a perimeter. Sinclair knew that one police officer cannot surround a house alone.

Sinclair stood there, hoping to hear Moore's footsteps racing through the house and out the front door or to see his face in a window looking for an escape. The smell of rotting garbage piled outside the door filled his nostrils. The silence in the house told him that Moore was still inside, possibly lying in wait for someone fool enough to come in after him. Or he could be quietly moving toward the front, hoping to slip out and escape before more officers arrived.

Sinclair was not about to let Moore get away. There was a fine line separating courage and stupidity with cops, and Sinclair knew he was straddling it. He pulled a small Surefire flashlight from his pocket and slid it onto the accessory rails below the barrel of his pistol. He slowly opened the door and slipped inside the dark house.

He flicked the light on and swept his gun and the light beam around the small kitchen and then turned it off and moved against a wall. The kitchen opened into a small dining room with a closed door to the left. Sinclair had been inside old houses like this in Oakland many times and knew the door probably led to a short hallway and two bedrooms.

The stale air smelled of mold and cat urine. He stood there and listened. The sirens were getting closer, but the house was silent except for Sinclair's breathing and his heart still pounding in his chest.

He took a deep, slow breath, held it for three counts, and slowly let it out, as he'd been taught years ago in the SWAT operator's course. The slow, full breaths lowered his racing heartbeat. He repeated the combat breathing technique several more times and felt the calming effect.

The floor in the dining room creaked.

Sinclair crept forward, shifting his weight softly from foot to foot. He held his gun with both hands at a low ready with the light off. Defused light came in through the windows—enough to see the doorway and walls now that his eyes had adjusted to the darkness.

Standing to the side of the doorway, he took three more slow, deep breaths and then moved quickly through the doorway, his gun up and sweeping across the room, the small flashlight mounted on his pistol illuminating the dining room.

A gunshot went off, its blast deafening due to the small room and its muzzle flash nearly blinding. Time slowed. Sinclair felt he was moving in slow motion.

He brought his gun up in the direction of the muzzle flash. Moore stood no more than five steps away and leveled his gun for a second shot.

Sinclair thrust his gun toward Moore and fired a double-tap, two shots as fast as he could pull the trigger.

The roar of his .45 was even louder than Moore's gun, and the muzzle flashes lit up the small room like a strobe light.

The gun bucked twice in Sinclair's hands from the recoil. He released the switch on his gun-mounted flashlight and the room became pitch dark.

He quietly moved across the room in the darkness and took another slow and deep breath. He awaited the onrush of pain, expecting to feel the warm, sticky, and wet sensation of blood oozing from his body.

Sinclair had been shot before and knew the adrenaline from the fight could mask the pain temporarily. Pain that would eventually come like a red-hot poker thrust deep into his body, every nerve ending screaming simultaneously, followed by a wave of overpowering weakness, and then unconsciousness as his body goes into shock.

He stood there for several counts, waiting for it.

It didn't come. He felt nothing.

Moore's bullet had missed.

Sinclair's eyes scanned the far wall for movement, but he felt blind in the darkness after the muzzle flashes. He wanted to turn on his light again to see where Moore was, but he dared not give away his position.

Although he knew Moore might be right in front of him in the darkness, lining up his gun for another shot, he also felt safe surrounded by the darkness.

Slowly his night vision returned, and the shapes of a dining table, a hutch, and a five-foot-wide opening that led to the living room materialized.

"You muthafucka. You shot me." The high-pitched voice came from the living room on the other side of the doorway.

"Alonzo, you shot at me first," said Sinclair. "I would have been, what—the sixth person you killed?"

"Sinclair, it's you who's the killer. The *Tribune* say you killed two dudes before. You gonna kill me too?"

"Throw out your gun and you'll live."

"You shot it out of my hand. I ain't got it."

"You're lying. Throw the gun toward me."

"I ain't fuckin' with ya, man. The gat's on the floor somewhere. It's dark. I can't see shit. I'm bleeding."

Sinclair heard two sirens getting louder and then go silent. He knew that meant two patrol cars were pulling up. He switched on the flashlight attached to his Sig Sauer and approached the living room doorway.

Sinclair crept across the opening, his light illuminating the room in small slices as he moved. First he saw two feet with black tennis shoes. He inched forward and saw blue jeans and the bottoms of Moore's legs on the filthy shag carpet.

Sinclair moved farther toward the center of the doorway.

At any second he expected to see the gun in Moore's hand pointing at him. As he shuffled to his right, he saw Moore's left hand resting on his belly, blood oozing through his fingers. Moore sat on the floor, leaning against a brown plaid sofa. The pistol was on the floor near his right knee. His right hand was on the floor an inch away.

"Don't move," ordered Sinclair as he stepped toward him, pointing his gun at the center of his chest.

Sinclair knew Moore could grab for the gun and get off a quick shot at him, maybe even before Sinclair could react.

Moore lay only two or three steps away. For a moment, Sinclair thought about taking those steps, reaching in with his left foot and sweeping the gun away. However, Moore could kick him as he moved, distracting him as he went for his gun, or just go straight for his gun as Sinclair moved and was off balance. Moore's eyes bored into his, and Sinclair sensed the wheels turning in his head.

"Don't move, Alonzo, it's over," said Sinclair, keeping the gun light trained on Moore's chest.

"Shit, Sinclair. You got nothing on me."

"How about attempted murder of a police officer and attempted murder of those two workers of yours you were about to kill?"

"Them boys ain't gonna testify. And you ain't in no police uniform. I tell the judge I think you some gang-banger trying to cap me. It's self-defense."

Sinclair kept his eyes on Moore's right hand as it slowly inched toward the gun. "It's over. Get your hands up."

"Sinclair, you got no proof I killed nobody. But you—you the killer. Even the papers and TV news say so."

Moore's fingers continued to inch toward the gun. "Maybe I take a plea, do one, two years. But that's all."

Moore's fingers stiffened—touched the gun. Sinclair waited for him to wrap his fingers around the gun but pulled the trigger before Moore could raise his gun.

★

Sinclair got up from his chair and walked to the hotel room window. The morning sun's rays hit his face. The sky was clear, not a trace of morning fog. He felt his heartbeat slow.

Walt said nothing until Sinclair finally turned around and looked at him.

"I take it the department did a full investigation," said Walt.

"The department and the DA's office both ruled my shooting justifiable."

Although the shooting was determined to be in self-defense, Sinclair's superiors reprimanded him for his unauthorized surveillance of Moore and pursuing him into the yards and the abandoned house at night alone. They said it was stupid, foolish, and dangerous. Sinclair couldn't disagree. If the media hadn't gotten hold of the story and made Sinclair out as a hero, he knew he would have faced major disciplinary action; however, it would have been a PR nightmare for the department to do anything other than accept the accolades from the community for taking a vicious killer off the streets.

"If you didn't shoot, he would've shot you," said Walt.

"I know."

"Yet you feel enormous guilt." Walt said it as a fact, as if he could read Sinclair's mind.

"What I feel guilty about is that I don't feel any guilt over it. Ever since that night, I've been asking myself whether I killed him because I had to or because I wanted to."

Chapter 53

Sinclair pushed open the office door and saw Braddock, Jankowski, and Sanchez sitting in a circle of desk chairs drinking coffee.

"I guess I'm late," said Sinclair.

"I think we can let you slide today," said Braddock. "How're you feeling?"

"My feet and knees are damn sore, and these new shoes don't help, but other than that, I'm great."

"SFPD called and gave us names of two people who might have seen the abduction of Melissa Mathis," said Braddock. "So I thought that once we finish our coffee, Dan and I could head over there and handle it."

"Because I'm still confined to the office per the chief's order."

"Sorry, Matt."

"I just got off the phone with an NYPD detective before you walked in," said Jankowski.

Sinclair dropped into his desk chair and spun it around to face Jankowski.

"The detective sat in on the interview with Jane's common-law after she killed herself. He was the one who found her."

"The common-law husband wasn't a suspect?" asked Sinclair.

"No, he was at work and it was no doubt a suicide. Anyway, they weren't married but had been in a long-term relationship. Says his name was Chris Olsen. Remembers him as being forty or forty-five, between six and six-two, and well-built, maybe one ninety or two hundred, with sandy blond hair and a beard."

"The same size as the guy who visited my apartment."

"Exactly my thought," said Jankowski.

"Is Olsen Samantha's father?"

"I asked, but the detective said he didn't know. He wasn't the primary on the case; he was just helping on the interview."

"Or he knew but wouldn't tell you. What did he admit knowing?"

"He told me an *s-o-n* spelling in Olson means the person could be from any Scandinavian country or the name was Americanized when the family immigrated. An *s-e-n* spelling means the name's Norwegian."

"So NYPD's an expert on Scandinavian surnames?"

"The guy they interviewed was Norwegian. It's why he remembers his name's spelled O-L-S-E-N."

Sinclair poked the on button to his computer and pushed the papers on his desk to the side. He pounded the enter key, even though he knew that wouldn't make the computer start quicker. Although he was a long ways from proving Olsen was the killer, everything felt right about him. Sinclair knew he was on the right track for the first time since he stood over Zachary Caldwell's lifeless body on the bus bench.

"What else did that detective say about Olsen?" asked Sinclair.

"He said that the case packet on Jane's suicide isn't in the unit files or archived, even though it should be closed, and he was told he had to get approval from his boss or partner before he said anything else."

"More secrecy," said Sinclair. "Who are they protecting?" Once the screen came up, Sinclair punched in his user name and password and clicked the icon to open RMS. If Olsen had any contact with OPD, he'd be in the department's record management system. It could be as insignificant as making a report for vandalism or witnessing a car break-in. He typed in Chris Olsen and searched from the date of Samantha's rape forward.

He got three hits. The first one was for a man twenty-six years old. Too young. The next one was a woman—Christine. The last record was for a Christopher Olsen who was forty-six. He brought up the report. A hit-and-run driver struck Olsen's car in East Oakland last month. Sinclair toggled to the DMV system and entered the name and the date of birth from the hit-and-run report.

The driver's license information popped onto the screen. Five-foot-eight and two-thirty. Not even close.

"Jankowski," Sinclair yelled. "You know anyone else at NYPD?"

"I got the cards of a couple of Polack detectives from the Bronx that I drank beer with at the last homicide conference in Reno."

"Dan, you can't . . . oh, never mind," said Braddock.

"I'm a Polack and proud—"

Sinclair said, "Can you get them to run Olsen in their version of RMS or DMV out there?"

"I doubt they're working on Sunday, but I'll give it a shot."

Sinclair turned back to his computer and pulled up the screen for CORPUS, the county arrest and criminal history system, and typed Olsen's name. Four pages of hits. He printed them out and scanned down the list, crossing out those younger than thirty-five and older than fifty. That left him ten entries on four different people. The first three didn't match the age or physical. The fourth one was six-one and two hundred pounds. He ran him out. This Olsen had a local arrest record going back twenty years with his first arrest in Fremont for disturbing the peace, followed by a succession of drug charges. It didn't look favorable. Sinclair couldn't imagine the killer spending time in the Bay Area until recently. The last arrest was six months ago. Sinclair scrolled through the entry and found the subject had remained in custody with a parole hold until his last court date when he pled guilty to a two-year sentence. Definitely not him.

"As I suspected, no one's in," said Jankowski. "But I talked to a precinct desk sergeant who said he'd try to call one of my old drinking buddies at home. While we're waiting, Braddock and I might as well head over to the city and do those interviews. Maybe we'll find someone who saw someone fitting the description of Olsen."

Sinclair went back to his computer and ran out all Chris Olsens with an Oakland address in DMV. He was ready to expand his search to surrounding cities, but he knew he was wasting his time. It was a long shot anyway. The Chris Olsen he was looking for wouldn't have a California driver's license, and if Olsen was the killer, as meticulously as he had planned the murders, he'd certainly be able to avoid police contact. He tried several websites and found more than a hundred Chris Olsens in New York. He eliminated some. It was appearing hopeless. Even if he were looking at the right Chris Olsen on the computer, he might not know it. He needed a birth date, a social security number, or some other identifier to bring up a driver's license, a criminal history, or some other record to be sure the Olsen he was viewing was the Chris Olsen he was looking for.

Chapter 54

The man sat at his hand-me-down desk in the windowless office scanning the Channel 6 breaking news on his desktop computer. The big news so far was the heat. Not yet noon and San Francisco was already in the mideighties, and Oakland was poised to tie the record high of ninety-nine degrees for the date, set in 1978. It showed one news team was in Marin County filming sailboats on the bay with the skyline of San Francisco in the background and another was interviewing a fire chief in southeast Alameda County about the risk of a wildfire. He pulled his smartphone from his jeans pocket, looked at the e-mails in the draft folder that he had previously prepared, and reviewed the first e-mail in the sequence:

To: Elizabeth.Schueller@channelsixnews.org
From: Oakland-BBK@gmail.com
Subject: Bus Bench Killer Interview

Hello Ms. Schueller:

I understand you were interested in interviewing the man whom you refer to as the Bus Bench Killer. If you are still interested in doing so, please advise.

Best regards

He pressed send.

Chapter 55

As he paced the homicide office in his stocking feet, Sinclair felt like the inmates he'd seen walking prison yards. He'd given up trying to find the right Chris Olsen among the hundreds on the Internet and spent the last hour reading reports from Melissa Mathis's murder, hoping for something that would tell him Olsen was the man responsible. But there were no witnesses to her abduction and none of the witnesses on the freeway got a look at the driver's face. He called the crime lab, and a criminalist in the fingerprint unit answered the phone.

"This is Sinclair down in homicide. What're you doing here on a Sunday?"

"Working your murder cases, Sergeant," she said.

"Any luck?"

"No, but I'm relooking at the evidence in all the cases to see if there's anything we can examine for fingerprints again, maybe through fuming."

"If you find anything—"

"You'll be the first one I call," she said.

Sinclair dialed the home phone number he had for Donna Fitzgerald and was surprised when she answered.

"I'm not calling about Jenny," he said before she could hang up. "What can you tell me about Chris Olsen?"

"I need to put this behind me, not only for Jenny's benefit, but for mine too," she said. "Please don't call me again."

At least she didn't slam the phone in his ear, he thought, as he called the phone number the woman at Berzerkeley Boutique had given him for the owner. Skye was the only person who had seen Olsen, assuming the man who bought all the medallions was Olsen. He got her voicemail and left another message. He entered her phone number into the computer, and it showed to be a landline with a Berkeley address. He called Berkeley PD and requested they send an officer by the address to see if Skye was there.

Ten minutes later, the Berkeley officer called. "The address is a big, old house filled with big, old hippies. Her housemates said she's away this weekend but should be home by around five this afternoon."

"Any way to locate her now?"

"They said she doesn't believe in cell phones, and the rumor is she's at a lesbian camp or commune somewhere near Guerneville."

Even if he could get the locals to look for her, there were hundreds of rustic camps along that part of the Russian River, and Skye would probably be on her way back long before anyone could find her.

Sinclair thanked the Berkeley officer and called Braddock. "How'd you do?" he asked.

"Big waste of time. We talked to two supposed witnesses, but neither really saw anything."

"I should've been out there with you."

"Jankowski's keeping me entertained."

"What's he bitching about today, the moral decline of the country's youth or the imminent collapse of the world economy?"

"Only the weather. Says if he wanted to sweat his butt off doing police work, he'd have joined LAPD. We're going to grab some lunch on the way back. You want to join us?"

Sinclair's watch read 11:55. "Nah, I had a big breakfast."

"Jankowski's waving at me. I'll put him on."

Sinclair pulled the phone a few inches from his ear as Jankowski's booming voice came on the line. "Sinclair, I just got a call from NYPD. I guess I rattled enough cages to get this pushed higher than the precinct captain. This deputy inspector bigwig claimed his cops misunderstood his directive. He only told them he didn't want anybody screwing with the Arquette family over bullshit or digging into shit that didn't concern them."

"Can this deputy inspector make the detective who handled the case call us?"

"He's on vacation. He's an old timer and only carries his cell phone on duty because they make him."

"Sounds like one of our old-timer homicide sergeants," said Sinclair.

"Fuck you too, Sinclair. I take my phone with me on vacation—I just don't turn it on. Otherwise, you young-sters bother me all the time."

"They're cops. Can't they find one of their own?"

"The detective's driving home right now from some-where in Pennsylvania and's expected to be home by seven or eight, their time. The inspector ordered someone to sit in front of his house and call us the moment he pulls up."

Jankowski gave the phone back to Braddock, and Sin-clair told her what he learned about Skye.

"We'll be back in an hour or so," said Braddock. "I guess we can go back into the reports and see if we missed anything."

"Or twiddle our thumbs until NYPD calls," said Sinclair. "Maybe he'll give us something that points to Olsen or at least give us all his info and maybe a photo."

"Then Jankowski and I can go to Skye's house by five and wait for her. If her description of the man who bought the medallions is anything like Olsen, we can show her a photo lineup."

"Sounds like a plan. Enjoy your lunch and don't worry about me. I'll just be here reading reports like a good little building rat."

Chapter 56

To: Oakland-BBK@gmail.com
From: Elizabeth.Schueller@channelsixnews.org
Subject: RE: Bus Bench Killer Interview

I would surely be interested in interviewing the Bus Bench Killer. Who are you and why do you ask?
                                    Elizabeth "Liz" Schueller

He brought up the next e-mail from his draft folder, pasted it into a reply, and hit the send button.

To: Elizabeth.Schueller@channelsixnews.org
From: Oakland-BBK@gmail.com
Subject: RE: RE: Bus Bench Killer Interview

Hello Ms. Schueller:

I am the one you refer to as the Bus Bench Killer. I killed Zachary Caldwell, Susan Hammond, Carol Brooks, and Melissa Mathis. I'd be willing to speak to you on camera and tell you why they needed to die if you are interested.

Best regards,
BBK

Chapter 57

Sinclair grabbed the next report on the stack, looked at the thirty pages stapled together, and flung it across the room. It sailed like a Frisbee until the pages opened up. Then it fluttered and fell to the floor. Sanchez stared at him but said nothing. He'd been reading reports and doing computer searches all morning. Still, no clues jumped out. Sinclair couldn't fathom how Sanchez sat at his desk all day reading reports and entering data into a computer. Sinclair could manage only a few hours at his desk on the best of days before he needed get out of the office and do something. Today, all he could manage was thirty minutes.

He pulled the stiff shoes onto his feet and took the service elevator to the basement, stopping at the heavy steel door that led to the indoor range. When he heard a lull in the gunfire, he swung open the door, grabbed a pair of earmuffs off the railing, and covered his ears. Two of the three bays were occupied with two officers each. They faced downrange, guns holstered, hands inches away. Sinclair heard a metallic click, and four silhouette targets mounted on metal rotating stands turned to face the officers. They drew their Glocks, brought them smoothly to eye level, and fired two shots each into the life-size depictions of an armed man's upper torso.

Inside the glass-walled office at the back of the range, Norris leaned toward a microphone. "Come back to the fifteen-yard line. Make ready with one, two-round magazine in your weapon, and another two-round magazine in your ammo pouch."

Norris gestured to Sinclair, who opened the door and stepped into the long, narrow office. Once inside, he removed his earmuffs.

"Hang on a sec," Norris said to Sinclair, then pressed the microphone button. "On the turn of the target, you will fire three rounds center mass. You will then change magazines and fire two carefully aimed headshots. This is to simulate a suspect who is wearing body armor and does not go down after successive shots to the torso."

Norris flipped a switch on the console and the targets turned. The officers fired the first three rounds in three seconds. Their pistol slides locked back and empty magazines dropped to the cement floor as the officers slid in fresh magazines and slammed them home. The final two shots rang out more slowly as the officers took their time to align their sights and press the triggers. One was still aiming when Norris flipped the switch to rotate the targets.

"Score each other's targets. Possible is fifty. I want to see any targets with less than forty-five holes. Jimmy, I'll score you."

The young, black officer who didn't get his last shot off brought his target into the office. Norris counted the holes, marking each with a pen.

"Forty-two," said Norris. "Passing is forty, but it's not good enough to survive on the streets. You missed both head shots."

"I jerked the first one and was aiming for the second when the target turned," Jimmy said.

"In the real world, you'd be dead. You need practice. The range hours for next week are posted on the door."

Sinclair removed his Sig Sauer from his holster, dropped the magazine, ejected the chambered round into his hand, and handed the gun to Norris. Norris disassembled it; inspected the barrel, springs, and firing pin; and then put it back together. He grasped the gun by the barrel and added a succession of weights to a rod that hooked over the trigger until the hammer fell. He did the same for the single-action trigger and wrote numbers into a steno pad.

"Three and a half pounds single-action and nine double," said Norris. "A little lighter than factory specs, but still okay."

Sinclair reloaded and holstered his gun. "You mind if I shoot some?"

"Actually, I'd like you to test fire a scenario I'm designing for SWAT training next week," said Norris.

Sinclair followed him to the third bay where the target stands contained two hostage targets. The paper targets were life-size cartoonish drawings of a light-haired ghoulish man holding a dark-haired woman around the throat with one hand and a gun to her head with the other. The woman shielded the man, leaving only half of his body exposed.

"Put on your ears and engage the one on the right," said Norris.

Sinclair pulled on his earmuffs, drew his .45, and put two rounds in the ghoul's head.

"Good," said Norris. "The body's the larger target, why'd you go for the headshot?"

Sinclair reholstered. "The man's pointing a gun at the woman and has his finger on the trigger. He wouldn't die immediately from a body shot and could still shoot. He could even pull the trigger involuntarily if the hand muscles contract. But a bullet in the head will short-circuit the brain."

"Exactly," said Norris. "I'll turn the targets when I run this for SWAT, and they'll have to figure it out instantly and go for the headshot. If they shoot in the torso, miss the head, or hit the hostage, they fail."

"Simple enough," said Sinclair.

Norris slid a sheet of plywood with a square hole cut in the middle in front of the other target. "This simulates the same hostage situation, but inside a house. The hostage-taker's peering through a window, holding his hostage as a shield in front of him. Instead of a six-inch-wide head to hit, less than half of the hostage-taker's head is exposed. More than an inch to the right and you hit the hostage. More than an inch to the left and you miss. I'll have the snipers shoot it with their scoped rifles at a hundred yards and the operators at fifteen yards with handguns."

Sinclair took several slow breaths, blew out most of the last one, aimed, and slowly pressed the trigger. The bullet creased the hair of the paper hostage.

"Just nicked her ear," said Norris. "What the hell, a good plastic surgeon can repair it."

Sinclair fired a second shot, this one hitting the ghoul in his left eye.

"Good shot," said Norris. "Not easy, huh?"

"I don't shoot as much as I used to, but the SWAT guys should be able to handle this," said Sinclair. "But here's the real solution."

He aimed two inches left of his last shot and fired three quick rounds.

Norris walked downrange, yelling, "Sarge, you shot my window frame."

Sinclair slid the bullet-peppered plywood away from the target to reveal three holes in the right side of the hostage-taker's head. "A window frame won't stop a bullet, so by ignoring it, I get a six-inch-wide target instead of a two-inch sliver. Easy shot."

Chapter 58

The man's phone vibrated on the desk in front of him.

To: Oakland-BBK@gmail.com
From: Elizabeth.Schueller@channelsixnews.org
Subject: RE: RE: RE: Bus Bench Killer Interview

Hello,

If you are truly who you say you are, I will gladly interview you and give you the opportunity to tell your side
of the story. However, I must be wary. Can you prove to
me you are the Bus Bench Killer by providing details of
the crimes that only you would know—details that have
not been reported?

Sincerely,
Elizabeth "Liz" Schueller

He had anticipated her demand for proof. Liz might be
ambitious, but she wasn't stupid, so he expected she would

vet him as an untested source before agreeing to meet. He replied,

To: Elizabeth.Schueller@channelsixnews.org
From: Oakland-BBK@gmail.com
Subject: RE: RE: RE: RE: Bus Bench Killer Interview

Hello Ms. Schueller:

I left a memento—a medallion of a peace sign—with each victim. I shot Ms. Brooks with a 9mm pistol, something the police can verify. I must warn you, however, that should you tell the police about our conversation or conspire with them to set me up, not only will you lose this interview, but you will force me to take other actions.

Best regards,
BBK

Chapter 59

Sinclair stepped into the office. Sanchez looked up from his desk. "That girlfriend of yours called. I think she might have tricked me into saying something."

"Liz? What did she want?"

"She said she had a source who mentioned the peace medallions and the murder weapon being a nine. She wanted me to confirm it."

Sinclair looked at his cell and noticed a voicemail from Liz. "Did you?"

"Of course not. I told her distinctly I would not confirm it; however, I told her that if she reported it on the news, it could jeopardize your investigation."

Sinclair shook his head and chuckled. "Yeah, she got you."

"Sorry."

"Don't worry about it. You actually put her on notice not to use it. She won't risk getting on homicide's shit list."

"Who do you think told her?" asked Sanchez.

"We put out those details to every department in the state, so that leaves a few thousand possibilities."

"Liz Schueller does have a way of getting men to talk to her."

That she does, thought Sinclair, as he walked to the window. Staring at the street below, he punched up her voicemail.

Hi Matt, I'm thinking about you. A source told me your victims wore peace sign medallions and the gun used on Carol Brooks was a nine millimeter. I'm trying to determine if my source is credible. Love you.

Sinclair brought up the Channel 6 News website on his computer. Blasted across the screen was: *Tonight at 5 and 10. The Bus Bench Killer: A Special Report by Liz Schueller and the Channel 6 News Team.*

Chapter 60

The man read the incoming e-mail.

To: Oakland-BBK@gmail.com
From: Elizabeth.Schueller@channelsixnews.org
Subject: RE: RE: RE: RE: RE: Bus Bench Killer Interview

Your information checks out. Would you like to come to
our studio?

Sincerely,
Elizabeth "Liz" Schueller

The man pasted text from the next archived e-mail into
a reply.

To: Elizabeth.Schueller@channelsixnews.org
From: Oakland-BBK@gmail.com
Subject: RE: RE: RE: RE: RE: RE: Bus Bench Killer Interview

Hello Liz . . . I hope it's okay for me to call you Liz. As
you surely understand, I don't feel comfortable coming

to your station. However, I have a location in Oakland that will suffice. You must follow my instructions if you want the interview. Within 30 minutes, you must be at The Bus Bench. Once there, have your camera operator film you doing an introduction to your interview with me. I will be observing. Once I am comfortable you are alone and there is no police surveillance, I will e-mail you further instructions. You have 30 minutes from now.

The man hit send and walked out of his office.

Chapter 61

Sinclair leaned back in his chair, propped his stocking feet on his desk, and studied his notes from the interview with the lawyers Phyllis Mathis and Russell Hammond. He grabbed the phone and dialed Hammond. "How'd you end up getting the referral from Horowitz?" he asked.

"A previous client referred it."

"Who was that?"

"A man named Darryl Tyson. I represented him on a medical malpractice claim a few years ago. He'd developed a medical condition from parasites while working on a clean water project in Sierra Leone that the Arquette family foundation financed. When he returned to Oakland, he went to Summit Medical Center. They misdiagnosed him and he nearly died."

"Jane knew Tyson?"

"They met in the Peace Corps in their twenties and stayed friends," said Hammond.

"Would he know Jane's father or Samantha's father?"

"He was quite close to the family from the way he talked."

"Describe him?"

"Medium height, slightly built African American man in his forties. Very bright. Degrees in engineering and chemistry, speaks English, French, and several other languages fluently."

As Hammond talked, Sinclair entered Tyson into RMS. No hits. He brought up the DMV screen and entered his information.

"Do you have an address and phone number for him?" Sinclair asked as he clicked on a DMV record showing a man matching the information Hammond provided.

"I'd have to go to my office to get his file, but I've been to his apartment several times. He lives in the high rise on Lake Merritt—Twelve Hundred Lakeshore."

Sinclair hung up. The DMV record on his computer showed the same address. He ran Tyson in CORPUS, CII, and FBI. He was clean at the local, state, and federal level. DMV showed a year-old Volvo sedan registered to him and a ticket for running a stop sign three years earlier.

He grabbed his phone and started to call Braddock just as she walked in the door. He closed his phone.

"I know who can lead us to Olsen."

"I thought the chief said—"

"Fuck the chief," said Sinclair. "The killer's close—I can feel it." Sinclair nearly bumped into Jankowski as he headed out the door. Jankowski was coming in with a thick Sunday *San Francisco Chronicle* under his arm.

Jankowski said, "Thought this would help us pass the time while we waited—"

Braddock cut him off. "Tell Matt we can handle the field work for him."

"What field work?" asked Jankowski.

"I'm going," said Sinclair. "You coming?"

"Are you sure you want to do this?" she said.

"Damn straight." Sinclair pushed through the door and headed down the stairs. "This is the Oakland connection to Olsen."

Braddock followed. "Let me and Jankowski bring the guy in and you can talk to him."

"There's no time." Sinclair crossed the sidewalk to his car.

"I'm coming too," said Jankowski, as he hurried to catch up. "Where're we going?"

"You're supposed to support me, damn it," she said to Jankowski.

"Ah, come on, it's his case," said Jankowski.

She shook her head in frustration and climbed into the passenger seat of Sinclair's car.

"Twelve Hundred Lakeshore," Sinclair shouted to Jankowski, who lumbered down the street to his car.

Sinclair pulled out of the parking space, accelerated through the light at Broadway, and caught the last second of the yellow lights at the next two streets.

Braddock sighed loudly. "Okay, Matt, so what's this hot lead all about that justified your escape from office jail?"

Sinclair shot through the Chinatown streets, blowing through red lights after slowing and looking both ways while recapping his conversation with Russell Hammond for Braddock. Exiting the Eleventh Street Tunnel, he turned right and followed the edge of Lake Merritt. He jerked the car to a stop in front of the apartment building and strode to the front door with Braddock and Jankowski hurrying to catch up.

"Que pasa?" a short Hispanic doorman said when he saw Sinclair display his badge.

Sinclair glared at him. "Does my badge say Federales?"

"Sorry, sir."

"How long has Darryl Tyson lived in the building?" Sinclair asked.

"I've been here two years. At least that long."

"When did you last see him?"

He shrugged. "Weeks, maybe a month. He travels a lot."

"Does he live alone?"

"Why you asking all this? Tenants expect privacy."

Sinclair stepped closer and glared down at the twenty-five-year-old man. "I'm working a homicide and if you impede me, I'll arrest your ass."

"He lives alone, but a friend's been staying with him," the doorman said. "Been visiting for a month or more."

"Does the friend have a name?" Sinclair asked.

"The manager would know. He'll be here tomorrow at eight."

Sinclair's phone vibrated. He saw it was Liz and pressed the button to send her to voicemail. "What's the friend look like?"

"Anglo. Bigger than you," he said to Sinclair. "But not as large as you," the doorman said with a sly smile to Jankowski.

Sinclair caught Braddock's and Jankowski's expressions, as they noted the description fit that of Olsen.

"Is he home?"

"Tenants usually take the elevator straight from the garage, so I don't see them in the lobby."

"You got cameras, right?"

"I don't watch them all the time. But the nightshift saw him."

"When?"

"He said Mr. Tyson's guest came in through the lobby around four yesterday morning and took the elevator up."

"Was that unusual?"

"Four in the morning and he wasn't out clubbing."

"How's that?"

"Had on cargo pants, a vest, and small backpack. Strange time to be hiking."

"What's his apartment number?"

"I'll show you."

A few minutes later, they got off the elevator on the seventeenth floor and followed the doorman down the hall.

"Knock and tell him you got a delivery or something," said Sinclair.

The three detectives stood to the side of the door as the doorman pressed the buzzer. After a moment, he buzzed again and yelled, "Mr. Tyson, this is Manny the doorman."

"You have a key?" Sinclair asked.

"I have a passkey, but I must call—"

"We don't have time for that. Gimme the key or we kick the door."

"Don't you think we should get a warrant and have patrol make entry?" asked Braddock.

"I'm thinking that Tyson hasn't been seen in a while and he might be held hostage inside, which would justify entry under exigent circumstances," said Sinclair.

"You're really stretching it," she said.

"Or maybe under the hot pursuit doctrine," said Sinclair.

"Too much time has elapsed," she said.

It would take two or three hours to type up an affidavit and warrant and another hour to track down the duty judge for a signature. If Olsen wasn't inside, something there might lead them to him. The safest course of action was to get the warrant to avoid having a judge later throw out any evidence they found inside. But Sinclair seldom took the safe route. He needed to stop the next murder. "Series of crimes that is still ongoing. We've been working them nonstop. He's likely preparing for another murder right now, which we won't prevent if we're delayed getting a warrant."

"Sounds like exigent circumstances to me," said Jankowski.

"What the hell," said Braddock.

Using the doorman's master key, Sinclair unlocked the door and pushed it open.

"Police—anybody home?" he yelled inside.

After announcing twice more and getting no response, Sinclair drew his pistol and crossed the threshold into the apartment. Braddock and Jankowski followed. Sinclair swept through the living room and dining room with Braddock at his side. He peeked over a counter that separated the kitchen from the dining area. No one hiding there. He and Braddock squeezed past Jankowski, who had been covering the hallway while they cleared the main room. Sinclair poked his head into a bathroom on the left and pulled back the shower curtain.

"Clear," he shouted.

He entered the first bedroom on the right. A queen-size bed, dresser, and two bed tables filled the room. Sinclair pointed his gun at the closet as Braddock slid the glass doors one way and then the other. Nothing other than clothes. Although the bed seemed too low to the ground for some-one to fit underneath, he still dropped to the floor and peered under it to make sure. He led the way down the hall into the master suite, where he and Braddock searched two closets in the dressing area, then the bathroom, and finally the bedroom. All clear.

When searching a house under exigent circumstances, they couldn't justify opening drawers or looking in any place where a person could not conceivably be hiding; however, any evidence they saw in plain sight was fair game, so Sinclair stopped for a moment to take in the master bedroom and glance in the closet again on his way out of the room. He saw nothing noteworthy.

When they returned to the main room, Jankowski was standing over a dining table covered with DVDs, papers, stacks of files, and a laptop computer.

"Look at this," said Jankowski, motioning toward the stack of file folders with the names of the four murder victims printed on the tabs. Alongside that pile were two more folders, one with Braddock's name and another with Liz's.

Braddock gasped and pulled out her phone. "I need to call Ryan. Get the kids, get them safe."

Sinclair clasped his hands over Braddock's phone and held her hand until she calmed. "He's not after Ryan and the kids, Cathy. He's after you."

"Me? Why?"

"Because of me."

It was apparent to Sinclair the moment he saw Braddock's and Liz's names. Olsen killed family members of the people he blamed for what happened to Samantha and Jane. Braddock and Liz were the closest thing Sinclair had to a family.

"You're safe with us," said Sinclair. "But we need to locate Liz. She's his next target."

"Matt," interrupted Jankowski, who was standing by a bookshelf in the living room. "Is this Samantha, your first victim?"

Sinclair and Braddock crossed the room to where Jankowski was looking at a framed photograph of Samantha, a man, and a woman.

"Oh, shit," said Sinclair.

"You recognize him?" asked Jankowski.

"That's Liz's cameraman."

Chapter 62

Kristoffer Eric Olsen told Liz that there wasn't any reason for them to be standing outside looking at the bus bench. "Why don't we get back in the van where it's cool?"

Olsen put his camera in the back of the van and climbed into the driver's seat. Everything was working according to his plan. Once he had sent Liz the last e-mail, he walked down the hall to the newsroom and strolled past Liz's desk just as she looked up from her computer. She asked if he was available for what she said was the story of the year. Of course he was, he replied. Liz never suspected he was anyone other than Eric, a photojournalist burned out from working in New York City too long, an easygoing guy who eagerly worked with her on assignments even when the other cameramen tried to avoid her, and the great listener during the countless hours they spent together when she talked endlessly about herself, her relationship, and her insecurities.

"We got video of the bus bench from every angle possible," said Liz. "As well as plenty of me talking that will work as teasers and a good introduction for our meeting with the man responsible. What now?"

330 | Brian Thiem

"I guess we just wait for his next e-mail. Did you tell the producer or assignment editor where we were going?"

The van's air conditioning blasted its icy air on Olsen and Liz. Wearing a tan photographer's vest over a polo top, Olsen was still sweating from his recent activity outside, but Liz was wearing a sheer blouse and chose to turn the vent away from her.

"Just that we're doing an interview that might require more than the five minutes they allotted to my special report."

"Would they have permitted this if you told them?"

"No way," she said. "They'd have called the news director at home, who would've insisted on talking to legal, and the thirty-minute deadline would have come and gone."

"Sounds like we might be in trouble?"

"You're just following my orders, and if we bag this interview, we'll be heroes."

"What about your friend, Sergeant Sinclair?"

"He'll be pissed. Matt doesn't see the work we journalists do as important. But I'll call him as soon as we finish and tell him where the killer is."

"How do you plan to do that?"

"I'm thinking that once he tells us where to meet, I can call Matt and . . . I won't tell him where we're going, but I can send him some place close and tell him to wait."

"What if he has every cop in the department search that area for our van? That would blow the interview and might put you in danger if the man thinks you betrayed him."

"Good point."

"Maybe once he tells us where to meet, you can tell Sinclair to wait at the bus bench." Afraid he just revealed more than he should, he added, "assuming the interview location is in that vicinity, but not too close."

He could see Liz smiling out of the corner of his eye. "You're good at this."

"Before I came to Channel Six, I spent years overseas. I was part of a film crew that did these kinds of meets with members of Hezbollah in Beirut, and later with a BBC team that did the same with Hamas in the West Bank."

"I didn't know that. I just thought you were a local news station photojournalist in New York."

"The overseas stuff was back in my younger years."

Liz smiled. "What's the secret to working with dangerous subjects?"

"Don't cross either side. If you cross the terrorists, they kill you. If you cross the authorities, they lock you up."

"Maybe I shouldn't say anything to Matt until we finish the interview and are safely back in the newsroom?"

Olsen thought for a moment. He was afraid Sinclair might talk her out of the interview if they spoke, yet he wanted Sinclair to know what she was doing so he'd go crazy worrying, just as Jane did when she raced to the hospital after the phone call about Samantha.

"I don't want to get on the wrong side of the police," said Olsen. "But if you never actually talk to him, he can't tell you not to do it. Can't you just leave him a message or shoot him a text?"

"That might work."

"I'm going to change batteries and put the one in the camera into the charger," said Olsen as he opened the door. "Happiness is two fully charged batteries."

He walked around the van and opened the back doors, slid his personal phone from his back pocket, and sent the next e-mail. He was climbing into the driver's seat when Liz's Blackberry chimed.

"Is it from him?" Olsen asked.

"Yeah."

"What's it say?"

"*You must follow these instructions or else you'll never see me. Turn off your phones, both yours and your cameraman's. All the way off. Place them on the dash. Drive to the Golden State Motel at Fifty-Fourth and San Pablo. Park in the rear of the lot. Send your cameraman, alone, into the lobby. The manager will give him an envelope with further instructions.*"

Olsen pulled his work phone from his belt and held down the power button until it shut down. "You best make your phone call," he said as he tossed his phone onto the dash.

Liz brought up a contact list on her phone and pressed *Sinclair.*

"I thought you were going to leave a message at his office," said Olsen.

"I owe him this much," she said.

"I hope you know what you're doing."

"Matt, damn you—answer your phone," she said into the air. After a pause, she spoke. "When you get this message, you won't be able to call me back, but I'm on my way to interview the Bus Bench Killer. Wait at the bus bench and I'll call you with his location when I'm done." She let out a deep sigh, switched her phone off, and placed it on the dash.

"You still want to do this?" Olsen asked.

"Damn straight. Let's go win our Peabody Award."

Olsen pulled the shift lever into drive and pulled away from the curb. He reached behind him and swung a six-pack cooler to the front. "I have some cold waters in there. Help yourself."

"Thanks," she said, unzipping the flap. "One for you?"

"No, I'm good for now."

Olsen made a left turn on Fifty-Fifth Street as Liz unscrewed the top off a bottle of water and took several swallows.

Chapter 63

Braddock was still staring at the photograph when Sinclair turned to her. "Just to be safe, you should call Ryan."

"I better call Liz." Sinclair pulled out his cell and listened to her voicemail.

"How fucking stupid can she be," he said.

He called Liz's cell. It immediately went to voicemail.

"She's got her phone turned off," Sinclair said to Braddock. He next called the assignment desk at Channel 6. They said Liz was with the cameraman, Eric, doing an interview related to her special but didn't know where or any other details. Sinclair was afraid to tell the station what was happening or ask for their assistance because if Olsen found out the police were on to him, he'd likely kill Liz immediately.

"Let's call dispatch and have them broadcast a comm order for all units to be on the lookout for the van," said Braddock.

"All the news vans have scanners," said Sinclair. "Olsen will kill her as soon as he hears the broadcast."

He turned to Jankowski. "Call Sanchez and have him get a search warrant for this place, but don't wait for it. Tear the place apart and find something that'll tell me where they're at."

"Let's go," Sinclair said to Braddock and ran to the elevator.

Some cars swung to the right, some stopped in front of him, and others just continued to drive down the middle of the street as Sinclair screamed down the street with his lights flashing and siren blaring. As he approached MacArthur Boulevard, he shut down his emergency equipment.

"I have no idea why I'm racing to the bus bench," said Sinclair. "No one's there."

"You're worried about her," said Braddock. "You need to do something, but we can't find her without help."

Sinclair called the patrol sergeant for the North Oakland District on her cell phone and gave her the run down. She had every patrol officer that wasn't busy on a priority assignment switch to a tactical channel that scanners couldn't monitor and, with the help of a dispatcher, assigned the six available officers a grid to search for the news van.

2L72 asked over the radio, "Can you see if any other agencies have a helicopter up today?"

"East Bay Regional Parks had Eagle One up earlier for the high-fire danger, Two-L-Seventy-Two," said the male dispatcher. "I'll make a call."

"If you reach them, make sure they understand they cannot broadcast on a main freq," said Sinclair.

"Copy that, Thirteen-Adam-Five," said the dispatcher.

"It's times like this that I really miss ARGUS," said Braddock.

ARGUS, which stood for Arial Reconnaissance Ground Unit Support, was OPD's helicopter and had been grounded for most of the year because of budget cutbacks. "Crime keeps going up, yet they take away resources every year and wonder why the bad guys are winning," said Sinclair.

"If it were easy, anyone could do it," she said.

The radio cracked with the voice of the patrol sergeant. "Can Thirteen-Adam-Five give us a hint on where we should be looking?"

"Some place where they could conduct an interview undisturbed—a house, an office," said Sinclair for the benefit of all officers on the radio channel as he pulled into the bus loading zone on MLK Jr. Way. "I know that's not much help."

"Two-L-Seventy-Two and Thirteen-Adam-Five," said the dispatcher. "Eagle One is going down for fuel right now. If there're no smoke calls after they refuel, they'll head our way. ETA about thirty minutes."

Sinclair thanked the dispatcher and listened as units reported areas they searched. He knew they'd be lucky to find the van in time. There were just too many miles of street to cover, and the van could be tucked away off the street or even outside their search grid.

★

"This guy might be watching, so make sure you don't touch your phone," said Olsen as he stepped out of the van and marched across the parking lot.

Patel was looking out the window at the Channel 6 van. The smell of curry was even stronger in the heat.

"Hello, sir, is there something I may assist you with?"

"Nothing at all." Olsen removed a hundred-dollar bill and slid it through the window. "I just wanted to thank you for respecting my privacy."

Patel smiled and bowed his head slightly. "You are welcome, sir."

Olsen pulled an envelope from his vest pocket and returned to the van. Once inside, he tore open the envelope and removed a room key and a note, which he handed to Liz.

Liz's lips quivered as she read the note. "Get all the equipment you'll need, go into the room, and set up. I'll be there when I'm certain you weren't followed."

"We can still back out," said Olsen, knowing that if she were indecisive, his suggestion would raise her bravado.

"No way." She swung open her door and stepped onto the cracked asphalt parking lot.

Olsen opened the van's rear doors and handed the tripod to Liz. Every reporter knew it was customary for them to carry the five-pound tripod while the cameraman handled everything else, and having her carry it would make her feel they were a team. He gathered his camera, light set, and cooler, and led the way to the room. He unlocked the door, pushed it open with his body, and let Liz squeeze by him into the dark room.

"It's like an oven in here," she said as she flipped on the light switch.

Olsen set his equipment on the small table under the window and fumbled with the controls on the air conditioning unit until it clanked and hissed and finally blew a stream of cool air. He began setting up his lights and tripod as Liz wandered around the room. She looked in the bathroom and turned toward Olsen, her nose scrunched in disgust.

"If the walls of this room could talk," she said.

Olsen grinned. "I take it you don't normally frequent places like this."

She laughed. "On assignment only."

Olsen pushed a chair against a wall and pulled the other toward the door so they faced each other. He positioned the lights and fastened the camera onto the tripod.

"I suggest we have the man sit in the far chair. He'll be the primary subject, but I can zoom out at times and get both of you in the frame to show the interaction. While we're waiting, I can get some cut-away shots of you sitting in your chair asking questions."

As Liz walked toward the chair, she stumbled, but caught herself by grabbing the dresser.

"Are you okay?" he asked.

"Feeling a bit lightheaded," she said. "Must be the heat."

"Why don't you just sit down for a minute? I'll get you another water." Olsen grabbed a bottle from the cooler and handed it to her.

★

"If you were a reporter, where would you conduct an interview with a killer?" asked Braddock.

"In my studio," said Sinclair. "But Olsen certainly planned this as carefully as he did the other murders. I'm sure Liz has no suspicion he's anything other than her coworker."

"Do you think he'll actually take her to a place he picked out for an interview—that he'll reveal his true identity there and go through with the interview?"

"Maybe he just tazes her like the other victims and takes her some place to kill her?"

"If so, we're already too late."

"He must have another place," said Sinclair. "He didn't park that crappy old van at the luxury apartment building, and he sure didn't take the Hammond woman there, past all the security cameras, to kill her."

"A house with a garage where he could come and go without anyone noticing," Braddock suggested.

"Or one of the transient motels or apartments where no one calls the cops even when someone's being robbed in front of them."

Sinclair radioed his hunch to 2L72, and she directed half of her units to the motels on West MacArthur, known for prostitution and drugs, and the other half to drug hotspots further south.

Sinclair wished Olsen hadn't torched the van. The inside would have contained clues as to where he frequented—maybe a fast food wrapper or a store receipt. The registration had been a dead end. Like many cars driven in Oakland, it hadn't been registered in more than a year. The last owner told SFPD he sold the van for cash to an elderly man who never showed him identification. The van probably passed through many people since. Sinclair remembered looking at the photos of the burnt van earlier this morning. He'd noticed several bumper stickers: *Oakland Raiders*, *Vote for Change—Obama 08*, and *Praise Baptist Church*.

"Ever hear of Praise Baptist Church?" he asked Braddock. She pulled out her iPhone. "Fifty-Six-Oh-Four Marshall."

"Let's check it out."

Sinclair turned onto Fifty-Third Street and headed west. He zigzagged through narrow residential streets until he hit San Pablo Avenue. Marshall Street paralleled San Pablo, one block west, so Sinclair made a right on San Pablo, heading to Fifty-Fifth Street. On his left was a hamburger joint with a walk-up window and a large parking lot where Sinclair remembered waiting many nights as a young patrol officer for the paddy wagon to pick up someone he had arrested. On the other corner of Fifty-Fourth Street was the Golden State Motel, where he had made a half-dozen prostitution arrests when he worked vice narcotics. He glanced at the motel. In the far corner of the parking lot sat the Channel 6 News van.

Chapter 64

Olsen rose from the chair and switched off the camera. Although he had planned a five-minute video presentation, he ended up speaking for nearly fifteen. He needed the extra time to ensure the public understood his reasons for killing the women and boy instead of those who were guilty—the doctors, lawyers, and Sinclair. Samantha and Jane were innocent, after all, and he had carried the pain of their deaths for what felt like an eternity. Sinclair and the others responsible would come to feel the same pain as their days, months, and years dragged on. It was as simple and as horrible as that.

He pulled the Beretta from his waistband and set it on the bed table.

He remembered how furious he became when he had learned that Samantha had been raped, and Sinclair would get to experience that same rage.

Olsen was glad the GHB he added to Liz's water was acting as the dealer had promised. Finding heroin in the Bay Area was easy compared to finding Rohypnol. After striking out in Oakland and Berkeley, he had eventually found a bouncer at a strip club on Broadway in San Francisco who explained that most of what is sold as roofie is not Rohypnol at all but usually a mixture of various drugs that might do anything from making the person agitated to causing a massive seizure. The best substance to "make a girl pliable," in the bouncer's words, was GHB, known as Liquid E. He said it was primarily taken by people to promote libido and lower their inhibitions but acknowledged that some might use it for drug-facilitated sexual assaults, not that he would ever provide it to someone for that purpose, the bouncer told Olsen with a wink. Olsen bought four doses for forty dollars.

Liz tried to sit up in bed but fell back down. "What's going on?" she slurred.

Her eyes bounced around the room without focusing on anything and then rolled upward. Her eyes looked at him confused.

"Just pretend I'm your drunken cop boyfriend."

"No," she moaned.

"I'll be quick," he said, as he slipped the open-toed heels off her feet and ran his hands up her bare calves.

"Eric, stop—"

She kicked at him, but Olsen grabbed her ankles and held them until she stopped. Her head, eyes glazed over, rolled to the side as she slipped in and out of consciousness. He hiked her skirt above her waist, grabbed her black thong with both index fingers, and slid it down her legs and over her feet. She didn't move. He put his hands on the inside of her thighs and pushed her legs apart.

He crawled onto the bed and cupped her face in his hands, trying to see if she was conscious, although at this point, it wasn't going to change anything. Her eyes shot open.

"No," she groaned.

He clasped his hand over her mouth. "Quiet," he ordered, then felt a sharp pain in his left hand.

He pulled a bloody hand from her mouth. "Bitch," he yelled.

Liz grabbed the lamp from the nightstand and swung it toward his head, as if her body got a jolt of adrenaline for one last fight. He grabbed it and flung it across the room. It shattered against the wall. She clawed at his face. He pinned her hand to her chest and smacked her across the face. The crack of his open hand against her cheek sounded like a gunshot in the small room. Blood from his hand and her busted lip ran down her chin. She collapsed on the bed and looked up at him. Her last bit of fight evaporated. He kicked off his shoes and reached down to undo his belt buckle.

Chapter 65

Sinclair made a U-turn on Fifty-Fifth Street and pulled to the curb just north of the motel, while Braddock got on the radio to report their location and tell responding units to approach without lights and sirens from the north. The district sergeant, 2L72, came on the air to order all units to stage behind the homicide car and wait for her before they moved in. The dispatcher said she'd notify the watch commander and have the dispatcher on the main channel send additional units to the scene and to include patrol rifle officers and a canine unit.

Sinclair grabbed the portable radio as he exited the car and closed the door quietly. He headed toward the motel. When he didn't see Braddock at his side, he turned and saw her standing by the trunk.

"Vests," she whispered.

He paused for several beats and then realized she was right and jogged back to the car and popped the trunk. He yanked off his suit coat, dropped it in the trunk, pulled the dark blue Kevlar vest over his head, and slapped the Velcro straps in place. He rapped his fist solidly on Braddock's chest, connecting with the solid metal trauma plate.

She punched him back in his vest and smiled. "Let's do this."

They drew their handguns and crept around the corner of the building. Sinclair counted four cars in the lot in addition to the news van. Ten rooms on the ground floor faced the parking lot. Two metal stairways led to ten more rooms that overlooked the parking lot. They slipped into the office at the corner of the building, and while Sinclair stepped up to the window with his gun at his side, Braddock stayed in the doorway and watched the parking lot.

An Indian man with jet-black hair appeared at the window.

"Hello, Officer, how may I help you?"

"That Channel Six truck—a man and a woman drove up in it. Where'd they go?"

He stared out the window as if he didn't know what Sinclair was talking about.

"Look," said Sinclair. "I don't have time to fuck around."

The desk clerk lowered his eyes. "I'm sorry, Officer. I always cooperate with police. The man is a registered guest in room five. With him is a reporter lady I see on TV. Very pretty."

"Key," said Sinclair.

The clerk pulled a brass key attached to a blue plastic tag from a row of boxes alongside the counter and slid it through the window slot.

"More police will be here in a moment. Don't even think about calling the room."

"No, sir, Officer."

Sinclair stepped behind Braddock and keyed the radio mike. "Thirteen-Adam-Five, they're in room five. The door and a window face the parking lot on the south side of the building. No windows at the back."

Sinclair handed the radio to Braddock, wrapped his left hand around his gun hand, raised his pistol to a low ready position, and crept down the walkway.

He stopped at the door to room five and listened. No sounds inside.

Beyond the door was a large window, but the drapes were drawn, and he dared not step in front of the window to look for a slit in the drapes for fear of announcing their presence. His tender feet burned, and his sweat-soaked dress shirt stuck to his chest like a second skin under the ballistic vest. He heard Braddock's ragged breathing and glanced over his shoulder to see her flushed face a foot away, beads of sweat forming on her forehead.

Sinclair heard officers announcing their ETA—two and three minutes—over the radio and was about to tell Braddock to turn down the volume when he heard Liz's scream. His muscles tensed. He crouched lower to get his balance. A male voice yelled something. The only word he could make out was "bitch," followed by the sound of something crashing inside the room.

Sinclair knew that containment and negotiation was normally the best strategy in a hostage situation. Making a dynamic entry against an armed offender carried risks even for a professionally trained and equipped SWAT team, but when a suspect was intent on killing, such as in an active shooter situation at a school, first responders couldn't wait.

He glanced back at Braddock. Their eyes met, and she nodded. Without a word, they both knew what they had to do.

He returned his attention to the door as Braddock spoke into the radio. "Thirteen-Adam-Five, he's preparing to kill her. We're making entry."

The radio squealed as ten officers tried to talk at once. Braddock turned down the volume.

Sinclair whispered, "I'll go left, you go right. Stay on my ass—no hesitation."

"Got it."

Sinclair stuck the key in the lock and turned it. The metallic click was barely audible. Braddock tapped him on his back, indicating she was ready. He twisted the doorknob, shoved the door open, and followed it into the room.

During high-risk entries, officers must pass through what's known as the fatal funnel. A gunman can guarantee hitting the officers making entry if he directs enough rounds into the doorway at the right time.

Like a running back carrying a football on fourth and goal, Sinclair crouched low and rushed across the doorway and into the room. He heard two shots but didn't stop. Once out of the fatal funnel, he scanned for movement. He caught a blur of Olsen dragging Liz toward the back of the room, his handgun aimed at the doorway where Sinclair passed a split second ago.

Sinclair's momentum carried him into the room off balance. With Olsen moving and holding Liz in front of him, Sinclair couldn't take a shot. Sinclair fought to remain on his feet as he crashed into a light stand and chair. Behind him, he heard a guttural yelp.

Sinclair twisted to orient his body and gun toward Olsen, but his foot caught a power cord and sent him crashing face first to the floor. He slithered on his belly along the floor. Stopped behind a bed, out of Olsen's line of fire. He glanced back to see Braddock crumpled in the doorway, silhouetted by the blazing sun outside. She moaned and looked at Sinclair. He saw the pain etched in her distorted face and knew she'd been hit.

He motioned for her to get out of the doorway—to crawl out of the kill zone—but she didn't move. He couldn't get to her without putting himself in the line of fire. Although he was behind cover for the moment, he too was vulnerable. All Olsen had to do was walk around the bed to shoot him as he lay there helplessly on the floor. Before he could rescue Braddock, he needed to eliminate the threat.

Sinclair sprang up into a kneeling position and thrust his Sig toward the back of the room, immediately focusing the front sight on Olsen as his eyes adjusted to the darkness in the back of the room.

Olsen stood in the doorway to the bathroom, his left arm around Liz's neck and his right hand holding a gun pressed to her head. The bathroom wall and doorjamb hid most of him, and Liz's body shielded the rest. Liz's head covered most of his, leaving only two inches exposed. Not enough for a shot.

Sinclair locked his eyes onto Olsen, trying to ignore Liz's face, her cheeks streaked with blood and tears, her huge eyes pleading with him to do something—anything.

Sinclair took several deep breaths. His pulse slowed. His index finger barely touched the trigger. As long as Olsen kept the muzzle of his gun at Liz's head, Sinclair's only option was an incapacitating headshot, but he needed more of Olsen's head exposed to do that.

"It doesn't need to end this way," said Sinclair. "Let her go and drop your gun."

"There couldn't be a better ending. You watching me kill your girlfriend right in front of you."

"If you hurt her, I'll—"

"You'll what—kill me? Maybe you'll get me before I shoot you. Maybe not, but either way, you'll watch both of your women die. That's what this is about, Sinclair, making sure you feel the same pain I've felt since mine were taken from me."

Sinclair aimed his forty-five at Olsen's right eye, just at the edge of Liz's head. To take the shot, he needed Liz to move her head just two inches to the right or Olsen to move two inches to the left.

Two inches was all he needed.

"All that's keeping you alive is the woman you're hiding behind," said Sinclair. "You shoot her and you're dead."

"And that'll take you back to the bottle like it did the last time you killed a man. I know you better than you know yourself. You're a killer just like me." A smile crept across Olsen's face. He chuckled. "Maybe I'll shoot your partner first."

Olsen moved his gun from Liz's head and waggled it at the doorway where Braddock lay.

Without hesitation, Sinclair shifted his aim to the left and fired into the wall. He continued firing until he had shot eight rounds.

Both Olsen and Liz dropped out of his view. He pressed the magazine release. The empty magazine fell to the ground as his left hand slammed a fresh one into the gun's butt in one smooth movement.

Once reloaded, he moved around the bed into the center of the room. Liz was crawling away from the bathroom. Sinclair crept forward until he saw Olsen lying on the bathroom floor, splotches of red on his right shoulder, chest, and forearm growing larger. The gun still clenched in his hand.

Liz scooted into a corner and pulled her legs to her chest. Her skirt was bunched above her waist. She sobbed hysterically. Sinclair kept his focus on Olsen and pointed his gun at the center of his chest.

"It's over," said Sinclair. "Let go of the gun."

"Go ahead and do it," said Olsen, pink foam bubbling from his mouth. "I won't go to prison."

Sinclair heard the sirens closing in, some going silent as the cars arrived outside.

"It doesn't work that way."

Sinclair heard car doors slamming on the street.

Olsen laughed and pink spittle sprayed from his mouth. "People had to pay. You, if anyone, should understand. You and me—we're the same."

Behind him, Sinclair heard Liz in a soft, quivering voice. "Kill him, Matt."

Olsen's right hand trembled as he tried to raise his gun. There was a gaping hole in Olsen's right forearm, jagged pieces of broken bone poking out of the ragged flesh. His arm shook as he tried to raise the gun. Olsen began to reach across his chest toward the gun with his left hand.

"No," Sinclair ordered.

"It's either me or you," said Olsen, as his left hand crept closer to the gun. "The Bus Bench Killer or Sergeant Sinclair. That's how it's supposed to end."

Sinclair heard police radios coming across the parking lot. Then he stepped toward Olsen and, with all his might, kicked his arm, aiming at the shattered bone.

Olsen let loose a long, anguished scream and his hand released the Beretta.

With his foot, Sinclair hooked the gun toward him and kicked it clear. "This is how it ends. You and I are nothing alike."

Chapter 66

The waitress cleared their plates and brought coffee. It was the first time Sinclair had seen Liz since the ambulance took her away three days ago. Their conversation over dinner had been cordial, but he sensed a divide as wide as the San Francisco Bay between them. In the candlelight, Sinclair could barely make out Liz's injuries under her heavy makeup, but her eyes showed fatigue and stress. He'd been waiting for her to announce what was on her mind ever since he received a delivery of flowers and an expensive box of cigars at the office earlier that day. The note asked him to join her for a late dinner and closed with, *Thanks for saving my life. I'll always love you, Liz.*

His final showdown with Olsen at the Golden State Motel three days earlier was still fresh on his mind. Once Lieutenant Maloney and the rest of the homicide unit arrived on scene and cleared him to leave, Sinclair had rushed to the hospital. The ER staff had taken Braddock downstairs for a CT scan, so he grabbed a nurse and inquired about Liz. The nurse said Liz had been examined, found to have no serious injuries, and signed herself out against medical advice. A few hours later, Sinclair sat alongside Braddock as she lay unconscious in ICU. He was staring at the TV on the wall when the five o'clock news came on, and he was shocked to see Liz sitting at the anchor desk. A dark bruise covered half her face, and her lower lip was so swollen she spoke with a lisp. She wore her battle wounds proudly, and Sinclair was sure it was the first time Liz ever declined hair and makeup before going on the air. She reported the harrowing details of her ordeal and heaped praise on him and Braddock for her rescue. She was on the ten o'clock news later that night and on a morning show Monday. They spoke several times on the phone, but she was too busy to meet. She flew to New York Monday night and appeared on *Good Morning America* Tuesday morning and another network talk show that afternoon.

Liz added cream to her coffee and slowly stirred it. "I've been offered a huge contract for an anchor-track position with CBS in Chicago."

"That's what you've always dreamed of."

She smiled.

"Will you take it?"

"I already have. Movers arrive tomorrow and I fly out tomorrow night. I'm hot right now, and they want me in place right away to take advantage of it."

"Congratulations. You earned it." Sinclair only half meant it. Most of the homicide unit thought the DA's office should have charged her criminally for what she did, and all were in agreement that any cop who did something that reckless would be fired. Sinclair wasn't so sure. Monday morning, Chief Brown had told the Internal Affairs to initiate an investigation for disobeying his order to stay in the office, but like after the Alonzo Moore shooting, the media made Sinclair into a hero, and along with Liz, he became a national sensation. Brown called IAD a few hours later and told them to close the case. In a news conference that afternoon, he joined the tide of public opinion and praised Sinclair.

"None of this would have been possible without you," Liz said. She pulled a tissue from her handbag and wiped her eyes.

Sinclair nodded and smiled.

"I need to get back. Prepare for the ten o'clock broadcast. They're doing a farewell segment on me."

Sinclair reached for his wallet.

"I already paid," she said. "My new job comes with a credit card and expense account."

Sinclair stood. "I'll walk you out."

"Finish your coffee." She stood and wiped her eyes again. "I'll lose it totally if I'm alone with you."

Liz leaned in, kissed his cheek, and whispered in his ear, "I'll always love you, Matt."

He watched as she walked away, the sound of her clicking heels growing faint until she disappeared out the door. A wave of sadness came over him, but at the same time, he felt as if a huge weight had been lifted from his shoulders.

Chapter 67

Sinclair sipped from a lead crystal tumbler of Perrier and leaned back in the leather club chair. Walt poured another inch of Scotch for Maloney, Jankowski, and Sanchez and replaced the bottle on a mahogany corner bar.

"What was the name of this again?" asked Maloney.

"Aberlour," said Walt. "It's a single-malt from the Speyside region of Scotland. Mr. Towers discovered the eighteen-year-old Aberlour years ago when in Switzerland on business. He had several cases shipped home, and although he no longer drinks, he'll be quite pleased to hear you enjoyed it."

"I'm more of a beer drinker, but this is good shit." Jankowski drained his glass in two gulps. "Sinclair says you can even smoke cigars in this room."

Walt flipped a switch by the door and pointed to a vent high on the wood-paneled wall. "Yes, the library is equipped with a high-volume exhaust fan, and if you're so inclined, we can return here after dinner for cigars."

Earlier in the week, Sinclair had moved into the guest-house, located across the mansion's back lawn behind the pool. It was bright, airy, and casual—a stark contrast to the formality of the main house.

Maloney removed a leather-bound Hemingway novel from a bookshelf, fingered through the pages, and put it back in its place.

"Where did we leave off with the story?" Walt asked.

"Cathy is lying in the doorway after being hit with two bullets," said Maloney. "And Matt just kicked the gun away from the Bus Bench Killer."

"I thought for sure she'd been shot," said Sinclair.

Braddock wiggled the fingers of her left hand through the cast that covered her arm from the elbow to the knuckles and set her glass of Perrier on an end table. "I was lying there, wanting to tell Matt I'm okay, so he can focus on Olsen rather than worry about me, but I was in a daze. I followed Matt through the door, but not being a super-duper ex-SWAT cop, I was a bit slow and stepped into the doorway just as two bullets came that way. Thank God, he didn't go for a head shot. Both rounds hit me square in the chest. Like I took two punches from a heavyweight champ. They knocked me off my feet, and I tried to break my fall with my left hand."

"Which didn't work very well, because not only did she break her wrist when she landed, but she still smacked her head on the doorjamb," said Sinclair.

"So Matt was thinking that I was down because I was shot, and I didn't even know where I was at because my brain's rattled."

"The Monday morning *Chronicle* reported that Matt fired eight shots into him right through the wall," said Walt.

"Rumors like that are how legends are born." Sinclair grinned. "Only three rounds hit him, but it was enough.

The most serious one went through his right lung, but the paramedics and ACH ER did their magic and saved him."

Braddock leaned back on the sofa. "So there I was, still in a daze, when every cop in Oakland arrives. They dragged me outside, stripped off my vest, and started unbuttoning my shirt to look for bullet holes. I was thinking, *Hey, I'm a girl, show some respect.* My chest hurt so bad I was sure the rounds either went right through the vest or missed it. After they did a CT scan, the docs were amazed there was no internal damage or broken ribs from the blunt trauma. Only the giant bruises that are still purple and yellow. While a dozen officers were taking care of me, others swooped inside, handcuffed Olsen, and wrapped Liz in a blanket. She was pretty much in shock, so they sent her away in the third ambulance."

"The officers handcuffed a wounded man with a broken arm?" said Walt.

"I know it might sound barbaric," said Maloney. "But that's standard protocol. The aftermath of a shooting scene is chaotic. Just because a man's been shot, it doesn't mean he's no longer able to fight."

"It sounds awfully painful, but it makes a lot of sense," said Walt. "Any chance of this guy getting off?"

"There's a ton of physical evidence that ties him to the murders," said Sinclair. "And with what we found in his apartment and the statement that he taped for Channel Six, the trial will be a slam dunk."

"Lethal injection is made for assholes like him," said Jankowski.

"Even if the jury decides on the death penalty, with all the appeals these guys are entitled to, he'll still be occupying a prison cell when I retire," said Sinclair.

"Has the DA made a decision on the officer-involved shooting yet?" asked Sanchez.

"They weren't comfortable with Matt kicking him," said Maloney. "It never looks good when a cop puts the boots to a man who's down—but they understood it was better than shooting him."

When Sinclair stood over Olsen in the motel room, it had felt like déjà vu. Despite what both Moore and Olsen had said, Sinclair knew he wasn't a killer. None of what Olsen had done mattered at that moment: not the lives he destroyed; not Braddock lying in the doorway; not Liz, bloodied and cowering in the corner; not whether a jury would convict him or set him free; not even Olsen's threats to kill Liz and Braddock. Sinclair realized that the difference with Olsen was that he didn't *need* to kill him.

"It still doesn't make sense," said Braddock. "He decides to kill innocent people because doctors didn't magically cure his daughter."

"I learned a lot about Olsen over the past week," said Sinclair. "NYPD came through and did extensive interviews with Horowitz and the Arquette Family. Olsen had met Jane when he was a cameraman doing a documentary with a BBC team in Africa and Jane worked there with the Peace Corps. She came home pregnant with Samantha. Jane's family was against her marrying him, and Jane didn't want to upset her father or risk losing her multimillion-dollar trust fund, so she had the baby, and she and Olsen lived together without marrying. He got a job as a photo-journalist in New York City but never mingled with the Arquettes.

"When Samantha died, Jane went into a deep depression. Olsen was convinced that if the man that raped her was brought to justice and the doctors who failed to save her were slammed in a lawsuit, Jane would feel a sense of closure and could move forward. We'll never know if that would've mattered to her. When Jane committed suicide, Olsen blamed us. After her death, the family learned that she'd rewritten her will and left her estate to Olsen, which pissed off old man Arquette, but he wanted to keep everything quiet to avoid the social embarrassment, so he reached out to NYPD to ensure the suicide investigation was closed and buried. That's why no one from NYPD would talk to us initially.

"Olsen found Channel Six was advertising for a part-time cameraman and figured that was a good way for him to move west and dig into Samantha's case. His friend, Darryl Tyson, was in Africa on a project and gave him the keys to his apartment. His coworkers knew him only as Eric, and no one had any suspicion he was connected to any of this. Once we arrested him and the story came out, a bunch of people came forward and told us that Olsen had nosed around in Berkeley, digging into Samantha's rape."

"I guess he didn't get anywhere with it," said Braddock.

"No, and maybe that's when he decided to kill the family members of those he blamed for Jane's suicide and devised the plan to use the peace medallions and the bus bench to play with us."

"How was he able to time it so that you'd get assigned his first murder?" asked Braddock.

"He volunteered to work whenever Liz was scheduled. It seems that Liz wasn't the most popular reporter among the cameramen, so when she went out on assignment, no one objected when he accompanied her. She talked to him about how my arbitration was progressing, and he was her cameraman when she reported I was returning to homicide. She even mentioned to him when I went back on standby, so he planned his first killing to be sure I got it."

"It's still hard to fathom someone killing all those innocent people for revenge," said Braddock.

"Murder isn't a rational act," said Sinclair. "There's only so much we can understand."

Sinclair had learned years ago to stop trying to make sense out of the actions of murderers. When he had met with the DA last week to review Olsen's murder cases for charging, the DA lamented about the difficulty the prosecution would have trying to make sense of the killings for twelve people on jury. But Sinclair knew it wasn't his responsibility to make sense out of their deaths.

All he could do when he returned to the office was take the number from Samantha's case packet and pin it on the board next to the numbers representing Zachary, Susan, Carol, and Melissa. Then he took a marker from Connie's desk and drew a red line through each of them.

Acknowledgments

It's been a long journey from the evening in 2008 when I sat in a fiction writing class and thought it might be fun to write a novel. A special thanks to all the people who helped along the way, from the writing teachers who encouraged me years ago when writing a novel was just a dream; to those in my writing groups who critiqued my attempts at writing and urged me to continue; to the amazing teachers, mentors, and fellow students in the MFA Program at Western Connecticut State University who patiently helped this old cop and soldier transform into a writer; to the cop-writers who showed me it was possible to write something beyond police reports; and to those police officers, reporters, and others who provided input and guidance that helped make this story and its characters as authentic as possible: Andy Alexander, Holly Azevedo, John Bates, Michael Capuzzo, Richard Cass, Jane Cleland, Brian Clements, Elizabeth Cohen, Rick Corbo, Ann Marie Cannon, Sharon Charter, Debra Devins, Roland De Wolk, Donna Doble-Brown,

Pamela Fitzgerald, Lauren Gallo, David Griffith, Phylis Iqbal, Dana Jenkins, Jeff Joorfetz, Joe Klemczewski, Alissa Kocer, Jack Lundquist, Derrick McCluskey, Patty Melara, Tim Nolan, Dan Pope, Lynn Paris-Purtle, Ian Peterkin, Jeanette Ronson, Arthur Roth, DeShea Rushing, Ron Samul, Becca Simas, Don Snyder, John Taylor, Rachael Van Sloten, Karen Veazey, and Tim Weed.

My deepest thanks to my amazing agent, Paula Munier; my supremely talented editor, Matthew Martz; his super assistant, Nike Power; and the rest of the team at Crooked Lane Books for your guidance, support, and encouragement.